TEEN

APR   2017

D0960837

THE BOOK JUMPER

MECHTHILD GLÄSER

FEIWEL & FRIENDS

NEW YORK

A FEIWEL AND FRIENDS BOOK

An Imprint of Macmillan Publishing Group, LLC

Feiwel and Friends books may be purchased for business or promotional use.
For information on bulk purchases, please contact the Macmillan Corporate and Premium
Sales Department at (800) 221-7945 x5442 or by e-mail at specialmarkets@macmillan.com.

Library of Congress Cataloging-in-Publication Data is available.

ISBN: 978-1-250-08666-2

Book design by April Ward

Feiwel and Friends logo designed by Filomena Tuosto

First American edition—2017

Originally published in 2015 in Germany by Loerve Verlag GMbH under the title *Die Buchspringer*.

3 5 7 9 10 8 6 4 2

fiercereads.com

Contents

PROLOGUE

WILL RAN. HE RAN AND RAN.

The island seemed bigger than usual, and he'd been running for so long his chest hurt. Across the moor, through the fields, down to the beach, past the graveyard and Lennox House, into the village, up to the stone circle, through the library, back to his cottage, and in and out of the last wisps of fog that hung over Macalister Castle.

Nothing.

The dog ran beside him. Its black ears streamed in the wind and its huge paws left prints on the moor. Why weren't there any other footprints? Why couldn't they find him? He would never have left the dog behind. So he must be here somewhere. What had he said just before he'd stepped outside? He'd only been going out for a walk, hadn't he?

They ran on, up the narrow path to the clifftop. The dog ahead,

Will behind. But there was nobody up here either. Of course not. Not in this weather. A storm had blown up and it had started to rain. They came to a stop at the end of the earth. Though, of course, it wasn't really the end of the earth, just the end of the island. The world carried on beyond this precipice—the water below stretched away to the horizon and beyond that to other islands. Was that where he was, somewhere out there? Beyond the horizon?

For a while the two of them gazed out to sea. With one hand Will scratched the dog behind the ears, and with the other he shielded his eyes the better to see through the rain. To no avail.

Sherlock Holmes had vanished without trace.

The monster had slept for many, many years.
Deep, deep in the darkest corner of its cave.
On and on it had slept, as time rolled over it in waves.
And it had dreamed of its awakening. It had slept for so long that
the people of the kingdom no longer knew it existed.
At first, perhaps, they had dimly remembered the terrible creature.
But over the years it had faded to a dark foreboding. Now, however,
as the fog of forgetting engulfed the people entirely—
now the time had come for the monster
to open its eyes once more.

ONCE UPON A TIME
THERE WAS AN ISLAND

ONCE UPON A TIME THERE WE STOOD, Alexis and me, chucking things into suitcases. Socks, sweaters, pants. I tugged handfuls of clothes from my wardrobe and flung them into the wheeled suitcase that lay open behind me, and Alexis did the same in the next room. We barely even registered what we were packing, whether we'd included our favorite clothes or not. The main thing was to get it done quickly. That's what we'd agreed. Because if we'd taken our time over the packing and made a list, the way we usually did, we would surely have realized that what we were doing was completely and utterly crazy.

Everyone in my family was crazy. That's what my mum, Alexis, always said anyway, when I asked her why she'd run away from her home in Scotland at the age of seventeen with nothing but a suitcase in her hand and me in her belly. She'd upped sticks and left for Germany—pregnant and not even legally an adult yet—and ended up in Bochum. I think she felt too young to be a mum, so she wanted me to call her by her first name instead, which I always had and still did. And now I was nearly seventeen myself (well, in fourteen months I would be) and it was starting to look like I'd inherited the "crazy" gene. That morning at breakfast—an hour ago now—I, too, had spontaneously decided to leave the country. We'd gone online and booked ourselves flights on a budget airline, departing that same afternoon. All we had to do now was pack. I rooted around in a drawer and hurriedly dug out a few bras and pairs of underwear.

"Bring your warm jacket with you, Amy," said Alexis as she wheeled her suitcase (stuffed to bursting with clothes) into my bedroom and tried to squish my pillow in on top. Inside the case I could see her organic cotton corduroys and a shirt from Etsy decorated with a brightly colored apple print.

"I don't really think I need a parka in July," I muttered. My suitcase was pretty full by now, too—although mainly with books. Clotheswise I'd packed only what was strictly necessary. The way I saw it, it was better to take one less cardigan than have to do without one of my favorite books.

"I think you're underestimating the weather over there," said Alexis, eyeing the contents of my suitcase and shaking her mahogany-brown locks. Her eyes were red and swollen; she'd been up all night crying. "Just take your e-reader. Won't that do?"

"But I don't have *Momo* or *Pride and Prejudice* as e-books."

"You've read both those books about a hundred times each."

"And what if I want to read them for the hundred-and-first time while I'm there?"

"They've got more than enough books on that blessed island, Amy, believe me. You have no idea."

I ran my fingertips over the cover of my well-thumbed copy of *Momo*. I'd often wished I had an enchanted tortoise like the one in *Momo* to guide me on my journey through life. I needed this book. It comforted me when I was sad. I needed it now more than ever.

Alexis sighed. "Well, make sure you fit the jacket in somehow, OKAY? It can get pretty chilly there." She sat down on the suitcase and tugged at the zipper. "I'm worried this whole thing is a bad idea anyway," she fretted. "Are you sure that's the only place you'll be able to take your mind off things?"

I nodded.

The tiny boat pitched in the swell, tossed back and forth as though the sea were playing ball with it. Lightning flickered across the sky, where dark storm clouds were massing, shrouding the ocean in a cloak of surreal gray pierced by sudden flares of light and ominous rolls of thunder. The water had turned the color of slate and the rain was coming down in sheets—heavy, biting gray raindrops that hammered down on the waves and sharpened their crests. What with the thunderstorm and the giant waves smashing against the cliffs that loomed on the horizon, Mother Nature was putting on a pretty formidable display. It was terrifying, awe-inspiring, and wonderful all at the same time.

On second thought, "wonderful" was possibly a bit of an overstatement. The problem was that I happened to be sitting in this tiny little boat, in the middle of this thunderstorm, clinging onto my seat

for dear life to keep myself from falling overboard. Spray shot into the air and into our faces. Alexis tried gamely to hold on to our luggage, while the man driving the boat cranked up the engine till it roared.

The rain had come down quite suddenly and within seconds I'd been soaked through. I was also freezing cold, and all I could think about was arriving—I didn't care where, as long as it was somewhere warm and dry. During our flight from Dortmund to Edinburgh, the sun had still been shining, in a bright, cloudless sky. And though a few clouds had appeared by the time we'd boarded the little plane to Sumburgh Airport on Mainland (the biggest of the Shetland Islands, off the Scottish coast), I certainly hadn't reckoned with this apocalyptic scene.

I blinked at the burning of the salt water in my eyes as another wave rocked our boat and nearly swallowed up Alexis's handmade felt handbag. It was getting harder and harder to hold on to my seat. The ice-cold wind had long since numbed my fingers to the point where I could barely control them. Reading about a storm like this in a book was a far more pleasurable experience. When I was reading—even when I was scared, when I shuddered in horror, when the story plunged me right into the midst of the most terrible disasters—I never entirely lost that warm, cozy tucked-up-on-the-sofa feeling. There was no trace of that feeling now, and I realized that real-life storms, unlike literary ones, were most definitely not my idea of fun.

The next wave was even more savage than the last, and it washed clean over my head. At the same moment I gulped frantically for breath—not the best idea, as it caused me to choke on a huge mouthful

of water. Coughing and gasping, I tried to empty my lungs of sea-water while Alexis landed a few hearty thumps on my sodden back. This sent her bag sailing overboard. Oh, crap! But Alexis seemed to have given up on the idea of bringing all our possessions safely ashore anyway, and didn't even spare a glance for this portion of her worldly goods.

"Nearly there, Amy. Nearly there!" she called—no sooner had the words crossed her lips than they were carried away on the wind. "We did want to come here, remember. I'm sure we're going to have a lovely holiday on Stormsay." It was probably supposed to sound cheerful, but her voice cracked with suppressed panic.

"We're here because we're running away," I replied, although too quietly for Alexis to hear. I didn't want to remind her or myself of the real reasons for our trip. After all, we were running away to forget. To forget that Dominik had broken up with Alexis and gone back to his wife and children. Completely out of the blue. And to forget that those stupid idiots in my year at school . . . No—I'd promised myself not to even think about it anymore.

The boat's outboard motor howled as if trying to drown out the storm, and the rain grew heavier, beating down on my head and shoulders and lashing at my face. It was literally impossible for me to get any wetter. But I was relieved nonetheless to see that the island seemed to be drawing nearer. Stormsay, the home of my ancestors. Through a curtain of wet hair, I squinted at the shoreline and hoped the skipper knew what he was doing and that we were not about to get smashed to smithereens on the rocks.

The cliff face looked immense, jagged, and deadly. It towered nearly a hundred feet above the slate-gray waves and at its summit, way up high where the raging of the wind was at its most treacherous . . .

. . . there was somebody standing at the cliff's edge.

At first I thought it was a tree. But then I realized it was a human being, leaning into the storm and looking out to sea. A figure with short hair, coat flapping in the wind, watching us from the clifftop. It had one hand raised to shield its eyes, and the other rested on the head of a huge black dog.

I stared back, shivering, as the boat hove to. We left the cliffs behind us and battled on, arcing around toward the eastern shore of the island. The figure receded into the distance, eventually disappearing from view.

And then, finally, we came to a jetty. It was half submerged and wobbled precariously, but our captain managed to moor the boat with a few deft movements and we tumbled out onto dry land. At last.

The embankment was slippery and the rain was still falling hard, but we'd reached our destination. Stormsay. The word tasted of secrets. It sounded somehow full of promise and slightly eerie at the same time. This was the first time I'd ever been to the island. For a long time Alexis had never even mentioned it to me—until at some point during primary school I'd realized that not all children learned both German and English from their parents, and that my name sounded different from everyone else's. Amy Lennox. And even then Alexis had been reluctant to admit that we came from Scotland. When she'd left, in fact, aged seventeen, she'd vowed never to go back. And now . . .

We trudged along a muddy street, the wheels of our suitcases sinking into the sludge. On either side of us, scattered at intervals along the road, were little houses—no more than a handful of cottages, really, with crooked roofs and cob walls and windows of bulging glass, some of which flickered with yellow light. I wondered which one my grandmother lived in, and hoped that the little houses were more weatherproof on the inside than they looked from the outside.

The man who'd ferried us across to the island mumbled something about the pub and beer and disappeared through a doorway. Alexis, however, plowed straight on past the last of the cottages. She seemed determined to leave even these meager remnants of civilization behind us, and it was all I could do just to keep up with her. My suitcase had gotten stuck in yet another muddy puddle and I had to tug at the handle with all my strength to get it out.

"Your mum does live in an actual, like . . . house, right?" I grumbled, wondering why I hadn't questioned Alexis more closely as to what exactly it was that was so crazy about my grandmother. After all, "crazy" might mean she ate tree bark and wore clothes made of pinecones and lived out in the wild with the creatures of the forest. . . .

Alexis didn't answer but simply gestured toward something in the darkness ahead of us and beckoned to me to follow her. At that moment my suitcase suddenly came unstuck with unexpected force. I was splattered from head to toe with mud. Brilliant!

While Alexis still looked gorgeous, even with her wet hair (as if she'd stepped straight out of a shampoo ad), I was starting to feel more and more like a drowned rat. I muttered away to myself crossly as I trudged on.

The road soon narrowed into a track and grew even muddier.

The lights were far behind us now. We could barely see the little village at all anymore, though the icy wind still blew alongside us like a faithful friend and wormed its way through all the little gaps in the knit of my woolly sweater. Raindrops whipped into my face as I caught up with Alexis. We really were heading out into the wilderness.

"There was somebody up on the clifftop. Did you see?" I said breathlessly, trying to distract myself from the feeling that any minute now I was going to freeze to death.

"On Shakespeare's Seat? In this weather? I'd be very surprised," murmured Alexis, so quietly I could barely hear her. Then, from the top of a steep little slope she'd just clambered up, she offered, "Here—let me take your suitcase."

I heaved the case into her arms and scrambled up after it. When I reached the top, I realized we were standing on a sort of plateau. In the distance I could see another cluster of lights, and towers that looked like the turrets of a castle etched against the night sky. And there were lights close by, too, in some of the windows of a huge mansion to our right. We were standing at a fork in the path. Straight ahead, the track carried on across the moor.

But Alexis took the right-hand fork and marched up to a wrought-iron gate between two hedges, behind which I glimpsed something like a park or a gravel drive with a fountain in the middle. These big houses (in the movies, at least) almost always had gravel paths flanked by crisply clipped shrubs, statues, climbing roses, and often a classic convertible for good measure. You had to have an imposing backdrop for the lovers' kiss, or the tracking down of the murderer. . . . The house behind the gate looked pretty grand, at any rate, even from this distance. The walls were studded with countless bay windows, and a whole host of little towers and chimneys jutted into the sky, grazing the storm clouds. Behind the windowpanes hung heavy curtains, with flickering candlelight shining through the gaps between them.

The rain grew heavier again now and the individual raindrops merged to form a veil as if trying, at the last moment, to hide the mansion from view. But it was far too late for that. We'd landed on the island, and there was no going back now.

Alexis laid her fingertips on the ornate handle of the gate and took a deep breath. *"All happy families are alike; every unhappy family is unhappy in its own way,"* she murmured at last, pushing open the gate.

"What?" I said.

"Oh—it's just the first line of a novel I often used to . . . read here." She sighed.

"I see," I said, though I didn't really. My teeth were chattering so loudly by this time that I could hardly think straight.

We hefted and hauled our luggage across a small park made up of gravel paths and crisply clipped shrubs, past a fountain and several climbing roses, and up a flight of marble steps. The only thing missing was the classic convertible. Without further ado, Alexis rang the doorbell.

A gong sounded loudly inside the house.

But it was still a long time before the oak door swung open and a large wrinkly nose emerged from behind it. The nose belonged to an old man in a suit, who eyed us keenly over the top of his glasses.

"Good evening, Mr. Stevens. It's me, Alexis."

Mr. Stevens gave a curt nod. "Of course, ma'am. I can see that," he said, stepping aside. "Were we expecting you?"

"No. But I'd like to speak to my mother," said Alexis. Mr. Stevens nodded again and helped her heave her battered suitcase over the threshold. When he reached for my case with his liver-spotted hands, I quickly sidestepped him. I'd lugged the thing this far, I could carry it the last few feet without dumping it on an old man who must surely be even more of a weakling than I was! But Mr. Stevens gave me such a stern and un-old-mannish look that in the end I let him take the suitcase and stuffed my hands in my jacket pockets instead. And indeed, the weight of our luggage seemed to give him no trouble at all.

"Wow," I gasped the moment we stepped in out of the rain.

The entrance hall to the mansion was bigger than our entire flat. When you stepped into our hallway at home, you found yourself in a dark, narrow tunnel with ancient daisy-patterned wallpaper peeling off the walls. Alexis had tried to spruce it up a bit with a beaded curtain and an indoor palm tree but the tower block apartment remained stubbornly unglamorous. The living room, which also served as Alexis's bedroom, the kitchen with its '70s tiles, the bathroom, and my bedroom, where the carpet had bunched up with age—they all felt like boxes. Concrete boxes with tiny windows, in which even bookshelves and colorful polka-dot teapots couldn't counteract the gray.

My grandmother's hallway, on the other hand, was incredible. The ceiling arched so high above our heads that looking up at the paintings on it almost made me dizzy. Instead of fat naked angels on clouds and other such popular motifs, the artist had painted pictures of people with books. Some of them were reading, some were pointing toward bulging bookcases, and others had placed open books across their faces. Interspersed with the pictures of people, the same coat of arms appeared again and again: a green stag with huge antlers, perched proudly atop a pile of books against a wine-red background. A chandelier hung at the center of the entrance hall, its arms made up of strings of golden letters. Matching lamps were mounted at regular intervals along the wood-paneled walls, and between them were more stag coats of arms. The floor was spread with brightly colored Oriental rugs, with letters woven into them that I'd never seen before, and on the opposite wall a staircase swept upward, its oak banister fashioned from carved books. It was just possible I'd inherited my love of reading from my grandmother, I reflected.

"Follow me, if you please. I shall attend to your luggage shortly," said Mr. Stevens. For a man of his age, his back was remarkably straight, and his polished shoes made not the slightest sound on the opulent rugs.

We, on the other hand, left a squelching trail of muddy footsteps in our wake. "Um," I whispered to Alexis, "do you think maybe we should take off our . . . ?" But she shook her head distractedly. Only now did I notice that her fists were clenched around the fabric of her woolen coat. She was chewing at her bottom lip and her eyes flicked nervously back and forth.

Oh well. We had to get a move on anyway, to keep up with the butler. But I still felt bad about making such a mess in the most beautiful hallway I'd ever set foot in, and I tried to pick my way around the edges of the rugs. At least the glossy wooden floorboards underneath would be easier to clean.

They were certainly a lot more slippery. I'd only gone a few steps when I lost my balance on the sheet of mud and rainwater beneath the soles of my sneakers and my feet slid out from under me. For a split second I teetered in the air (one flailing arm grazing Mr. Stevens's pomaded coiffure, and ruffling its cement-like surface), before landing heavily on my bum. Oh, *crap*!

The butler turned to inspect me through his now wonky glasses, eyebrows raised, but said nothing. The hair on the back of his head stood up in spikes like the feathers of a cockatoo.

"Sorry," I mumbled.

Alexis, without a word, put out a hand to help me up. She was used to my frequent accidents and liked to console me, at times like this, by calling me her "little giraffe," because it sometimes seemed as though my arms and legs were simply too long for me to control. And I did often feel like a giraffe compared to all the other girls my age, who'd gotten curvier over the past few years instead of taller and thinner like I had. A giraffe with roller skates strapped to its clumsy feet.

I let Alexis pull me to my feet and refrained from rubbing my bruised bum, trying to preserve the last shred of my dignity. Mr. Stevens (whose hair, incredibly, had already regained its former bombproof glory) carried on walking. We'd crossed the entrance hall now and he led us through a door set into the wood paneling, onto a long corridor, up some stairs, along another corridor . . . I was just starting to think that if I ever got lost in this house I'd never be able to find my way out again, when we finally arrived at a sitting room containing a silk-upholstered divan.

"Please." He motioned to us to sit down and busied himself lighting a fire in a large grate. But we didn't sit down because the fire, which was soon crackling merrily, was far more inviting. Alexis and I stationed ourselves as close as possible to the hot flames, while the butler disappeared from the room. The heat almost sizzled as it met my skin. It sank slowly into my hands and face in what felt like a series of tiny little electric shocks. I closed my eyes and relished the reddish-orange glow that shone through my eyelids. But where the heat of the fire met my wet clothes it bounced off as if from a suit of armor. Only in one or two places did it manage to work its way— slowly—through the fabric.

I don't know how long I stood there willing the heat to filter right through to my bones. Perhaps it was only a few moments. Mr. Stevens returned much too soon, at any rate. "Mairead Lennox, Lady of Stormsay," he announced.

I forced myself to open my eyes and turn away from the fire.

Like all the women in my family, it seemed, my grandmother was tall. She was even taller than Alexis and me. Or did she just look taller because her white hair was drawn up into an imposing knot on the top of her head? She had the same dark eyes as me and Alexis, anyhow, shining in a nest of fine wrinkles. Her nose was a little too long, her lips a little too thin. But she must have been very beautiful once upon a time. In her dark green silk dress, fastened at the neck by a white collar and a brooch, she seemed—like her house—to belong to a different era. On a ribbon around her neck hung a slim pair of reading glasses, the frames set with tiny red stones.

For a while, she and Alexis looked at each other in silence. Alexis, standing there in her very wet, very colorful clothes, kneading the fabric of her coat so hard she wrung little droplets out of it. I'd always thought of Alexis as a sort of vegan reincarnation of Pippi Longstocking. Strong, brave, different from everybody else. A friend who I called by her first name. A mother who didn't give a crap if people snorted contemptuously to see her walking along the top of a wall, singing loudly, as she took her five-year-old daughter to kindergarten. It wasn't like her to be nervous. But she was now.

Alexis moistened her lips as my grandmother's gaze shifted to me. She looked searchingly at me, and an unspoken question hung in the air between us, although I had no idea what it was. Alexis, too, remained silent. I swallowed, and Lady Mairead raised her eyebrows expectantly. The fire behind us crackled, and outside the rain drummed against the windowpanes. The climbing roses and the manicured shrubs rustled, bracing themselves against the storm that was howling around the house. My grandmother's nostrils flared as she breathed in. The water from our hair and clothes trickled off us and formed puddles at our feet.

Still Alexis didn't say a word.

This was unbearable!

"Um—so—I'm Amy," I ventured finally. "Nice to meet . . . er . . . to make your acquaintance," I stammered, and then, as no response was forthcoming, I added a "Mi . . . lady?" for good measure. Everyone knows aristocrats can sometimes have a bit of a thing about their titles. At the same time, entirely of their own accord, my legs twisted themselves into a kind of mangled curtsy. It wasn't exactly the pinnacle of elegance. I felt the blood rush to my face.

The ghost of a smile played around the corners of my grandmother's mouth. "Is this your . . . ?" she asked Alexis. "Can it really be true?" She took a step toward me and ran her fingertips down my cheek and along the line of my chin.

Beside me, Alexis nodded. "I got pregnant very young."

"Indeed," said Lady Mairead, and now she smiled in earnest. "Well then, Amy—I suppose I must be your grandmother," she declared, adding, in a language I assumed was Gaelic, "*Ceud mìle fàilte!*" Luckily she switched straight back to English. "A thousand welcomes to Lennox House, Am—"

"Don't get your hopes up," Alexis interrupted her. "That's not why we came back."

"No? Why, then?"

Alexis took a deep breath, as if speaking to her mother was a great effort. "We needed to get away for a bit and we didn't know where to go," she began. "Perhaps we were being a bit hasty, but . . . Anyway, we just want to stay here for a while and . . . recover, that's all. It's Amy's summer holidays. We have to go back in a few weeks."

Alexis knew perfectly well, of course, that I hated my school now. I never wanted to see my so-called "friends" again. But when we'd decided to flee abroad we hadn't talked about how long we should stay. And I supposed we might have to go back to Germany at some point. After all, I was still planning to do my A-Levels there and study medicine afterward. But I didn't want to think about that right now, and my grandmother too batted away Alexis's objections with a sweep of her slender hand. "If you want to stay, you know what my condition is. She has to read. As long as you are here, she will read, and when the holidays are over, she can decide for herself."

"Read? What do you mean?" I asked. "Why do I *have* to read?"

Alexis sighed. "It's a long story, treasure. It's to do with our family, but it's not important. We—"

"She doesn't know," said my grandmother flatly. "She doesn't know." Her lips tightened as if she'd just bitten into a lemon.

"What don't I know?"

Lady Mairead was about to explain, but at that moment Alexis finally overcame her uncharacteristic nervousness. "Not tonight, okay?" she told my grandmother. "I'm just not up to it right now. Amy's soaked and frozen half to death, as am I. Things haven't been easy for us these past few weeks and getting here in this storm definitely wasn't. We'll talk tomorrow."

At first it looked as though my grandmother was about to object, but she seemed suddenly to realize that I was still shivering. "Very well," she said. "Mr. Stevens will make up your rooms and run you a bath."

A little while later, Alexis and I were lying in a bathtub the size of a swimming pool. When I stood up the water reached all the way to my waist, and if I tucked my legs in tight enough, I could even swim one and a half strokes from end to end. But as it was we were far too tired to do anything remotely sporty. Instead we just bobbed about in the hot water, thawing out our numb toes. Fragrant drifts of bubbles floated between us. From the ceiling of the marble bathroom hung another chandelier made of golden letters.

As we'd negotiated the mansion's intricate web of corridors, I'd asked Alexis why she and Lady Mairead had such an issue about whether I should read or not. It was a no-brainer, after all—I certainly wasn't going to *not read* for the whole of the holidays. For years now, working my way through the contents of the city library had been my favorite pursuit. But Alexis had only shrugged and said, "This entire family is crazy, Amy—you know that."

Now we relaxed wearily into the heat of the water, which felt almost painful against my cold skin. Its warmth spread slowly through my body, right to my core. I let myself sink just below the surface and, without moving a muscle, watched my long, thin hair as it wafted and coiled through the water in slow motion. Its rusty sheen was only a pale echo of Alexis's wild mane; when my hair was wet, you could barely even tell it was red. Still, I did feel a little bit like a sea anemone on a tropical ocean floor. That must be a nice life—nothing to do all day but sit around being caressed by the warm current.

It had just occurred to me that on second thought I was quite glad I wasn't a sea anemone because I'd probably get bored pretty quickly down there on the seabed without any books, when the gentle lilting of the water grew choppier; Alexis was on the move. First she paddled all the way across the bathtub; then she took a deep breath and dived down under the water. She crouched on the bottom of the tub for nearly two minutes, and when she resurfaced her eyes looked as if she was trying hard not to cry. She was probably cursing the day she'd twisted her ankle on the pasture of the organic farm where she worked, and had a splint put on it by a good-looking doctor in the ER. Dominik had found his way into her heart, and our family, far too quickly. The two of them had been together less than a year, but he'd become part of the family straightaway. He'd cooked steaks for himself and me, in our otherwise vegan kitchen; he'd come ice skating with us. . . . I missed him. He was the only one I missed.

"I'm sure we're going to have a lovely holiday on Stormsay," I said, quoting Alexis. And I meant it. Because anything was better than sitting around at home, where everything reminded you of everything. Where Alexis had had her heart broken and where I risked running into kids from school—a school where people were not very forgiving toward a girl with straight As and a flat chest.

Alexis blinked back her tears. "Yes," she said. "Yes, you're right." She looked at me for a few moments. Suddenly she grinned and scooped some of the bubbles toward her. "Hey, Amy, could there be any more perfect start to a holiday than a full-on bubble fight?"

I smiled and started stocking up on soapy ammo.

Later, as I lay in bed cocooned in a warm quilt, I listened to the storm outside my window. Through the howling and raging of the wind, I was sure I heard another sound, like a child sobbing. Was somebody crying out there on the moor? No—it must be my imagination.

The princess lived in a castle with silver battlements
and stained-glass windows. It stood on a hill
from which the whole of the kingdom could be seen.
Every day she climbed to the top of the highest
tower and looked out across the land.
She knew her kingdom, knew it well.
But only from afar, for she never set foot outside the castle.
Since her father the king and her mother the queen
had died, she no longer dared venture outside.
She thought the meadows and lakes too dangerous,
the forests too impenetrable. An old fairy tale,
which her subjects had long ago ceased to believe,
told of a monster lying in wait somewhere,
hidden deep in a cave.
The princess feared the monster.

THE SECRET LIBRARY

The next morning I woke with a start from a nightmare in which I'd been pursued by photos and laughter. The pictures had shown me in the swimming pool locker room without my bikini top, captured on the camera phone of a so-called friend. Posted on our year's Facebook page. "This is your before picture on *Extreme Makeover!*" Paul had commented on one of the photos, as if I needed a whole load of plastic surgery in front of rolling TV cameras just to be able to lead a normal life. In the dream I'd shut myself in the school bathroom where no one could hear me, and cried.

Just like in real life.

Jolina really had taken the photos, and she really had shared them on Facebook and WhatsApp so that people with nothing better to do could look at me naked and laugh about it. It was stupid and childish.

But it still hurt.

Especially because I'd thought Jolina and I were friends. But now it seemed she preferred to fit in with everyone else than keep hanging out with me—the geek, the bookworm, the nerd. Alexis had told me time and time again how wrong they all were, that it wasn't true what they said about me, that I was pretty and likable and a lovely person. I knew it was mainly because they were jealous of my good grades and my fluent English that they were always looking for something they could use to upset me. But part of me secretly believed them nonetheless. However stupid it was, there was a sore spot in my soul, a tiny hole through which my self-esteem was trickling away.

But I wasn't going to let it—I'd promised myself. I was just going to forget about the photos and the laughter. And Stormsay was going to help me.

Resolutely I blinked back the images of the night and found myself lying in a four-poster bed. A swath of red-checked fabric was draped above my head, overflowing into four thick walls of curtain. My bed was like its own little room within a room. A cocoon with only me in it—and the e-reader by my pillow, of course. It reminded me of when I was little, when I used to make caves out of old blankets and hole up inside them with my favorite books. I lay there a moment longer gazing at the slivers of light that slipped through the chinks in the fabric here and there, painting patterns on the embroidered quilt. Then I got up.

The guest room Mr. Stevens had put me in wasn't particularly big, but it was magnificently furnished, just like the rest of the house. The wallpaper was made of dark red silk with a shiny floral pattern, and there was an armchair with gilded legs, a chest of drawers with a mirror mounted above it, and a deep window seat covered with cushions where you could sit and look out over the grounds and the moorland.

My muddy suitcase stood in the middle of the room like a foreign object. I'd been much too tired yesterday to unpack it. And even now it was all I could do to fish out a few pieces of clothing—a pair of jeans, a shirt, and a long cardigan would have to do. My wardrobe wasn't particularly varied at the best of times: unlike Alexis, I wasn't keen on brightly colored, patterned clothes and stripy tights. I preferred earthy colors, khaki, or black.

Directly opposite the four-poster bed was the door to the bathroom, which I was to share with Alexis. Environmentally friendly creams and pots of makeup, hair clips with flowers round the edges, and batik hair bands were already lined up along the edge of the sink and on the shelf above. Alexis had settled in, then. She was probably already having breakfast.

I was pretty hungry by now, too—after all, I hadn't eaten since yesterday morning apart from a couple of sandwiches at Dortmund Airport. I had a quick shower, threw on my clothes, and tied back my wet hair in a ponytail. Then I went out into the corridor in search of something to eat.

I soon struck lucky. I'd only gone a few steps when the raised voices of Alexis and my grandmother showed me which way to go. Unfortunately, they seemed to be yelling at each other. At first it was just unintelligible shouting, but the closer I got the more words I could distinguish.

". . . can't force her!" cried Alexis. ". . . never have even *come* here if I'd known . . . !"

". . . did you think . . . ?" replied my grandmother. ". . . our family's birthright . . . can't stop her from . . . !"

". . . give a shit about our birthright!"

"If you want to stay here . . . !"

". . . argh!"

I went up a spiral staircase and onto another corridor: the voices grew clearer. They seemed to be coming from a room at the end of the hallway.

"She likes reading, doesn't she?" asked Lady Mairead. "So why are you so against it? I'm sure she'll enjoy it."

"Have you forgotten what happened with me?"

"No, of course not. But you ended up with the wrong book, that's all."

"Still. It was horrible. I don't want that for Amy. She doesn't need those books."

By this time I was outside the door of the room where the voices were coming from, and I pushed it open. I found Alexis and Lady Mairead seated in a sort of conservatory. Between them was a table laden with toast, sausages, eggs, bacon, and jam. I also spotted a stack of pancakes. My stomach rumbled audibly. But first I had to find out what Alexis and my grandmother were arguing about.

"What's going on? What books don't I need?" I asked.

Alexis gave a start and almost dropped the piece of dry toast she'd been nibbling on. Lady Mairead smiled. "Good morning, Amy. How was your first night at Lennox House?"

"Good," I said. "I—um—like my canopy bed."

"I'm glad. Would you like some breakfast?" My grandmother motioned toward an empty chair. "We can't offer you a German-style breakfast, I'm afraid. We have ordered supplies in from Lerwick, but they won't be here until tomorrow. How about some toast in the meantime?"

"Thanks," I said, helping myself to some sausages and bacon. "I'm not a vegan." Alexis didn't particularly like it when I ate meat, but she knew my body needed more calories than hers because mine seemed to burn them the instant I swallowed them. That was why I lived my life by a simple motto: never pass up an opportunity to eat anything greasy.

But at the moment Alexis didn't much seem to care what I was eating anyway. She was still glaring at my grandmother. Her jaw tightened.

Lady Mairead, on the other hand, looked on approvingly as I shoveled the food into my mouth. "Your mother hasn't told you this, but we have a very special library here on Stormsay. It's very large and very . . . secret," she began at last. "Some of the texts are over two thousand years old and come from the famous Library of Alexandria. Our ancestors rescued them from the fire there before building the library on Stormsay. Might you like to see it? Some of the volumes are priceless."

I looked inquiringly at Alexis, but she was too busy casting withering looks at her mother to notice. She didn't reply, anyway. And I couldn't see what was so wrong with having a little noncommittal look around a library, especially when it belonged to your own family.

"Um, yeah," I mumbled between mouthfuls. "Definitely."

"Excellent." Lady Mairead nodded. "In that case, Mr. Stevens will take you straight there."

"Okay." I helped myself to another pancake as Alexis almost burst a blood vessel.

"Fine," she cried. "She can try it. But only on one condition."

Lady Mairead raised her eyebrows. "And what would that be?"

Alexis gripped the edge of the table so tightly her knuckles went white. "That you give her a children's book," she declared. "Something completely harmless. A story where absolutely nothing can happen to her. I mean it. Give her a children's book or we leave here right now."

"Oh, good lord," muttered my grandmother, and to be honest I was thinking the same thing: good lord, the crazy gene of the Lennoxes strikes again. This time Alexis seemed to be the one feeling its effects.

The library in question was not located at Lennox House—or in a house at all, in fact. When Mr. Stevens (who, to judge by the glossiness of his hair, had applied an extra helping of pomade today as a precaution against further assaults by clumsy houseguests) had led me out onto the moor, I'd thought at first that he was taking me to the castle on the other side of the island, which my grandmother had told me was home to a family named Macalister. But in the end he'd stopped at the bottom of a sort of hill. At the top of the hill were a number of enormous stone slabs piled one on top of the other. They formed a circle made up of several gateways, similar to Stonehenge, and their porous gray bodies were covered with moss and lichens. Mr. Stevens pointed not to the ancient monument, however, but to the mouth of a cave at the foot of the hill.

"Here it is," he said, lifting a flaming torch from a bracket set

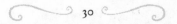

into the rock. "We are now entering the *Secret Library*, ma'am," he declared solemnly.

"O . . . kay?" I said skeptically, but Mr. Stevens's stern face brooked no dissent. Plus, I liked being addressed as ma'am.

At first the stone passageway led uphill for a few yards, but it ended abruptly at the center of the hill and gave way to a flight of steps carved into the rock, leading deeper and deeper underground. I ran my fingertips along the rough walls as I followed Mr. Stevens into the darkness.

The steps were steep.

And there were lots of them.

We went down and down, step by step by step, for what felt like an eternity. The library was not inside the hill where the stone circle was, as I'd assumed. It was *underneath* it. Deep, deep underground. We must have been right down inside the bowels of the island by now, maybe even below sea level. From far away I thought I could hear the booming of the waves. Whose idea had it been to build a library in a place like this?

The flight of steps ended as suddenly as it had begun and I was met by the smell of old paper. This was where the bookshelves began. They were made of dark wood and were around ten feet tall. There were narrow ladders at regular intervals that could be slid from side to side. The shelves groaned under the weight of folios and leather-bound books, and in among them I could also make out paperbacks and yellowed scrolls. Aisles branched off everywhere from the rows of shelves. Lady Mairead had been right: this library was both enormous and ancient.

It was full of whispered words, the lure of stories waiting to be

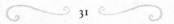

read, a rustle of promise that hung in the air. How many adventures were hidden here in paper and ink, how many great love stories, how many epic battles? I'd fallen in love with the place already. I would have liked to just stand there stroking the books, maybe taking one of them in my hands and leafing through it, perusing the deeds of some tragic hero. My steps began to slow, but Mr. Stevens led me inexorably onward into the heart of the library with its labyrinth of aisles.

Despite the many lamps that glowed between the shelves, it was too dark to make out the full extent of the cave system. And the aisles became more and more tightly interwoven the farther we went. But at last the walls of books opened out onto a space that looked a bit like a classroom. A rather old-fashioned classroom, to be sure, containing worm-eaten wooden desks with lids you could lift up to store books in the compartment beneath. But, yes, it was definitely a classroom, and what worried me most of all was that it wasn't empty.

In the front row sat a boy and a girl of my own age, and at the blackboard stood a bald man in a monk's habit. An invisible fist gripped my stomach and squeezed hard. I had to force my feet to keep walking.

"Good morning, Glenn. I have brought you Amy Lennox. The Lady would like her granddaughter to attend lessons. Had you been informed?" asked Mr. Stevens, and the man at the board nodded. "Ah yes, thank you. We've been waiting for you."

Lessons? The word set off alarm bells in my head. So this really was a school. And I was the new girl. And in the summer holidays too. Fan-fricking-tastic. There was a bitter taste in my mouth.

Stormsay was supposed to help take my mind off school, not . . . the girl in the front row had blond hair just like Jolina's. I swallowed hard.

The teacher beckoned me over to him. His eyebrows were so bushy it was almost as if they were trying to compensate for the lack of hair on his head. On his forehead was a jagged mesh of raised scars that stretched across his bald pate like a spider's web. He wore a patch over his left eye. He pretended not to see the dismayed expression on my face, and shook my hand. "My name is Glenn, and I've been teaching members of the Lennox and Macalister families for many years. It's good to have a Lennox among us once more." He gestured toward his two students. "These are Betsy and William Macalister, the Laird's daughter and nephew. This is Amy Lennox, the Lady's granddaughter."

"Hi," I mumbled.

"Hello." The girl was wearing a satin headband in her perfectly shiny blond hair; her eyelashes were long and thick with black mascara. She looked me up and down. The boy, however, merely nodded and smiled briefly and went on writing in his exercise book. He had dark hair that stuck out in all directions, as if he'd spent the night outdoors in the thick of the storm.

Leaving them both to underline something in a Shakespeare sonnet, Glenn and I withdrew to one of the bookshelves in the far corner of the classroom. At last I was able to get a closer look at some of the books. My gaze ran along the leather spines, embossed with gold lettering. There was *Alice in Wonderland* alongside *Ronia, the Robber's Daughter*; *The Wizard of Oz*; and *The Neverending Story*, and a red leather-bound book, which turned out to be *The Jungle Book*.

"Your two clans have been reading books since time immemorial, but they read in a different way from other people," Glenn began. "In your families, ever since ancient times, a special gift has been passed down from generation to generation. That is why they share this library."

"Uh-huh," I said, and Glenn sighed.

"Yes—I know you have no idea what I'm talking about. The Lady tells me your mother kept all of this a secret from you. So it's probably best that I show you what I mean. And I shall do so directly; but first, there is one thing you should know. The Macalisters and the Lennoxes have not always lived so peacefully together on this island. Once upon a time they were locked in a bloody feud that lasted from the Middle Ages until about three hundred years ago, when the hostility reached its peak. Their strife led to a fire, and one of the things destroyed in that fire was a particularly valuable manuscript. It was the only written record of a legend that is now lost forever. Ever since then, the families have observed a truce and devoted themselves to protecting literature and preserving the books you see here. That is why we built the library so deep underground and why we tell nobody of its existence unless they belong to one of the two families, or have earned their trust. Everything we do, and everything you will do from now on, must be done for the good of the world of stories. You must make that promise before we begin, because . . ."

The red leather binding of *The Jungle Book* shone out at me enticingly. *Read me!* it cried. *Read me!*

"Amy?"

My hand was drifting toward the books. At the last moment I

managed to stop myself from reaching out and grabbing one. I withdrew my arm abruptly, pretending I needed to scratch my cheek, and shifted my weight awkwardly from one foot to the other. As I did so, however, I managed to bump into one of the ladders propped up against the shelves, and it toppled over and fell to the ground with a deafening crash. My face turned red, and a derisive snort could be heard from the direction of the desks.

Glenn's lips twitched as if suppressing a smile, but a moment later he met my eye with the same stern friendliness as before.

He cleared his throat and continued as if nothing had happened. "Well, Amy?"

"Y-yes?"

"Do you vow that whenever you read you will strive to protect stories and to do nothing that might destroy or alter them?"

"Um—of course," I said. How on earth was someone supposed to destroy a story just by reading it anyway?

"Good," said Glenn. "Your mother wants you to choose one of these books here. Have you seen anything you might like to try?"

Half an hour later, Glenn, Betsy, William, and I entered the stone circle at the top of the hill. *The Jungle Book* lay red, smooth, and heavy in my hands. Naturally I'd slipped on the wet grass climbing the hill, but I'd just about managed to keep the book from falling into the mud. The knees of my jeans, on the other hand, now sported a pair of greenish-brown stains, and I felt clumsier still in comparison to Betsy—who went trotting elegantly up the hill—and William, who tagged along at the back of our little group as if he were just out for a casual stroll. I wondered why exactly we had to come out here to read, when the wind had turned so cold again. Betsy and William were carrying books under their arms, too, and Glenn had brought along a moldy-looking woven beach mat that he spread out in the mud beneath one of the gateways in the stone circle. "Will, would you go first?" he asked.

"Sure," said the boy. His voice was deeper than I'd expected, his eyes the color of the sky above us. Stormy blue. He was also tall and thin, like me, but his body looked muscular, as if he was strong despite his skinniness. He strode purposefully over to the mat and lay down on it so that his head was positioned directly beneath the stone arch. Then he opened his book and laid it over his face. On the cover I could see a picture of an enormous dog. *The Hound of the Baskervilles* was the title: it was a Sherlock Holmes novel. I knew the story—I'd been given it for Christmas four years ago. But the dog on the front of my book wasn't quite as scary as this one. As I looked at the cover, the book suddenly dropped through the air and landed on the mat. The pages glowed for a moment.

I blinked. No—it couldn't be! I blinked again, unable to grasp what I was seeing. But it was true: Will had vanished. Only the book remained in the stone circle. "What?" I exclaimed.

"These stones form the *Porta Litterae*," Glenn explained. "They are the entrance to the world of stories."

"But . . ." I still couldn't get my head around the fact that Will seemed to have disappeared into thin air from one moment to the next.

"He's inside his book now," said Betsy, with a condescending smile. "No need to panic—it's totally normal for us."

I opened my mouth and then shut it again because I didn't know how to reply. Glenn placed a hand on my arm. "I know it is hard to believe. But this is the special gift possessed by your two families. Between your fifth and twenty-fifth birthdays you have the ability to jump inside literature and check that everything is in order. Each of you takes special responsibility for one book in particular until the time you finish school. After that you use your skills to protect the whole of the literary world. Betsy, for example, has been looking after this book of fairy tales since her tenth birthday. She is about to jump into *Snow White and the Seven Dwarfs*."

Betsy swept her bangs out of her eyes. "One of the dwarfs is causing trouble—he's taken it into his head to go off on his own and open an ice-cream parlor. I've been trying for weeks to make him see sense. *Snow White and the Six Dwarfs* just sounds ridiculous."

"Um . . ." Was this a joke?

Betsy settled herself serenely on the mat and opened her book. "Well, here we go again," she said. "Don't worry, Amy. You might not even be able to do it. No book jumper in history has ever left it till your age to start training. It's probably too late by now."

"Well—we'll see soon enough, won't we, Amy?" said Glenn, smiling at me encouragingly.

Betsy shrugged and laid the open book of fairy tales across her face. In a heartbeat, she too had disappeared. All that was left was the rustling of the pages as they landed on the mat. My mouth went dry.

"Book jumpers?" I breathed. "Did they really jump *into* the books?" It sounded too absurd. It couldn't be true.

"Yes," said Glenn. "And now it's your turn. Simply open the book at the page where you want to jump in, and do as the others did."

"I don't know," I said. Was this some kind of stupid prank? An initiation ritual? Were Will and Betsy actually lying in the bushes with their camera phones, waiting to film me making a fool of myself?

Glenn interpreted my hesitation differently. "You can do it, I'm certain of it. I think Betsy is mistaken. After all, you are a Lennox. And you can come back straightaway if you're frightened—all you need to do is return to the page you jumped in at."

"But how . . . And for how long? And what should I . . ." I stammered helplessly. This was crazy! People couldn't just vanish from one moment to the next and reappear as a book character!

"I can't explain it either, Amy," sighed Glenn as I remained rooted to the spot. "But your families have been doing it for centuries—it just works, somehow. And nobody has ever failed to come back before," he added with a smile. "You really have no need to be afraid; your mother has even made sure your first jump is into a story which is absolutely safe. Give it a try, have a little look around and come back to the point where you started once you've had enough. Then we'll see what you think of it."

I looked first at the mat under the arch and then back at Glenn, scanning his good eye for evidence that he was lying. But I found none. Was he really serious about this whole thing? Did the members of my family really have a special gift? Did I have it, too—the ability to jump inside literature? The idea was ridiculous and at the same time . . . tantalizing. Until now I'd only ever visited the world of stories, that world that held such fascination for me, in my imagination. But if there was a way of entering it for real . . . I ran my fingers over the soft red leather in my hands and the delicate depressions formed by the imprint of the title. *The Jungle Book*. I'd never been in a jungle before. Especially not one that was home to Baloo the bear. A smile stole across my face.

Glenn nodded. "Just give it a try." He pointed to the mat.

I lay down on it as I'd seen the others do, with my head directly below the stone arch. I could hardly believe I was actually doing this. It was utterly insane, and I caught myself giggling nervously. But I opened the book and laid it across my face. The paper slid smoothly over my cheeks and along the bridge of my nose until it covered my eyes. The letters were far too close up to read. They swam before my eyes, melting into an inky whirlpool. They swirled around one another; they changed shape. Words flexed and twisted apart to form bushes and foliage. And then they came pattering down like rain-drops: a shower of words raining down on me.

In the space of a heartbeat, I found myself lying among the roots of a gigantic jungle tree. Around me was an explosion of greens of every shade imaginable. Vines snaked around tree trunks and ferns sprouted between them. The air was warm and humid and filled with the sweet fragrance of exotic flowers. Somewhere close by I heard a child laughing.

I sat up, flicked an oversized ant off my knee, and began to creep through the bushes in the direction of the voices. The vegetation was thick, but I'd only gone a few yards when, through the curtain of ferns, I spied a group of wolves. The group consisted of two adult wolves with silver-gray fur, talking quietly to each other, and a whole heap of cubs at their feet, frolicking happily with a naked human child who couldn't have been older than two. Mowgli!

This was the beginning of *The Jungle Book*! The wolf family had just found Mowgli alone in the jungle and decided to bring him up as one of their own—and I was right in the middle of it! I felt dizzy. I'd never read the book, but I knew the Disney version of the story. It had been one of my favorite films as a child. Was Bagheera the panther about to show up? Or Baloo the bear? Would he sing a song, like in the film? Would he take me to the monkeys' lost city? Would I be able to understand the language of the animals and speak to them? Oh, man—I had really and truly jumped into a book! My thoughts tripped over one another as I crawled closer and closer to Mowgli and the wolf family. Unlike the Disney Mowgli, this Mowgli had curly hair and was not wearing red trunks.

But just as I was about to burst from the undergrowth and greet the wolves with a friendly "Hi, how's it going?" I suddenly felt something settle upon my back. I froze; the something was soft and warm and heavy and felt suspiciously like a paw of some kind. Slowly, very slowly, I turned around . . .

. . . and found myself face-to-face with a predator. It was Shere Khan, the tiger. His yellow cat's eyes blazed and all of a sudden I remembered that the main storyline in *The Jungle Book* was about this very tiger trying to hunt Mowgli down and eat him. Because he was afraid of men and their guns. And because he was a tiger, and in the wild tigers do have a tendency to eat humans.

Shere Khan bared his teeth. The stink of his breath hit me square in the face. Now I understood why Alexis had insisted on me jumping into a harmless children's book. Unfortunately, however, even those didn't seem to be entirely risk-free. If I called for help, would the wolves be able to save me? I drew a deep breath, but before I could make a sound the tiger put a claw to his lips.

Put a claw to his lips?

"You must not interfere with the plot, Reader," whispered Shere Khan. "If they see you, they will not keep the man's cub. Then you will be lumbered with the brat, and our entire story will fall apart."

I stared at the tiger. He could talk. "Herghm," I said.

The tiger cocked his enormous head to one side. "Not so loud," he murmured. "I just told you. Come with me."

The big cat moved off, and after a moment's hesitation I followed him into the jungle thicket. What was the likelihood that Shere Khan was only luring me away from the tumbling wolf cubs so he could devour me in peace somewhere else in the forest? Was it even possible for me to die inside the story or, as a visitor from the outside world, was I invincible? Powerful bands of muscle rippled beneath the tiger's striped coat as he prowled noiselessly onward. I, on the other hand, kept treading on snapping branches and rustling leaves, a far cry from the graceful elegance of my companion. If he really was planning to attack me, I didn't stand a chance.

But with every step I took, my fear dissipated a little beneath the jungle canopy. I was reassured by the thought that Shere Khan could have killed me by now if he'd wanted to, but he hadn't. And somehow I just couldn't imagine being eaten by someone I'd been having a conversation with a few minutes earlier.

The tiger led me to a clearing where there was a fallen tree lying on the ground, and I sat down on it. Shere Khan lay down beside me, head on his paws. His tail whisked to and fro among the ferns.

"I am Shere Khan," he said.

"Amy," I replied. "I'm sorry. I've never been in a book before and I didn't know . . ."

"It's all right," returned the tiger. "I would say it's the law of the jungle, but it's the same everywhere in the book world: Readers are not allowed to intervene. Under no circumstances. You must always stay in the margins, between the lines."

"Kind of like—in the subplot?"

Shere Khan nodded.

"Okay," I said, and a fresh wave of excitement washed over me now that I was fairly sure the tiger wasn't going to hurt me. "What should I do, then? I'm very pleased to meet you, by the way. Do you know where I might find Baloo and Bagheera? Which way is the monkey city? Are you really so terrified of fire?"

The tiger sighed and stood up. "You had better ask someone in the outside world. In a few pages they are going to take Mowgli to the Pack Council. Then I will have to sit in the thicket and demand that they hand him over to me," he explained. "This is the way back to the plot and to the tree that will take you home again." Even as he spoke the last few words he had disappeared into the tangle of the undergrowth.

I stayed seated on my tree trunk for a moment. Should I go after Shere Khan and return to Stormsay? Or . . .

As if of their own accord, my feet carried me off in the opposite direction. This trip was far too exciting to turn back now. I'd spoken to Shere Khan the tiger. The whole thing was unbelievable. Unbelievably awesome! Perhaps one of these days I really would have Momo's tortoise Cassiopeia as my guide, I thought, as I made my way deeper and deeper into the jungle. There were so many stories I would have liked to jump into and so many characters I was desperate to meet. But coming face-to-face with a dancing Baloo in the monkey city would do for starters.

There were no footpaths in the jungle, of course, so I clambered over tree roots and boulders and battled my way through ferns and vines until the vegetation gradually began to thin out. But the trees gave way not to a lost city or an indigenous village, as I'd expected, but to a different landscape altogether.

All at once the air was drier and cooler. A sandy road wound its way through fields and meadows. In the distance I could see a windmill and a knight galloping toward it, lance lowered. Before me lay a crossroads with a towering signpost at its center. *The Jungle Book* was written in ornate, squiggly letters on one arrow, pointing in the direction I'd just come from; another pointed to *Shakespeare's tragedies*. Other roads branched off to *Don Quixote*, *Alice in Wonderland*, and *The Strange Case of Dr. Jekyll and Mr. Hyde*.

Wow! It looked as though I'd reached the edge of *The Jungle Book* and could now decide which story I wanted to travel to next. I'd just resolved to pay a visit to the murderer with a split personality, Dr. Jekyll/Mr. Hyde, when I spotted another arrow. It was smaller than the rest, and somebody had written a single word on it in a spidery hand as if it had been painted on in a great hurry: *Margin*. I'd never heard that title before. Seriously, since when had there been a book called *Margin*?

The sign pointed to what could scarcely be called a road: it was more of a dirt track flanked by craggy rocks. It was littered with rubble, but hey—I had just successfully navigated a jungle thicket, after all, and I was also exceedingly curious. Without further ado I set off along the track, the strange title going round and round in my head. I made surprisingly good progress. Normally I would've been bound to stub my toe or fall over or trip on a loose stone. But this literary rubble seemed to be on my side.

The rocks on either side of me loomed higher and higher until they formed a ravine, which I was now walking along the bottom of. The sand crunched under my feet and my footsteps echoed off the walls. After a while I thought I heard voices in the distance. Was I getting close to the next story? How long had I been walking? Was it only five minutes ago that I'd been talking to Shere Khan, or an hour?

Eventually I reached a bend in the path. As I turned the corner I saw a man sitting on the ground—though it took me a while to establish that he *was* a man, because he was wearing silk stockings and heeled shoes and had his hair tied back in a ponytail with a velvet ribbon. He'd buried his face in his knees and flung his arms over his head in an attempt to protect himself from three old women who were flying through the air around him, hooded cloaks flapping. They were scratching at his arms with their long fingernails.

"Hail to thee, young Werther," screeched one.

"Thou shalt find happiness with Lotte," called the second.

"Thou shalt wed her by and by," shrieked the third.

The man curled up into an even tighter ball and his shoulders quaked beneath his embroidered waistcoat. A sob could be heard amid the jeers of the old women flitting around Werther's head. "Go away," he pleaded, a choke in his voice.

But this had no effect whatsoever on his tormentors. "Hail to thee," repeated the first, flying closer to the man. Her voice rang out across the ravine and made the crags tremble. Here and there, showers of dust and stones cascaded down the rock face. Her victim made himself even smaller, not even attempting to fight back.

"Hail to thee, young bridegr—" began the first.

I was so fixated on the scene that I forgot to look where I was going, and caught my foot on one of the larger rocks. I almost fell headlong into the midst of the whimpering man and his tormentors but managed to steady myself just in time. The old women immediately fell silent and turned their watery eyes upon me. Their hair snaked out from beneath their ragged cloaks as if it had a life of its own.

I cleared my throat, gurgled something that sounded vaguely like "Hello," and swallowed hard. The three old women hissed menacingly, and the man sobbed. Now that their attention was turned on me I felt somehow obliged to try to help the poor wretch at the roadside. "C-can't you see he's upset? Just leave him alone."

The old women grinned.

"Thou art brave," rasped the second.

"Thou art a Reader," snarled the first.

"Yes," I said, squaring my shoulders. "And who are you?"

They laughed.

"Thou wouldst know who we are?" screeched the third. "Come, sisters, 'tis time for our potion."

They were still laughing as they spiraled up into the air and flew away.

The man squinted out from between his elbows. "Thank you," he mumbled.

"You're welcome. I hope I haven't messed up the plot," I said, remembering that I had only recently been warned by a massive tiger not to interfere with the progress of any stories. I bit my lip.

But the man waved aside my anxieties. "No, no—this is no-man's-land. I was on my way to the Margin when you found me. To all intents and purposes they are harmless outside of their own play. But they take pleasure, you see, in reminding me of my sorrows."

"Why?"

"Oh, because I am easy prey, I suppose." The man clambered effortfully to his feet, brushed the dust from his silk stockings, and pulled out an embroidered handkerchief. He blew his nose and gazed at me from under his long eyelashes. "Forgive me, but would you happen to be Miss Amy?"

"Er—yes. How do you know my name?"

"Half the fairy-tale forest is looking for you, truth be told. They say your friends in the outside world are afraid you might not have survived your jump."

"Oh." I tucked my hair behind my ears. "I'd better set them straight, then."

Soon afterward, when I jumped back to Stormsay from the giant jungle tree and landed in the stone circle, the first thing I saw was the anxious faces of Betsy and Glenn. Will stood apart from the others on the brow of the hill. He was strikingly pale and his hands gripped *The Hound of the Baskervilles* so tightly that the veins showed blue under his skin. He was staring off into the distance and didn't even seem to register my arrival.

But the other two came rushing over to me straightaway.

"At last," Glenn exclaimed. "Did you get stuck? Are you hurt?" His eyes examined me from head to toe.

"Um, no, I—"

"It's too late, simple as that," Betsy broke in. "She's too old to start training. A Macalister might be able to do it, but a Lennox . . ."

"Betsy," admonished Glenn, but Betsy was undeterred.

"It doesn't do anyone any good to have her stuck at her jumping point for hours, not even able to move. How is she ever going to learn how to speak to the characters? She should just stay here till the holidays are over and then go back to Germany. You can't force these things."

"Um—actually, I didn't get *stuck*," I said, picking my book up off the mat. "First of all I talked to Shere Khan the tiger. Then he had to go back to the plot, so I went on by myself and eventually I got to the end of the jungle and I found a signpost and—"

"You left *The Jungle Book*?" cried Glenn.

"Students aren't allowed to do that." Betsy wrinkled her nose. In her eyes was a flicker of something I'd seen before on the faces of my classmates in Germany. Jealousy. But she did her best to hide it.

Glenn folded his arms. "Well, you do seem to be very talented. But I have to agree with Betsy in this instance: it is still far too soon, and far too dangerous, for you to explore the book world outside of your practice book."

Betsy nodded vigorously, and now at last Will did look over at us—and eyed me with interest.

The monster crept out of its cave.
Softly, softly.
Nobody noticed it.

CHEWING GUM FOR
OLIVER TWIST

THE COTTAGE ON THE MOOR WAS SMALL. It consisted of a single room, just big enough to hold the sofa with its holey cushions and the cast-iron stove. The thatched roof reached almost to the ground; mold had set in among the stalks and let the rain in the moment it came knocking. In a storm the wind whistled through the cracked windowpanes. But in spite of all this Will liked his home.

Of course, it wasn't really his home—Will was after all the nephew of Reed Macalister, Laird of Stormsay, whose ancestral home was Macalister Castle in the north of the island. But the castle was scarcely less drafty than the cottage and when Betsy and her old nanny launched into one of their frequent tirades about Will's father and what a failure he was, what a disappointment to the clan, Will vastly preferred the bubble and gurgle of his own little stove to the griping by the fire in the great hall of the castle. Not to mention the presence of the Laird, whom he went out of his way to avoid.

Some time ago Will had transported all of his treasures from the castle to the cottage. He now kept his favorite books in a chest sandwiched between the sofa and the wall, along with the album full of photos from his past. His memories were hazy; they felt like the fading fragments of a dream. He'd been five years old when his parents had left. That was twelve years ago now.

But today Will had no desire to recall the distant past. He just wished he could remember more of the details of the previous day. Because yesterday something had happened—possibly even something terrible.

His gaze was riveted to something that had been daubed on the wall above the stove. The color bloomed red, far too red, against the plaster. A few drops had trickled down the wall like tears not wiped away in time. But this liquid wasn't water. Will didn't want to think what it was.

It formed words on the wall, the letters turning brown at the edges.

I HAVE AWOKEN

It had appeared suddenly yesterday afternoon. Will had dozed off on the sofa and when he'd woken up from his nap, there it had been. Was it supposed to be a warning? A threat? Who had painted the words on the wall? Had they already been there before he'd fallen asleep? What did they mean?

Will had run to the stone circle to fetch his best friend.

Holmes.

It was forbidden, but it wasn't the first time he'd done it.

And Holmes seemed to have a hunch. He had stared long and hard at the writing, and at last he'd murmured, "It wasn't Moriarty." Then he'd gone out into the storm, perhaps to organize his thoughts. Will hadn't seen him since. He and the dog had searched for Holmes all evening before eventually giving up. They'd hoped Holmes had gone home to play his violin or experiment with anesthetics or engage in another of his favorite pastimes.

But today during lessons when he'd jumped inside the book, Will had found it empty. He still couldn't believe Holmes hadn't returned to the book world. But the great detective did seem to have vanished into thin air.

And now Will sat here alone, staring at the wall.

"Do help yourself to another, Amy," said Lady Mairead, sliding the plate of biscuits closer to me. "They are a little old, but if you dunk them in your tea they taste almost freshly baked."

We both knew she was lying. The biscuits between us were massive—not dainty little cookies like the ones we had in Germany, but dry, inch-thick slabs as big as the palm of my hand. I took a second biscuit, even though the first was already lying like a stone in my stomach and weighing it down. Ever since my journey into *The Jungle Book*, Lady Mairead had been remarkably kind to me, and I was far too polite to spurn her biscuits. A cloud of dusty crumbs filled my mouth as I took a bite.

My grandmother smiled contentedly and leaned back in her chair. We were having afternoon tea in the conservatory where we'd eaten breakfast. A tabby cat named Macbeth had curled up on Lady Mairead's lap and was purring loudly. "We don't get to the shops as often as we used to, unfortunately," my grandmother explained, tickling Macbeth behind the ears. "But the main thing is just to get some proper food into you. Your mother's fruit and vegetable diet doesn't seem to agree with you." She glanced at my wrists.

I was about to reply that my figure was not due to my mum's vegan cooking but to a cruel freak of nature, when I found that the dust-biscuit had cemented my tongue to the roof of my mouth and was now threatening to block my windpipe as I attempted to swallow it. I eventually managed to wash the thing down with the help of two cups of tea. Then I had a coughing fit that lasted a full minute.

Lady Mairead, meanwhile, was chatting away again about the Secret Library. As I'd discovered on the way back to the classroom, Glenn had two colleagues at the library named Desmond and Clyde, whose job it was to maintain order among the chaos of the books. They, too, wore monk's habits and had scars on their faces. Clyde cataloged the library's holdings and Desmond was a bookbinder and only a few years older than me. Twenty at most, I reckoned.

"Ah, those were the days. When I was young, I jumped into hundreds of stories." Lady Mairead smiled to herself. "Our gift is very precious, Amy. Make the most of it while you can."

"Was it an accident?" I asked once I was able to speak again.

Lady Mairead raised her eyebrows. "What?"

"The librarians—Glenn's eye and their injuries, I mean."

She looked down at her teacup. "Ah, yes. Yes, it was." Macbeth raised his head and stared at me.

My grandmother seemed to have no intention of revealing anything more, so out of politeness I took another bite of my biscuit. The volume of biscuit in my mouth seemed to increase the more I chewed, and I felt another choking fit coming on. I was such an idiot! My jaws worked overtime.

As if sensing that I was in urgent need of a refill to wash down the biscuit crumbs, Mr. Stevens entered with a pot of freshly brewed tea. The cat settled back into Lady Mairead's lap.

As I'd made my way from the stone circle back to Lennox House, I'd been in a euphoric mood. I couldn't wait to tell Alexis about the experience I'd had. My feet seemed to fly across the moor. As I arrived at the mansion I ran into Alexis in the entrance hall, muffled up in her coat and scarf. The words came tumbling out of me. "I was inside *The Jungle Book*. I spoke to Shere Khan—"

"I'm going for a walk, Amy," she'd interrupted, stemming my torrent of words. "Let's talk about it later." The next thing I knew she'd disappeared outside. I'd been waiting for her to return ever since.

As Mr. Stevens poured the tea, I glanced at my watch. Alexis had been gone nearly three hours now. The island wasn't *that* big. Perhaps she was doing more than one lap?

"It's not easy for your mother to come to terms with you jumping," said Lady Mairead, noticing the glance.

I shrugged. "She agreed to come here. And anyway, I don't understand why she's so against it. I think the whole thing is absolutely brilliant." Again and again I thought back to my encounters with the tiger, the young man and the three old women, who I now supposed must have been witches. I'd been to a new world. A better world, one where dreams came true. And I was annoyed that I couldn't tell my closest confidante about it. When Lady Mairead had tried to question me soon after I'd arrived back at the mansion, I'd simply shrugged. Despite my mum giving me the cold shoulder earlier, I still wanted her to be the first to hear about my experiences in the book world.

My grandmother stirred a dash of milk into her tea. "I think that for many years Alexis was in denial about the fact that you might have the gift, too—until she almost came to believe her own self-deception. She is afraid of what might happen to you in the book world."

"Why?"

"Well—her own experiences as a book jumper were not entirely positive," said my grandmother quietly, as if she didn't want anyone else to hear.

"Really?" I leaned forward.

"Do you know the novel *Anna Karenina*?"

"Sort of," I said. "I haven't read it. But I know it's about a woman who jumps in front of a train at the end."

Lady Mairead nodded. "Alexis chose the story as a practice book and—"

At that moment, Alexis entered the conservatory and Lady Mairead fell silent.

"I just wanted to let you know I'm back, and I'm going to go and have a lie-down. I think I've got a migraine coming on," said Alexis. And off she went again.

But I wasn't going to let her get away so easily this time. I stuffed the remainder of the second biscuit into my pocket "for later" and hurried out into the hallway after Alexis.

She was already one and a half flights of stairs ahead of me. When

I caught up I found her leaning against a window with her forehead pressed to the glass, looking out across the moor.

"Is everything okay?" I asked. My irritation at her disappearance suddenly evaporated, to be replaced by concern.

Alexis jumped as if I'd caught her doing something she wasn't supposed to be. "Oh, er—Amy," she stammered. "Yes—I've just got a headache."

I moved a step closer to her. She did look pale, and there were dark circles under her eyes that I hadn't noticed that morning, perhaps because they'd been hidden under a layer of makeup. Her arms hung down limply at her sides. Even her colorful knitted dress looked as though somebody had covered it with a gray veil. She wasn't okay. Of course she wasn't. How could I have forgotten that?

It was only three days since Dominik had left her. Her world had fallen apart, just like mine had that Wednesday afternoon when Jolina had posted the photos online. And the fact that I'd spent a few hours in a dream didn't change that.

I put an arm around Alexis's shoulders. "Let's forget about all that," I said. "That's why we came here. Stormsay is going to help us forget."

Alexis said nothing.

I dreamed about the naked photos again that night. This time, however, they weren't being sent from phone to phone but were printed on a poster on the wall of the Secret Library. Instead of Jolina and Paul and the rest of my class, it was Betsy, Will, and Glenn looking at the pictures. Will was snorting with laughter, while Betsy and Glenn argued.

"She can't really look like that. The photos must have been doctored," said Glenn. "No normal human being looks like that."

"Rubbish. I took the photos myself in the locker room. She's a Lennox, what do you expect?" retorted Betsy. "Just look at her sticky-out ribs. I told you, she'll never be a book jumper. She's nothing more than a dry twig."

Will's laughter grew louder now, and even Glenn began to grin.

"If you ask me we should just throw her on the compost heap," added Betsy, pointing to a miniature rubbish pile that had suddenly sprung up in the corner of the classroom.

"Yes," said Glenn, ripping the poster off the wall. As he did so I realized that I wasn't standing behind the other three, as I'd thought, but inside the pictures. I seemed to be trapped inside them.

"We shall have to tell the Lady that Amy is not worth training," Glenn continued. He tore the paper into tiny pieces, and me with it. First he ripped my face in half, then my body, my hands, my fingers. I screamed, but nobody could hear me. The poster disintegrated into smaller and smaller scraps; my arms and legs turned to confetti. My head was shredded. All that was left of me ended up on the stinking heap of muck.

I was woken by my own scream.

The sheets were drenched with sweat and clung to my body. Panting, I stared into the darkness of the canopy above my head. It wasn't real. Nobody on the island except Alexis and me knew about the photos. My subconscious had been playing tricks on me again, and it had all been just a stupid nightmare. I'd had a lot of those recently.

But it still took a while for my breathing to slow. I didn't dare

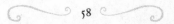

close my eyes. Who knew what crazy dream I would have next? Instead, I fumbled for my e-reader and switched it on. The screen lit up, bathing my face in its comforting glow.

I scrolled through the library and came across a book I had out on loan from the public library back in Germany: *Oliver Twist*, by Charles Dickens. I'd almost finished it, but now I went back to the beginning and skimmed through a few sentences about Oliver's life in the workhouse without really taking them in. I knew now, after all, that reading wasn't the only way to get inside a story. There was another way—a much more exciting way. What would it be like to jump into Oliver Twist's story? To join him on all his adventures in Victorian London—the journey to the big city, the time spent in the clutches of the band of thieves? I'd never been to London before.

I laid the e-reader carefully over my face. This was no easy task, since there was no fold down the middle and only one page, which I had to balance on my nose and forehead. I pictured the scene from that afternoon, the way I'd jumped from the stone circle into the book world, the way the letters had slowly started to warp before my eyes. I remembered how the blackness of the words had expanded and contracted, how the sentences had swirled and merged. The memory was so vivid that the lines of text on the screen in front of me suddenly seemed to be moving too.

At first the lines grew longer and longer, and then the letters began to trickle across the screen and melt into one another. The gray shades of the text gave way to brown. It was the brown of a table made of coarse wood.

Suddenly I was sitting underneath this table, wedged in among a gaggle of thin boys' legs in heavily patched trousers. I ran my fingertips across the dirty floorboards in disbelief. I could smell sweat and unwashed bodies.

"I'm still so hungry," came a voice from somewhere above my head.

"Course you are—we all are. Who could ever be full after three spoonfuls of gruel?" declared another.

"If it goes on like this, I shan't be able to guarantee anything—I may end up eating one of you tonight in your sleep," said a third. "That's it—I'm going to ask for a second helping."

"You wouldn't dare."

"No. But one of us must, else we'll waste away and die."

"Yes."

"Before we all croak."

"We'd best draw lots."

There was no longer any doubt in my mind: this must be Oliver Twist's workhouse! I crawled through the forest of legs until I found a spot where I could wriggle up onto one of the long benches. By now the boys were busy drawing matchsticks, and didn't notice me. I was shocked to see how gaunt their faces were. They looked almost ageless—not like children, at any rate. The skin was stretched tight over their cheekbones, and most had greasy hair that hung raggedly down over their foreheads and into their eyes. They all had empty bowls.

This row of tables was not the only one in the room: there were three other rows full of scrawny children. And not a single one of them was eating, even though a grubby man stood in the corner stirring an even grubbier pot from which I could clearly see steam rising.

"Oliver Twist," murmured the boys around me. "Oliver must ask."

A small, watchful-eyed boy gulped nervously. His fingers were almost as thin as the broken match they held.

"Go on, Oliver!" prompted a buck-toothed boy not much older than him. "We'll starve to death on the spot if you don't."

But the little boy hesitated. There was fear in his eyes. Trembling, he rose slowly from the bench.

I looked over at the grubby pot and the man standing behind it. His fierce expression would have put me off too. Why didn't he just give the boy a bit more of the sticky grayish gruel he was slopping round and round in the pot? It would probably only end up having to be turned into dust-biscuits tomorrow anyway (Lady Mairead's favorite).

Oliver swung his leg over the bench, then shrank back as the cook glanced in our direction. Fortunately, he didn't see me.

"Wait," I said—I'd had an idea. "If you're that hungry, I might . . . I might be able to help."

Thirty heads turned to look at me. Oliver Twist gazed at me hopefully.

"She's a Reader," somebody whispered.

"A Reader," came the echo from farther down the table. "From the outside world."

"What does that matter? As long as she's got some grub for us!"

"Just a second," I murmured. "Wait here, okay?" I dived back under the table and crawled back to the spot I'd arrived at. The next moment I found myself back in my four-poster bed on Stormsay. The thought that I'd just jumped from my bedroom into a book exploded in my head like a firework. I'd done it—I'd gone to visit Oliver Twist in the middle of the night! I—

No: I'd have plenty of time to celebrate later. Right now I had to help the half-starved boys in the workhouse. On my bedside table I found the plate of biscuits Lady Mairead had sent up that evening. (She was evidently very keen to get rid of them. Well, that wouldn't be a problem now!) I dropped the biscuits into my pajama pockets, then quickly fished a packet of chewing gum out of my backpack. A moment later the e-reader was balanced on my face once more.

I jumped back under the table and tugged at one of the boys' trouser legs.

Oliver Twist ducked his head under the table.

"Here," I said, pressing the biscuits and the chewing gum into his hand. "That's all I can rustle up for the moment. These are biscuits and this is chewing gum. You can munch on them till you get something else to eat. But don't swallow the chewing gum. I hope it helps a bit."

"Thank you," he mumbled.

Above my head, boys quickly set to sharing the food out equally between them.

I heard somebody say: "But tomorrow Oliver will have to ask, if they keep giving us such tiny portions."

And then I found myself back in my bed in the twenty-first century.

"I choose you," said the princess. "Kneel."

The knight did as he was bid.

"Do you swear that you will hunt and kill the monster
and that you will not rest until I, your princess,
am safe once more? Do you swear it upon your life?"

The knight looked up at the princess's face,
her dainty nose, the arch of her eyebrows, her rosy cheeks.
Her beauty was flawless. He would be happy, he thought,
to look upon this face and nothing else until the day he died.

It was like looking into the eyes of an angel.

No harm must ever come to this angel.

"I swear it upon my life," he said.

BETWEEN THE LINES

THE NEXT MORNING'S LESSON began disappointingly. I'd hoped to be able to jump straight back into *The Jungle Book*. Instead, Glenn gave us a two-hour lecture about the book world. He talked about our duty as book jumpers to protect literature—a duty that was both an honor and a burden. He told us it was possible, in an emergency—although strictly forbidden otherwise—to bring characters back with us to the outside world (in order to rescue them in a crisis, for example) and to let them find their own way back into their stories afterward. He also explained in detail how all books bordered on other books in certain places, and that there were paths between stories that would take you from one to another and, if you were lucky, to the so-called Margin. This was a place outside the lines where lots of book characters liked to hang out when they weren't currently appearing in their own plots. His explanations were interspersed with anecdotes about some great-great-uncles of ours who had made various stupid mistakes. And he gave us an emphatic warning about the consequences of altering a story—such alterations, he said, would immediately appear in every printed copy of that story. *In every printed copy?*

Betsy and Will must have heard all of this a thousand times already. As Will stared dully at the cover of *The Hound of the Baskervilles* (was it just my imagination or had the book got thinner overnight?), Betsy seemed to feel the need to emphasize every word Glenn said. She spent the whole time nodding and saying things like "Exactly," and "Yes, that's right," and "You probably won't be able to manage that for a while yet, Amy." Her lips were so shiny with lip gloss this morning it looked like she'd eaten a tin of sardines in oil for breakfast.

"Lady Mairead, for example, jumped into *Macbeth* once when she was younger and—" Glenn broke off. "Yes, Amy, what is it?"

I put my hand down. "Is it bad—" I began. "I mean—um— would it do any harm if somebody were to jump from somewhere other than *Porta Litterae?*"

Glenn furrowed his brow. "What do you mean?"

"Well—yesterday you said we could only jump into books from the stone circle. Why is that? Would it be bad if somebody was, say, reading in bed, and then . . ." I'd had a guilty conscience ever since I'd woken up that morning, and it had been bothering me more and more as Glenn's speech had gone on. I'd simply jumped into *Oliver Twist* without a second thought, and as if that wasn't bad enough I'd interfered with the storyline by giving the boys dust-biscuits and chewing gum. The longer I'd listened to Glenn the more it had dawned on me that I didn't really know anything about the book world and that it might not be such a great idea to go tinkering about with it however the fancy took me. "If something like that happened—would it be a problem?"

Betsy rolled her eyes and quietly sighed. "Oh, Amy." She looked almost as cruel as she had in my dream.

Glenn, however, shook his head. "No," he said. "It wouldn't be a problem. It just wouldn't be possible. Your gift only works within the stone circle."

"Really?" I looked over at Will and Betsy. "Have you ever tried to jump from anywhere else?"

"I've got better things to do with my time than make an idiot of myself," said Betsy. "Now if you'll excuse me." She pulled out a makeup bag and sailed from the room, while Will looked at me properly for the first time that day. He was still as pale as if he'd seen a ghost, and his hair was just as unkempt as yesterday. He looked hard at me.

"Of course," he said at last, and smiled, a little bit more with the right-hand side of his mouth than the left. "I often tried when I was a kid. But it never worked."

"Hmm," I said. Had I only imagined my excursion into *Oliver Twist*? Had the whole thing been just another dream?

Glenn's lecture continued for another hour and a half before he finally led us up to the top of the hill. One after the other we jumped into our practice books: Will (whose task was to try to find out why his book really did only have a few pages left), Betsy (who was going to negotiate with the ice-cream-parlor dwarf and had touched up her eyeliner especially for the purpose), and me—who knew nothing about anything and was bursting with curiosity.

It began almost as soon as I'd slid the book over my face. Again I was greeted by the hot, humid jungle air; the letters exploded into plants before my eyes, and I heard Mowgli and the wolf cubs playing together. The roots of the giant tree creaked softly as I landed in them. This time, however, I immediately slipped off in the opposite direction from the voices.

"You're back," observed Shere Khan, who was crouched in the thicket nearby.

I nodded to him. Glenn had tasked me with trying to get an overview of Mowgli's story. But any child capable of watching TV knew what happened in *The Jungle Book*, surely? I left the tiger behind me and went tramping off toward the edge of the jungle.

The signpost was still there, as was the ravine where I'd come across the tearful young man with witch issues the day before. Today, however, I did a surprisingly good job of clambering over the boulders and rubble. So much so that I was almost disappointed when the path grew wider and straighter and eventually turned into a road. The steep walls of the ravine still towered into the sky on either side of me, but they grew farther and farther apart before eventually curving inward and meeting in the middle to form a kind of natural amphitheater. At the base of this amphitheater was a town.

It wasn't a big town. It consisted of only one street, in fact. But this one street was packed full of shops of all shapes and sizes, newsstands, cafés, and pubs. In the window of a chemist's shop was a sign advertising a cure for weak verbs, and a fat woman with a hawker's tray was shouting something about a miracle powder that could apparently be used to concoct a happy ending in a matter of minutes if you didn't happen to have one handy. On a market stall I spotted a tub of self-service periods and commas (there was a special offer on—three quotation marks for the price of two). The shop next door had cloaks, swords, and wands on display. The sign above the door read: *Hero Outfitters—from classical drama to science fiction epics. (We also cater to secondary characters).*

And everywhere you looked there were throngs of book characters, dressed in clothes from every era imaginable: a man in a toga surrounded by a gaggle of girls in dresses with enormous crinolines and ruffs, soldiers marching past them with laser guns, magicians in colorful hats, businesswomen in court shoes and trouser suits, and orcs with grotesque misshapen faces. Fairies with dragonfly wings buzzed in and out of the crowd. A goose with a tiny boy riding on its back pecked at the instant happy endings, and was shooed away loudly by the fat lady.

Then I spotted a tomcat wearing a pair of riding boots and walking on its hind legs, and followed it through the crowd until it disappeared into a pub called the Inkpot. Not really fancying the "ink cocktail" being advertised on a board outside, I decided to keep walking. But just as the door to the pub was swinging shut, I caught a glimpse of a familiar face bent over a glass at the bar.

I went in and sat down beside the young man, who cut just as wretched a figure as he had at our last meeting. "Are you still not feeling better?"

He looked up, his eyes red from crying and glittering with tears. "Ah, Miss Amy. How nice to see you again."

"Nice to see you too. Have the old women been bothering you again?"

"No, no," he said, downing his half-full glass in a single swig.

And if his glazed eyes were anything to go by, this glass was not his first. "I am merely full of sorrow," he mumbled, flinging out his arm so wildly that the tabby cat on the bar stool next to him narrowly avoided a blow to the face. "About life, you understand? About the world, about love, about fate. Cruel fate! O, a thousand emotions rage within my breast!" His voice grew steadily louder.

The cat got up and moved seats.

"Ah, yes," I said. "I understand." Unhelpful sentences like *But you won't find the answer at the bottom of a glass* hovered on the tip of my tongue. I bit them back, however, and instead pushed away my stool and stood up. "I've never been here before, and I don't know anyone apart from you. Would you be so kind as to . . . show me around?"

The man gazed wistfully into his empty glass, then nodded and stood up. He swayed a little at first, but soon regained his balance. "I can refuse nothing to such a pretty young lady," he declared, tucking his shirt back into his breeches and a few loose locks of hair back into the velvet ribbon that fastened his ponytail. Then he bowed, almost falling over forward in the process. "Allow me to introduce myself. My name is Werther."

The title of a book we'd read last year in school flashed through my mind, the letters bright and vivid: *The Sorrows of Young Werther* by Goethe. Lots of things suddenly started to make sense. So the guy was drinking because he was unhappy in love—so unhappy, in fact, that at the end of the book he committed suicide. And those weird witches had been tormenting him by prophesying that there was still hope for his doomed love. Poor man!

"Er—pleased to meet you," I said, putting out my hand. Werther did not shake it but planted a boozy kiss on it instead. I forced a smile. "Very busy in here, isn't it?"

Werther nodded. More and more characters were crowding into the pub; most had gathered at a table in the corner where they put their heads together and whispered.

"How much gold is missing?" asked a man whose head was covered with scales instead of hair.

"They'd been slaughtered, just like that," said the tiny boy on the goose's back to a woman with a fish's tail, who reached for a jug of water every few seconds and poured some over her face. "The whole stable was full of blood—away from the plot, thank goodness."

"And have you heard about Alice?" murmured a man with gray-ish skin and a briefcase under his arm.

Werther drew me outside. There he took a few deep breaths, as even more people streamed past us into the pub. "There is something afoot. The rumor mill has been turning for hours now. Something seems to have gone awry in our world."

"In *Oliver Twist*?" My heart beat faster. "Has the story been messed up?"

"What? No." Werther rubbed his nose with his thumb and fore-finger. "Apparently, gold has been stolen from *The Arabian Nights*. And Alice is rumored to have missed the White Rabbit this morn-ing, and to have been unable to find her way to Wonderland. I know no more than that—I have spent the past few hours . . ."

"Drinking?" Werther was swaying dangerously, and I linked arms with him to stop him from falling over.

"Thinking," he corrected me. "At any rate, people are up in

arms—nothing like this has ever happened here before. Alice has never once missed the rabbit, you understand. Such a thing is simply unthinkable. She must be reproaching herself very severely."

"Does that mean . . . could some tiny little change have set off a chain reaction?" If all stories were connected somehow, could introducing a harmless packet of chewing gum into Oliver Twist's workhouse have led to repercussions like this?

"It looks more as though somebody has been intentionally interfering with parts of the affected stories," said Werther, his face suddenly turning pale. He leaned weakly against a market stall and closed his eyes.

"I'll get you a drink of water," I offered.

But Werther shook his head. He pulled out an embroidered handkerchief and pressed it to his mouth and nose. "No, thank you," he said. "But . . . perhaps tomorrow I could . . ." He wheezed. ". . . show you around? If you would be so good as to excus—"

He vomited into a crate of fresh exclamation marks. Feeling rather nauseated, I decided to head home.

That afternoon the sun was shining over Stormsay for a change, reminding us it was July. Alexis made the most of the good weather by going for another walk, and I felt the urge to be outdoors too. After combing the pages of *Oliver Twist* for a while looking for changes in the story (I found none—Oliver must simply have asked for a second helping of gruel the day after I'd seen him), I gathered together my art materials. There was a lot I hadn't been able to bring with me; my acrylic paints had been left at home to make room for more books, as had my paintbrushes, easel, and canvases, which wouldn't have fitted in my suitcase anyway. But I had packed a sketch-book and a few pencils. Tucking them under my arm, I headed off across the moor and up the hill to Shakespeare's Seat. The cliffs looked just as steep as they had on our arrival. From up here, in fact, they felt even higher and more treacherous.

I sat down on a rock and began to sketch the vegetation at the edge of the cliff and the ocean beyond. The waves were dove-gray and ebbed lazily against the foundations of the island with an ancient soughing sound. The wind had died down over the past few days too. It was still blowing my hair all over the place, but at least I actually felt warm in my sweater now. There was a smell of salt and freedom; the sunlight danced across my fingers. With quick strokes I sketched the movement of the waves and the pattern of the few clouds reflected on their surface. I wished I hadn't left my paints in Germany now. This was the most beautiful view I'd ever seen.

I felt like I was sitting at the end of the earth. There was no wireless or cellular signal here—it didn't matter who posted what on social media. Jolina was far away. All that mattered was the sweep of smoky blue sky overhead, stretching away to the horizon and caressing the sea. I'd never felt so much space around me before—space to breathe, space to think. Space for the heather that dangled curiously over the edge of the cliff to peer down into the depths.

I was busy sketching the tiny blossoms when a shadow fell across the paper.

"Pretty," said a voice behind me.

I clung to my pencil and the magic of the moment for a second longer, then let out my breath and turned around. "Hi."

Before me stood Will. He pointed to the sketchbook on my lap. "I didn't know you liked drawing."

I raised my eyebrows. "Well that's hardly surprising, is it? You don't know anything about me." It came out more brusquely than I'd intended.

"Well," said Will, "I do know your name. And I know you must be a talented jumper because you got to the edge of a novel on your first ever visit to the book world."

"Hmm." I bent over my drawing again. "Still not a massive amount, all things considered."

"True."

The wind caught my hair as I reached for a softer pencil to shade in the waves.

Will stood beside me a little longer and studied my drawing, watching me shade in the sky. After a while he cleared his throat. "But it looks like you want it to stay that way. I get it." He leaned closer to me. "I'll get out of here and leave you in peace, then, shall I?"

I didn't answer. He was right—up to now I'd only spoken to Betsy and Will when absolutely necessary, and in lessons I usually tried to avoid meeting their eyes. It wasn't that I didn't want to make new friends. I was just more cautious now. Hypercautious.

And anyway, it wasn't like my new classmates had exactly been falling over themselves to make me feel welcome. Will in particular gave the impression most of the time that his thoughts were somewhere else entirely.

He obviously interpreted my silence as an answer to his question, and turned to leave. His feet were stuffed into battered leather boots and his shaggy hair flew out behind him. Only now did I remember where I'd seen hair flapping in the wind like that before.

"You were up here the night before last, weren't you?" I said just as he reached the path that led back across the moor.

Will stopped. "Yes," he said.

"What were you doing outside in that storm? And what was that massive dog you had with you?"

He came back and sat down beside me on the rock. "I was looking for someone. A . . . a friend. It's his dog."

"Did you find him?"

"Unfortunately not." He put his head in his hands. "I've turned the whole island upside down. But he's disappeared."

"Has he gone away?"

"You could say that."

We looked out over the sea. "Aren't you going to carry on?" asked Will.

My sketch was nearly finished, but I laid down the sketchbook and pencils on the grass and snuck a sideways glance at Will. His nose had a very small bump in it, as if it had once been broken, and his face was a little too angular to be perfect. But in his blue-gray eyes was a clarity like that of the sky over Stormsay. They were stormy-sky eyes.

"Did you manage to find anything out? About why your book has suddenly got thinner?" I asked.

"Yes," he replied, dropping his voice to a whisper. "It's because Sherlock Holmes isn't there anymore."

"Oh," I gasped. "Might he be in a different book? There's a whole series of Sherlock Holmes novels, isn't there?"

Will sighed. "Yes, and none of the other Sherlocks have seen him."

"I heard today that some gold has been stolen, and there's been some kind of misunderstanding in *Alice in Wonderland*."

"He's my best friend," said Will, who didn't seem to have heard me. "He has been since I was five years old. He always used to think up riddles and cases for me, and I helped him outside of the plot. He practically brought me up."

"And now you're looking for him on Stormsay?" I was confused by this sudden overlap between the literary world and the real one. "What would he be doing here in the outside world?"

Will tipped his head back and closed his eyes in the sunlight. His eyelashes cast shadows on his skin, like dark moons. But he wasn't as relaxed as he made out. I could see that his lips were pressed tightly together. He'd dug his fingers into a tuft of grass.

"You brought him here, didn't you?"

"We're not allowed to do that."

"Didn't you?"

"It's not allowed, Amy. As Glenn explained at great length this morning."

"I gave chewing gum and biscuits to Oliver Twist."

He blinked. "Really?" The beginnings of a smile crept onto his face. He scrutinized me for a moment, as if wondering whether I could be trusted. "Amy Lennox," he murmured. "Our families don't like each other very much, did you know that?"

I remembered Betsy's remarks. "I had noticed."

He grinned at me, and a dimple appeared in his right cheek.

"Well—I was going to go and have another look for my friend in the village and on the beach. Perhaps Holmes is testing me and I just need to find the vital clue. Or else he's drinking himself into a stupor at the pub. Do you want to come with me?"

I nodded. I'd had enough of drunken book characters for one day, but I had nothing against a walk. Especially in such charming company.

The beach extended along the east coast of the island all the way to the Macalisters' castle. This beach was no white-sanded bathers' paradise out of a glossy travel magazine. It was covered in pebbles and fragments of seashells and other broken things; in the shallows, huge rusty bits of metal coated in flaking green paint jutted up out of the water. Will told me they were the remnants of a submarine fleet that had been torpedoed during the Second World War. The crew had all been killed and for days bits of the wreckage had washed up on the shore of Stormsay and sunk deep into the silt.

Holmes was nowhere to be seen.

I amused myself by letting the waves lick at the soles of my sneakers. Will poked about with a stick in clumps of seaweed and a washed-up plastic bag. But still there was no trace of the great detective and the closer we got to Macalister Castle, the slower Will advanced. Ahead of us, meanwhile, the castle's turrets loomed higher and higher into the sky. Will eventually came to a standstill a few yards from an imposing quarried stone gatepost.

"Nice pad," I said, looking up at the Macalister coat of arms over the gateway. It showed a dragon against a green background, blowing books from its nostrils instead of flames.

Will hurled the stick into the sea with surprising force. It sailed through the air and landed a long way out. "Bit uncomfortable if you ask me."

"But perfect for playing the lady of the manor."

Will grinned. "You mean like Betsy does all the time?"

"Well, I don't know about that—she spends most of her time putting makeup on, doesn't she?"

"Also true." He laughed, but immediately afterward grew serious again. "I've searched this dump multiple times already. I think we should try the village next."

"Okay," I said, tilting my head. "You don't like your home very much, do you?"

Will didn't answer.

A quarter of an hour later we came to the little hamlet Alexis and I had passed through the evening we'd arrived. The village that could scarcely be called a village. Now, by daylight, I could see that almost all the cottages were standing empty. They looked derelict; most of the windowpanes were broken. Wooden beams jutted like ribs from the crooked roofs, and some of the doors were nailed shut. Only two of the houses looked even remotely habitable.

One was small and shabby, with a patch of weeds out front enclosed by a rotting picket fence. The clay and straw walls of the cottage looked as though they might have been whitewashed once upon a time, but now they were just covered in muddy handprints. Here and there a creeper sprouted from the plaster, causing it to crumble. On the broken steps leading up to the front door sat a boy, his lips moving soundlessly. Or was he a man? He was burly and broad-shouldered and dressed in blue dungarees. His face was covered with an uneven layer of fuzzy hair. But his gaze was that of a child, and it was glued to a sandbank on the shoreline that was covered with gray bodies.

"Hello, Brock," Will greeted him as we passed.

The man-child didn't respond. He carried on mouthing words, his brow furrowed in concentration. Then he cried suddenly, "Seventeen!"

I jumped. "Pardon?"

But he was still staring at the sandbank. His mouth opened and shut as if he were talking to somebody only he could see.

Will nudged me onward. "He's counting seals," he whispered in my ear. "It's his hobby."

"Counting seals?"

"Twenty years ago, when Brock was little, he got washed up on the beach here. We think he must have hit his head somehow." Will tapped his forehead. "He must've been floating around at sea in his life preserver for ages, all alone."

Goose bumps stole across the back of my neck.

The second house was the one where the ferryman had disappeared in search of something alcoholic the night of our arrival. It was bigger and nicer than Brock's. A chalkboard was propped up on a bench outside, announcing that stamps, lettuce, and toilet paper were currently on special offer. Frilly curtains hung in the windows. A little bell tinkled as we went in.

Inside there was indeed a bar, with three stools standing in front of it. The walls were lined with shelves where spools of thread were stacked alongside boxes of tissues and tins of corn. An umbrella stand held several spades, a crutch, and two badminton rackets.

"Is this a pub or a shop?" I asked.

"Both," said a man I hadn't noticed amid all the clutter. He was sitting at a table in the corner stuffing his pipe. His hair was red. "I'm also the local post office. Welcome to Finley's."

"Hello," I said. The man looked familiar, somehow. "I'm Amy."

"I know," said the man, pipe between his teeth. "News travels fast here. I'm your uncle." He struck a match.

"Oh. Er . . ." I didn't know how to reply, and gnawed at my lower lip. Alexis had never told me she had a brother.

Will was wandering around the room peering under tables and behind shelves. "Has anyone been in today?" he inquired.

Finley raised his eyebrows, exactly the same way Alexis did. "No, why?"

Will pulled a spade from the umbrella stand and weighed it in his hand as if considering whether to buy it or not. "Doesn't matter," he murmured.

I still didn't know how to react to the fact that this man was claiming to be my uncle. Why had Alexis never told me about him? On the other hand . . . she had kept pretty much everything about our family a secret. She'd always refused to tell me who my father was, most importantly. It shouldn't really surprise me to learn that I had more relatives kicking about on the island. What I didn't understand was why Alexis hadn't told me all this in the first place.

"How many people live here?" I began once Will and I were back outside in the sunshine. "Altogether on the whole island, I mean?" It looked as though I was going to have to find a few things out for myself.

"Not many. There's Lady Mairead and Mr. Stevens at Lennox

House, Brock and Finley and a guy called Henk here in the village, and Betsy, her nanny Mel, and the Laird at Macalister Castle. And me, of course, and now you and your mum."

"You forgot Glenn, Clyde, and Desmond."

"They live in the library."

"Aha." Fourteen people, then. That wasn't just "not many"—it was *hardly any*. There were five times that many people in my apartment building alone, back in Germany. This island really was at the end of the earth, and it obviously did something strange to its inhabitants. Something that either kept them here irrevocably or drove them away completely, like Alexis. Something I didn't fully understand yet. I eyed Will's leather boots, his tattered trousers, and the ancient sweater he wore. With the best will in the world, I couldn't picture him in a city like Bochum. "Have you ever been to the mainland?" I asked.

He laughed. "Of course I have," he said. "Many times."

*"The monster's poison works quickly.
It causes spasms in the bowels
of its victims, rendering them helpless,"
explained the king's counselor. "And most
of the time, it kills them."
The princess shuddered.*

IN SEARCH OF THE
WHITE RABBIT

I N CLASS THE NEXT MORNING, when I jumped back into *The Jungle Book*, Werther was there waiting for me. He was wearing a knee-length coat made of red silk and an old-fashioned hat. A vine had sunk its thorns into one of his silk stockings and laddered it. He was struggling to free himself from the plant's grip when I landed.

"Good day, Miss Amy. My sorrows are great indeed," he greeted me.

"I know," I said. "I've read your book."

"But today I suffer more cruelly than ever. My head feels as though it had been trodden under a horse's hoof." He grimaced. "I have the Inkpot to thank for that. Never again shall I set foot in that den of iniquity. I almost missed my own suicide last night," he cried indignantly. "Can you imagine?"

"Not really," I admitted. "But are you sure you're feeling up to showing me around today?"

"Barely," said Werther, finally wrenching himself free of the thorns. His stocking was in tatters, revealing a pale calf decorated with red scratches. "But I would willingly suffer a thousand sorrows for a young lady such as yourself."

In the undergrowth nearby, Shere Khan rolled his eyes.

"Um—cool," I said. "So, I was thinking: I saw the Margin yesterday, so I'd prefer to visit *Alice in Wonderland* today to see if everything's back to normal there. Shall we?"

"Your wish is my command." He gave me his arm and I took it. But it proved almost impossible to make our way through the dense jungle arm in arm, and I soon attempted to extricate myself. Werther's grip on my arm, however, was unshakable. In true gentlemanly style he insisted on escorting me across the rough terrain, and so we stumbled on clumsily over roots and undergrowth and squeezed along narrow tracks side by side, treading on each other's toes, until at last we reached the edge of the story. At the crossroads with the signpost we turned left.

We hadn't gone far before the sandy road turned into a garden path made of flagstones that led across a meadow. On either side were beds of brightly colored flowers; the air had the scent of a summer's afternoon. From somewhere ahead of us came the quiet murmur of water. Werther and I passed through an archway covered with climbing roses, and then the path ended as suddenly as it had begun. Now the garden was split in half by a stream, and on the banks of the stream sat two girls in pinafores. One was reading a book and seemed not to notice our arrival. The other was wearing several daisy chains in her hair, and burst into tears when she saw us.

"I've missed him again," she sobbed, and the cat in her lap mewed piteously. "The White Rabbit simply doesn't come anymore. Or if he does, it's when I'm not looking."

"But—but—my dear Miss Alice," said Werther, fishing out his handkerchief. The little girl blew her nose.

"Could the rabbit be ill, maybe? Have you been to look for him?" I asked.

Alice shook her head, dislodging the daisy chains. "I can't. I have to stay here until he comes. Otherwise the whole story will get into a muddle." Tears ran down her cheeks and dripped onto the cat's back. "What if I never find my way back to Wonderland?"

"Then you can read my book with me," said the other girl.

Alice made a face. "That book's far too dull," she said. "It hasn't even any pictures in it. We'd rather carry on making daisy chains, wouldn't we, Dinah?" She tickled the cat behind the ears, then bent to pick some more daisies.

I turned to Werther. "We have to find the White Rabbit," I said. "Perhaps that'll help us find out what's going wrong?"

He gave me his arm again. "Indeed," he said. "We had better skip forward a few pages."

"Is that possible?"

"Well—as a Reader, you must know that. Or do you only ever read one page of a book at home?" said Werther.

"No."

"You see." He marched straight into a flowerbed and tugged at a daisy.

The world folded up around us; the sky tilted sideways. Where the horizon had been, the garden—stream and all—was now suspended in midair, and the water was flowing upward. I craned my neck to see where it was going, but Werther pulled me forward with a jerk. We tumbled through the wall of meadow as if it were mist, and found ourselves in a cave whose walls were lined with a tangled web of tree roots punctuated by kitchen cupboards and shelves. Though it wasn't so much a cave, really, as an enormous hole. Beneath us was a yawning chasm, and we were falling into it feetfirst. I only vaguely recalled the story because it was a while since I'd read the book. But I did remember that at the beginning Alice had spent quite a long time falling down a rabbit hole. Despite the fact that there was no ground beneath my feet for miles, I felt a surge of excitement. I still couldn't believe I was actually *inside* a novel. My gift was so new and surprising that I still hadn't considered all the possibilities that came with it. It looked like I was about to enter the *real Wonderland*!

I blinked, and when I opened my eyes I found the cave had turned into a long corridor full of doors. At the end of the corridor I saw something white scurrying away from us.

"There he is, over there!" I called, pointing to a tiny door half hidden by a curtain. "He hopped through there." Unfortunately, the door in question only came up to my ankles. "We have to go after him. Can you skip forward?"

Werther waggled his head from side to side. "Yes—but we must be sure not to miss him. And we must alter our size for the next part of the story." He massaged his temples—his head must still be pounding.

"Oh yes," I said, "of course." I remembered that on her journey through Wonderland Alice was forever eating and drinking things that made her grow and shrink.

Werther handed me a little glass bottle filled with what looked like cough syrup. The label read "Drink me."

"Well then—cheers!" I said, and gulped down some of the liquid, which didn't actually taste that bad. It was a bit like Black Forest cake . . . But before I'd had time to think, my legs contracted like elastic bands, my arms shortened, and my hands grew so tiny that I could no longer hold the bottle. I was shrinking. Just as I was about to be crushed to death by the bottle, Werther picked it up again and drank from it himself.

"I hope it will help with my indisposition, too," he muttered. His voice went booming through the cave. He was a giant.

By this time I was the size of a grasshopper. The toes of Werther's shoes towered above me like two hills and I retreated a little way to make sure he didn't accidentally trample on me. Fortunately, however, he now began to shrink, too.

A few moments later, Werther pulled at the handle of the tiny door and the cave turned upside down. This time he skipped both forward and backward: first we found ourselves surrounded by a gaggle of animals swimming in a lake, then suddenly inside a house, then out in the open again. Somewhere in between the pages floated the Cheshire Cat's mouth, grinning—the rest of its body was invisible. But the White Rabbit was nowhere to be seen.

We stopped at last in front of a mushroom, on top of which lay a fat blue caterpillar. The caterpillar had a kind of hookah pipe clasped in its numerous little arms. Smoke rings coiled into the air above its head. I had to stand on tiptoe to see over the top of the mushroom. The caterpillar stared at us for a while. Its face creased as it took a drag on the mouthpiece of the pipe.

"Um—excuse me? Has the White Rabbit been by here recently?" I asked.

The caterpillar blew a smoke ring over the top of our heads. "Who are you?" it asked in a raspy voice. "Where is Alice?"

"Ah! My sincerest apologies!" Werther bowed. "My name is Werther and this is young Miss Amy. We are delighted to make your acquaintance."

"Alice can't come because she missed the White Rabbit again. We're trying to find out why," I explained. The way the caterpillar was staring at down us from on high was starting to annoy me. "So—have you seen him?"

The caterpillar crawled down off its mushroom. As it slid past us through the grass we were engulfed by the smell of tobacco. "Yes—he came by here earlier. But he seemed to be in a great hurry."

"Which way did he go?"

"I believe he was on his way to tea with the Hatter and the March Hare," the caterpillar replied before vanishing into the undergrowth.

Werther sighed and put his head in his hands. "I should be glad to rest a moment," he said. "The hooves are pounding against my poor brow from the inside out now."

I laid a hand on his arm. "I know—but if we're ever going catch up with the White Rabbit, we've got to keep going. We've got to find the Hatter."

Werther nodded sorrowfully. "In that case, we should eat some of this mushroom to return ourselves to our proper size." He reached up and broke two chunks off the top of the mushroom. No sooner had we bitten into them than we started growing—just large enough to comfortably drink tea with a rabbit.

Again, Werther skipped forward and backward through the pages of *Alice in Wonderland*. Colors, landscapes, and characters whizzed past us in quick succession. I saw the eyes of the grinning cat, and at one point we hurtled past a queen in a heart-patterned dress screeching, "Where is Alice? Off with her head!"

We arrived at last at a little house in the woods. In front of the house was a long table, set for tea. And at the table, all crowded together at one end, sat a hare, a dormouse, and a little man with buckteeth. He wore a top hat with a price tag attached.

The Hatter and the March Hare were drinking their tea with the dormouse wedged in between them, so deeply asleep that it had no idea it was being used as an armrest.

"Tell me: what do a raven and a writing desk have in common?" asked the Hatter, the instant he spotted us.

"Um . . . they both begin with an *r* sound?" I guessed.

The Hatter wrinkled his nose. "Hmm," he said. "That could be it. What do you think, March Hare?"

"I think my watch has stopped again. Even though I put the best butter in it. It really was the very best butter," said the March Hare. "And why are you two sitting down, may I ask? We didn't invite you to sit down. This is outrageous!"

But Werther and I stayed seated. "I beg you, sirs—there is enough room here for all of us," said Werther, visibly cheered by the winged armchair he had flopped down in. The March Hare snorted.

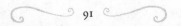

"Both begin with an *r* sound . . ." murmured the Hatter. "That's good! That may well be the answer! Will you take some tea?"

Before we could reply he'd poured us both a cup of tea and deposited a slice of cream cake on each of our plates. "Dig in," he urged.

"Thanks," I said. The cake looked delicious. But it would have to wait. "We're looking for the White Rabbit. Have you seen him?"

Hare and Hatter exchanged a glance.

"He is not well," said the March Hare.

"He is much changed," said the Hatter.

"So he was here? Where did he go?"

"Nowhere." The Hatter opened the teapot and pulled out a dripping wet rabbit that must once upon a time have been white. Brown rivulets of tea trickled down its legs. It looked around fearfully at the occupants of the table.

I raised my eyebrows. "*That's* the White Rabbit? He looks . . . pretty ordinary." The rabbit wrinkled its nose, affronted.

"We've tried butter too, but we simply cannot put him to rights," declared the March Hare. "He has lost the ability to talk. And his watch and waistcoat have disappeared. So he keeps crawling inside our old teapot to hide."

"Strange," murmured Werther. "It is almost as though his idea had disappeared."

"His idea?" I asked.

"The author's idea that this story should feature a talking rabbit with a pocket watch and a waistcoat, which leads Alice into Wonderland," he explained. "Could somebody have . . . no, it cannot be."

"What?" I asked.

"Well—it seems almost as though somebody had stolen the idea."

"Is that even possible? Who would do something like that? And *why*, more to the point?" I didn't understand how you would even go about erasing an idea from a book.

Werther shrugged.

"Who knows?" The Hatter stuffed the rabbit back inside the teapot and seemed instantly to forget that it existed. "But both begin with an *r* sound! Isn't that wonderful? Come, eat your cake, drink your tea!"

Unfortunately the cake didn't taste nearly as good as it looked. A bitter taste filled my mouth the moment I bit into it. It rolled across my palate and down my throat. I coughed and took a sip of tea to take the taste away. But it didn't help.

The bitter taste persisted long after I had jumped back to Stormsay. At lunch I could hardly eat a thing, and gulped down glass after glass of water instead. My grandmother kept shooting inquiring glances at me, but I ignored her. A big row about how I'd wandered into a story I wasn't supposed to be in was the last thing I needed right now. At last I slipped into my four-poster bed and lay staring at the fabric overhead. I took the smallest breaths I could manage. The taste of the cake had formed a lump in my throat, and it was now sliding up and down my gullet like a slimy rubber ball. At the same time a knot was forming in my stomach, tightening into a ball of iron and gurgling loudly. I panted, drew my knees into my chest, shut my eyes for a moment, and then leaped out of bed and lurched to the bathroom.

I was only just in time.

Three hours later, Alexis found me lying on the bath mat. She brought me a pillow and a blanket. The walls were spinning: it felt as though the sink and the toilet were dancing around me, laughing at me. Alexis crouched down beside me and mopped my forehead with a washcloth.

"I don't feel well," I whispered. My lips were chapped. "There was something wrong with the cake in Wonderland."

"You were in *Alice in Wonderland*?"

"Yes." I wanted to tell her about Werther and our search for the White Rabbit, but I was too weak.

"I went there, too, when I was younger," said Alexis. She stroked my hair. "I played croquet with Alice and the Queen of Hearts. It was wonderful."

"I thought . . ." I wheezed. The lump in my throat was threatening to surface again. ". . . I thought you hated the literary world."

"Not at all," said Alexis. "I loved it. I loved it far too much, unfortunately."

Her words sounded muffled, as if I was hearing them through a wall of cotton wool. "Really?" I whispered as the bathroom began to spin even faster and dark clouds crept across the edges of my vision.

"Yes. But going away was my only option. Especially once I found out about you, little giraffe. I—"

It was as if somebody was turning the volume lower and lower. Everything went black.

When I next opened my eyes I found myself back in bed. Alexis was bending over me, trying to feed me some lukewarm tea, while my grandmother paced up and down the room. Macbeth was dozing on the window seat.

"I don't understand it. Literary food never goes off! Either it is already rotten because the plot requires it, or it is fine. But nothing ever goes moldy inside a book," said Lady Mairead. "Stories never go out of date."

"Perhaps somebody *wanted* her to get ill," suggested Alexis.

"But why? Amy has only just started jumping." Lady Mairead pursed her lips. "Simply to go wandering off into Wonderland! I hope you realize, Amy, that it was completely against the rules, and I very much hope it will not happen again. You see what can happen. We must face facts, however." She put her hands on her hips. "Nobody in the book world would have been capable of turning *Alice in Wonderland* so topsy-turvy as to end up with an inedible cake at the Mad Tea-Party."

"Hmm," said Alexis. She gently lifted my head and held the cup to my lips. "We need to get some fluids into you."

I sipped at the tea and forced myself to swallow some of it. A trace of the bitter taste wormed its way back down my throat. Perhaps I should head for the bathroom just in case? I sat up. The room immediately started to spin.

"Are you feeling sick again?" asked Alexis.

I nodded, shook my head, swung my legs out of bed, and tottered a little way across the carpet. My knees were shaking. The nausea was starting to subside again now, though, and I went and flopped down onto the window seat next to Macbeth.

Alexis hurried after me with the teacup. "Take one more sip. And these." In her hand were several little tablets.

"Later," I said, looking out across the moor. I could see three figures moving toward us. A woman in an apron with an old-fashioned white cap on her head was pushing a man in a wheelchair across the uneven terrain. Both of them looked rather surly—probably because the chair's wheels kept getting jammed despite the fact that there was a third person helping them lift it over the largest of the rocks and puddles. At first I thought it was Will, but then I recognized the gray habit and blond hair of the young bookbinder with the scar on his cheek. The weight of the wheelchair didn't seem to trouble him in the slightest.

"Oh no—Mel and Desmond are on their way with the Laird," Lady Mairead said with a sigh, following my gaze. "I completely forgot to ask Mr. Stevens to prepare a snack." She hurried out of the room.

Alexis squeezed in between me and Macbeth on the window seat and waved the hand that held the tablets in little circles under my nose. "Take us, Amy," she said in a squeaky voice. "We'll make you better. We're maaagic!"

I smiled. "I'm supposed to eat something that can talk to me?"

"Yes—we want to die!" squeaked Alexis. "Please, Amy! Eat us."

"Fine." I picked the tiny white globules out of Alexis's hand and put them in my mouth. "Happy now?"

"Good," said Alexis in her normal voice again. "I'd be even happier if you could make this tea disappear as well."

"No way." Just the thought of it made the rubber ball rise into my throat again.

The figures outside were still battling across the moor. The closer they got, the angrier the woman and the man in the wheelchair appeared. "What's the Laird doing here? I thought the two families didn't like each other."

"They don't. But our two clans are the only ones in the world with the gift of book jumping, and we have to share this island, and the library. So they have to consult each other about certain things," Alexis explained. "Once a month the heads of the families meet to discuss how to manage and finance the library, and anything else that needs arranging. Today your grandmother is probably going to have to explain why she sent you to lessons without having introduced you to everyone on the island first."

"Like my uncle, you mean?" I looked Alexis straight in the eye.

She blushed. "Oh, little giraffe. How was I to know I'd end up bringing you back to this godforsaken island one day? I didn't think you'd ever meet them anyway, so what did it matter if you didn't know about them? And quite frankly there are some people you're better off not knowing. Like the Laird. He thinks he can control everything and everyone on this island." She snorted. "The Macalisters have always thought their family was better than ours. They claim they were already living on Stormsay long before the Lennoxes, and that our family is just descended from a branch of theirs. But they've got no proof."

"Well—their castle does look a bit older than this house. . . ."

"That's because the Macalisters torched our castle hundreds of years ago."

"Oh."

Alexis nodded. "Crazy family. Most of them are, and always have been, idiots. The whole argument about the library and whose gift is more powerful is idiotic," she said. Then she suddenly started waving and put on a fake, sugary-sweet smile. "The worst thing is the annual banquet in August, where everyone has to pretend to like one another."

The Laird had reached the grounds by this time and was looking up at our window. He wrinkled his nose as he caught sight of us.

I spent most of the weekend reading—reading in the traditional sense, that is, without jumping into the book world. I was itching to jump, but I felt much too weak to go clambering through jungles or chasing after white rabbits or even to spend the day at a magical boarding school. Though the prospect was hard to resist, I was in no fit state for adventures right now.

Despite having to fight off dizzy spells and jelly legs, I was relieved to find that the bitter taste in my mouth soon abated. On Saturday I was able to eat a bowl of chicken soup and on Sunday afternoon I even ventured out of doors.

The sunlight was the perfect color for a love story, and danced across the backs of a handful of sheep grazing on the edge of the parkland attached to Lennox House. One of the animals was munching an unsymmetrical hole in one of the geometrically trimmed hedges, while the others sampled some flowers. Mr. Stevens would not be happy. Only yesterday I'd looked out of the window and seen him slip across the grass with a little pair of scissors to trim the edges of the lawn. Alexis said he couldn't sleep at night unless the grounds were up to his "very British" gardening standards.

I left the sheep to their munching and walked across the moor a little way, the light now dancing on my shoulders, too. I took the path that led down to the beach, and the air immediately grew colder. The wind tugged at my ponytail and my scarf. I wandered out across the broken seashells and, hoping to drive away the last remnants of the bitter taste, drank in a deep breath of the salty air that was filtering into every pore in my body.

Some distance away I caught sight of Will. He was playing with a gigantic dog (the Hound of the Baskervilles?), throwing a tennis ball into the sea for it to fetch. The dog bounded eagerly after it.

With my feet safely clad in a pair of my grandmother's dark green wellies, I too waded out to sea, letting the surf slosh around my ankles as I made my way toward the wreckage of the submarine fleet. The metal was old, the paint blistered. From afar the pieces looked sharp and jagged, but the passage of time had long since blunted their fangs. I leaned against one of the heavy bits of wreckage, ready-warmed for me by the sun. Now I had a good view of Will and the dog, who were still playing fetch and didn't seem to have noticed me.

The dog retrieved the ball and dropped it at Will's feet. Then it shook its shaggy coat and showered him with water before jumping up and down in front of him wagging its tail. Will laughed and threw the ball again. The dog sped off in pursuit.

Only now did Will look in my direction. I raised a hand to wave at him, then let it drop again because I'd just spotted something out of the corner of my eye that I hadn't noticed until now. I turned to face the open ocean. The waves rolled inexorably toward me and broke on the remnants of the warships. And on the surface of the waves, I saw something floating. Something large, snagged on the metal husks.

It was a human being.

"Will!" I yelled, and then again, "Will! Come here! Quick!"

The man was floating facedown. A clump of seaweed was stuck to the back of his head, and his leather shoes bumped gently against the wreckage.

"Hey, Amy!" called Will from the shore. He was still laughing. "Are you feeling better?"

I stared at the seaweed. It formed a nest in the man's dark, wet hair. It had worked its way in and taken root. And it didn't seem to want to leave. A lone strand wound cautiously down toward the shirt collar around the man's neck, wanting perhaps to glimpse this strange island it had washed up on.

"What is it?" shouted Will, splashing through the water toward me.

The jacket was checked, with corduroy patches at the elbows. The legs were encased in tweed trousers. I looked at the seaweed again.

Will was beside me now. He gasped. "Shit!"

"Shit," I echoed quietly. My mind only gradually understood what I was seeing, as if I was afraid even to think what I knew to be true: a man was floating there, and he was dead.

Will grabbed the body by the shoulders and dragged it onto the beach. As he did so, a pipe fell out of the inside pocket of the jacket and landed in the water. I fished it out and followed Will ashore, where he was rolling the dead man onto his back. The seaweed loosened its grip and slid off. I gripped the pipe.

The man's face was bloated and pale, his eyes sightless. Under the jacket he was wearing a waistcoat, and under that a shirt. Both looked threadbare and a little old-fashioned. Both were stained with a red blot that had spread from a hole in the man's chest.

Will sank to his knees beside the body, burying his hands deep in the seashell shards that littered the beach. He closed his eyes. "Sherlock," he said tonelessly. "It's Sherlock."

The knight bowed down before the princess.
"You can rely upon me," he vowed.
"I will put an end to the beast. It will be
a bloody end. A long, painful end.
An end worse than a thousand deaths.
And I will laugh and think of you, Princess."

THE GREAT FIRE

THE WORLD AROUND WILL FADED AWAY into the mist. The mist crawled out of the sea in thick swathes, lay heavy on his chest, blotted out everything else. Everything but the inert face of his oldest friend. A single word hummed in Will's head: dead.

Dead, thought Will. Dead. Dead. Sherlock was dead.

Suddenly he was five years old again, standing in a room of the house on Baker Street. Through the open window came the clatter of horses' hooves and the sound of loud cursing—somebody, obviously in a great hurry, was shouting something about having to get to the other side of London by the end of the day. On the massive desk in the middle of the room were piles of cards and notepads, some dirty crockery, and some bizarre measuring instruments with lots of cogs. A pipe and a scattering of brown crumbs lay on the Oriental rug. An acrid smell emanated from a test tube on the mantelpiece.

It was the first time Will had ever been here, and he could only just see over the edge of the desk. He didn't know whose house this was or how he had ended up here. It must have something to do with his gift—the one the Laird had told him about. A gift that Will didn't understand. A gift that could send him to strange places . . .

He liked the big magnifying glass. The lens—a circle of glass with both faces ground into a funny curved shape—glinted in the sunlight as he lifted it off the desk. It was heavier than he'd expected. Rainbow-colored streaks danced across the walls as he turned it this way and that. Will sat down cross-legged on the crumb-strewn carpet. The magnifying glass caught the light and transformed it into brightly colored flecks that darted around the room. Or were they little fairies?

All of a sudden, a pair of checked trouser legs appeared beside him.

"That's my magnifying glass, young man," said a voice from somewhere above the trouser legs.

"I was just having a look at it. Look what I can do!" Will sent the fairy flecks whirling across the ceiling. He looked up.

Above the trouser legs was a jacket, and above that was a head with a long, crooked nose and bright blue eyes. "Aha! This looks to me like a scientific discovery," said the owner of the head, and laughed.

Will blinked. The Holmes in front of him wasn't laughing.

He would never laugh again.

Will heard himself speaking as if from far away. "We have to get help," said his voice. He saw himself stand up and turn to face Amy. "We need help," he said again as the dog curled up beside Holmes and buried its nose in the crook of his neck.

Amy replied, but he didn't hear what she said.

They ran across the moor.

Later Will could hardly remember how they'd made it to the

Secret Library, how Glenn, Desmond, and Clyde had come rushing over, how he'd explained what had happened, how they'd all raced back to the beach, how Desmond and Glenn had helped him carry Holmes up to the stone circle, and how Will had taken the detective back into his book so that the other characters could bury him. The dog had disappeared back into the story along with his dead master.

At last, Will found himself sitting on the threadbare old sofa in his cottage wondering whether it had all really happened. Whether Holmes was really dead. Night had fallen by now and the cracked windowpanes were dark. A fire crackled in the stove in the corner.

"I am a detective," said Holmes.

"What's a dective?" asked Will, making the fairy flecks slide up and down the checked trouser legs.

"I solve criminal cases. Most are difficult puzzles, and I have to do rather a lot of thinking in order to solve them."

"Do you solve the puzzles with this?" Will held up the magnifying glass.

"Sometimes. You can help me, if you like. At the moment I am engaged in the search for a very large dog."

"I like dogs."

"Tea?"

Will turned his head. Amy was holding a steaming mug out toward him. A few strands of hair had escaped from her ponytail and hung down into her face, giving her a disheveled look. Will had never seen anyone who was so pretty without even trying.

"Thanks," he said, taking the tea. The warmth of the mug felt good. It brought him back to the here and now.

Amy poured herself a mugful, too, and sat down on the sofa beside him.

"Do you live here?" she asked.

"No," he said. "Well—yes, actually."

Amy nodded. "Interesting wallpaper, by the way." She cocked her head at the red letters above the stove. "What does that mean—*I have awoken?*"

"What? Oh." Will shrugged. "No idea," he said. "I . . . don't know, I—" He broke off.

"Sorry. I didn't mean to be nosy," said Amy. She pulled her knees up to her chest, wrapped her slim arms around them, and rested her chin on them. She looked at him intently with her large, bright eyes. "It must be awful to lose such a good friend."

Will felt himself nod jerkily.

"Should I . . . go?" asked Amy.

"No," he said quickly, banishing the last of the fairy flecks from his thoughts. "I . . . thanks for making the tea."

"No problem."

They sipped at their tea.

"Do you think it was an accident? D'you think he fell off the cliff during the storm?" asked Amy.

"Did you see the hole in his chest?"

"Yes."

"Looked more like something else, don't you think?" He turned cold at the thought.

"So somebody . . . killed him?" she whispered. "But he was a book character! Who would do something like that? *Why* would anyone do something like that?"

Will shrugged. "Perhaps because he found out something he shouldn't have?"

"But what?"

He pointed to the writing daubed on the wall. "He was looking at this just before he disappeared."

"Oh," said Amy.

Will took a big gulp of his tea, which was far too hot. It scalded his throat, but he didn't care. He didn't care about anything. He'd known Sherlock nearly his whole life. The master detective had been more to him than just a character in a book. He'd been his friend, his confidant, and his adviser. Will, for his part, had been responsible for Sherlock; it had been his job to protect Sherlock's story. And now the great detective was gone. Will had failed—failed miserably. He hurled his mug to the floor as hard as he could, and it shattered into a thousand pieces. Tea splattered across the room. "I should have been more careful! I should never have brought him to the outside world!"

"It might have been an accident," murmured Amy, without even batting an eyelid at the sight of the broken mug. "And anyway, you weren't to know something like that would happen, were you? This whole book-jumping thing has never seemed all that dangerous to me. Exciting yes, but not dangerous."

"It *isn't* dangerous," said Will. "Books are a wonderful thing. But what happened to Sherlock never should have happened, and it was all my fault. I brought him here." He kicked out at the rickety coffee table, which collapsed with a crash.

Amy laid a hand on Will's arm, but he couldn't bear to be touched. He didn't deserve consolation. Instead he reached down over the far end of the sofa and fished a well-thumbed copy of *Peter Pan* out of his chest of books. The book's spine was cracked, its pages yellowed. He tossed it to Amy. "The first book I ever jumped into," he explained.

That was where it had all started. The whole chain of events that had led to his best friend washing up dead on the coast of Stormsay, thought Will bitterly. Perhaps he should burn it. Yes—he should throw it in the stove right now!

Amy ran her fingertips over the plain cloth binding. "It's beautiful," she whispered.

"Even though I could have jumped into it whenever I wanted, I still must have read it the normal way about a hundred times." Why couldn't he have just left it at that? Why had he insisted on jumping and messing up the book world?

"Some stories are like that. I'm like that with *Momo* and *Pride and Prejudice*," said Amy. "I prefer the characters in those books to real people, to be honest." A shadow flitted across her face. The way she was sitting there huddled up on the sofa with her knees close to her chest and the book clasped in her skinny hands, she reminded Will of a butterfly whose wings somebody has tried to crush.

"Is it true your mum never told you about your gift?" he asked. "That you didn't find out about it till you came back to Stormsay?"

"Mmm," said Amy. "Though we haven't exactly *come back*— we're just spending the holidays here." The shadow in her eyes darkened.

"It is kind of weird how you two turn up here out of the blue and—"

"Next thing you know someone's dead?" She folded her arms across her chest. "Are you saying me and Alexis—"

"No," he interrupted her. "That's not what I meant. I—"

"It's okay." She sighed. "Today is not a good day." She breathed deeply for a while until the last of the shadow had vanished from her face. Then she opened the book and, in a pure, clear voice, began to read aloud the opening sentences of *Peter Pan*. Will rested his head on the arm of the sofa, closed his eyes, and listened to the stream of words that told of Peter, of the lost boys, of the evil Captain Hook, and of the fairy Tinker Bell with her magic fairy dust.

Lennox House was dark and silent by the time I tiptoed back to my room a little after midnight. I'd left Will asleep in his cottage; now I, too, needed somebody to comfort me. Lots of strange things had happened over the past few days. But the death of Sherlock Holmes was more shocking even than my experiences in the book world. I couldn't get my head around the fact that we really had found the great detective's body on the beach of Stormsay. Whether he'd been murdered or killed in an accident, it was a terrible thing to have happened. A man had died, albeit a fictional one. Although I was completely exhausted I had no intention of going to sleep. I slipped into my pajamas and through the tiny bathroom into Alexis's room.

I needed to talk to her about what had happened. The image of the seaweed caught in the dead man's hair had burned itself into my memory, and so had the sloshing noise the waves had made as they'd washed his feet repeatedly against the wreckage. I'd never seen a real dead person before. I'd only ever seen dead bodies in thrillers, and there'd been something immensely reassuring in the knowledge that all the blood coming out of them was just movie blood. The red stain on Sherlock's chest, however, had not been the work of a makeup artist. . . .

I padded across the room, tripping over bits of furniture and clothing that lay strewn across the floor, until I reached a four-poster bed very similar to mine. I carefully drew back the curtains. "Alexis?" I whispered into the darkness. "Alexis? It's me, Amy. Something bad's happened. I really need to talk to you."

Alexis didn't answer.

"Alexis?" I tried again, a little louder. I felt for the edge of the bed and my hand grazed the sheet. The quilt lay flat and cool on top of it. I bent down, groped my way up the bed to the pillow, and stopped short.

There was nobody there.

In three quick strides I was back by the doorway, but when I switched on the light the room was still empty. My first thought was that she might not have been able to sleep. So I went out into the hallway and prowled around the house for a while, checking the sitting room and the conservatory and hoping eventually to find her in my grandmother's library reading a book. But there was no sign of her there either. Unfortunately, my next thought was that this was how it had started with Holmes. He, too, had disappeared without a trace.

When I came down to breakfast the next morning, however, after a sleepless night of anxious tossing and turning, I found Alexis sitting at the table talking to Lady Mairead.

"Where were you?" I burst out.

Alexis put her head to one side. "Good morning, little giraffe," she greeted me. "What do you mean where was I?"

"Last night. I went to your room and—"

"Ah." She waved her hand dismissively.

Now Lady Mairead looked curiously at her, too, eyebrows raised.

Alexis sipped her coffee and pretended not to notice. "Mr. Stevens has just told us what happened to Sherlock Holmes. It's awful!" she said, without looking at me.

"Yes," I murmured as I sat down. What was going on with Alexis? Her hands jittered as she spread jam on a slice of toast, which she then wolfed down in a couple of mouthfuls before jumping up from the table. "Have a nice day, Amy," she called, still chewing, and disappeared through the door.

Lady Mairead and I exchanged a puzzled glance.

In the Secret Library, too, the sole topic of conversation that morning was the death of the famous detective. Betsy and I looked on as Glenn gave Will one hell of a telling-off, stressing again and again how irresponsibly Will had behaved in secretly bringing Holmes through the stone circle into the outside world. "This is a dark day for the venerable book-jumper clans," he declared at last, for the third time. "You are here to protect the literary world. You are supposed to prevent accidents, not be so reckless as to *cause* them," he admonished us.

Betsy, of course, nodded all the way through Glenn's lecture with an expression on her face that made it clear she'd been about to say exactly the same thing herself. Will, on the other hand, sat pale and silent at his desk as he endured the sermon.

"The other Sherlocks from the rest of the Holmes books will take over Holmes's duties in *The Hound of the Baskervilles*. The worst possible outcome, the destruction of an entire story, has thus been avoided," Glenn went on. "From now on, however, you will have to work twice as hard to compensate for your mistake. Other book jumpers before you have failed, but the death of a literary character remains a particularly grave sacrilege. I hope you know that."

"Of course I do," said Will. Those were the first words we'd heard him speak all day. He cleared his throat and stood up. "I know that," he said in a firm voice. "And that's why I made a decision last night: I'm stopping. I'm not going to jump anymore."

"What? No—you . . . you have a duty to use your gift!" cried Betsy. "You were born a book jumper—you can't just cast that aside."

"My parents did."

Betsy had leaped out of her seat now too. Two red spots appeared on her cheeks. "Your parents abandoned you. They went away and left their only child behind. Have you forgotten that?"

"I remember the day they left quite clearly. They wanted to take me with them. But I chose to stay behind."

"Because you chose your gift! You have to carry on, Will. You—"

"I stayed because I knew it was the right thing to do. Just like I know what I have to do now. It's the only way, if I ever want to be able to look myself in the face again," said Will, reaching for his jacket.

"The Laird will not agree to this," Glenn added.

But Will merely shrugged. Then he left the classroom.

Betsy was about to go after him, but Glenn motioned to her to stay put. "He will calm down once he is over the shock," he said, heaving a huge tome onto his desk. "And we must not let this prevent us from concentrating on the work we still have to do, must we? This is the family chronicle of the Lennox clan, which is what we are going to look at today."

"Oh, great," muttered Betsy, rolling her eyes.

"Come here." Glenn opened the fragile cover and unfolded something that looked like a map. As we moved closer, I could see that it was in fact a family tree. A family tree in the shape of a pair of antlers, whose prongs looped across the paper in countless little squiggles, illuminated in gold and various shades of green that must have been applied with an extremely thin paintbrush. In between the antler prongs were tiny painted portraits. The words *Eoghan of Lennox, the Great Reader* captioned a picture of a man with a red beard and a bald head right at the bottom of the tree. From there, the main stem branched off toward Ronald of Lennox—a rather fierce-looking man swinging an ax above his head—and Aidan of Lennox, who was dressed in a ruff and a shimmering robe. It went on to depict a whole series of redheaded men and women ending, at the top of the tree, with the portrait of a young and beautiful Lady Mairead. But no, wait—Glenn was unfolding another piece of paper featuring a picture of Alexis, her face framed by her dark red hair. From there, a thin branch led on to a portrait of a young girl with large eyes and shining hair. The words *Amy of Lennox* had been written with a flourish underneath. The little painted Amy was even wearing my navy woolly sweater!

"Desmond finished it yesterday," said Glenn. "Do you like it?"

"Er—yes, yes of course I do," I stammered. Desmond had been

pretty flattering in his depiction of me, it had to be said. I looked almost pretty.

"Good," said Glenn. "And now I would like you to observe the terrible consequences that can result from a failure to take your role as protectors of literature seriously enough." He folded the chart up again and began to leaf through my family history, stopping at a chapter headed *The Great Fire*.

Betsy and I were soon lying side by side in the stone circle on the hilltop. We'd both tried to protest when we'd realized he wanted us to jump together, but Glenn had been implacable. "Senseless conflicts between your two families have done enough harm already. It is time you finally realized that you can achieve far more by working together. Now off you go!" With these words he'd heaved the weighty tome containing my family history onto our faces. The letters swam before our eyes and the story took hold of us. By now I was used to the strange feeling I got at the moment of jumping.

We landed in a very old, vaulted cellar. The musty smell crept up my nose and I was still trying to get my bearings in the dim room when Betsy stood up and brushed the dust off her dark red minidress. I, too, got slowly to my feet, swaying slightly.

"Have you been here before?" I asked.

Betsy put a finger to her lips and shook her head with a reproving frown.

We looked around. The cellar was pretty dark—the only light came from the fire in the hearth, over which a suckling pig was roasting on a spit. A young man with a red beard was dozing in a carved armchair by the fireside. He wore a kilt and an old-fashioned shirt. A pair of boots lay on the floor beside him, and his grubby bare feet were stretched out toward the flames. His eyes were half closed and he had a pile of books balanced on his stomach.

We were about to go closer when a door flew open with a crash at the other end of the cellar, and in burst two boys with dark eyes and tousled hair. They were wearing kilts, too, but with a different pattern. They looked to be about fourteen or fifteen years old and extremely pissed off.

Betsy and I retreated silently into the shadows.

"Malcolm Lennox!" roared one of the boys, drawing his sword. The blade flashed in the dancing firelight. "What possessed ye?"

The man in the armchair sat up with a jolt. "Cailean! Tevin! Who let ye Macalister rats in here?" he murmured. "And what do ye mean by this foolish swordplay, Cailean?"

The two boys were upon him now, and pulled him to his feet. The pile of books clattered to the floor. "Stand an' fight like a man," Cailean demanded, holding the tip of his sword to the man's throat. "Or die like a coward."

Malcolm Lennox quickly made up his mind in favor of the first option, and now he, too, drew his sword. The two blades clashed, and metal rang against metal. Malcolm and Cailean dueled their way across the room.

"Might I ask why ye are trying to kill me? Did yer Ma drop ye on yer heads again?" asked Malcolm nonchalantly.

"Ye have sinned. Ye did it. Ye brought them here!" hissed Cailean.

"What?" Malcolm almost forgot to parry a thrust, raising his sword hastily at the last second. He staggered back a few steps toward the fireplace. "Brought who where?"

"Don't play the innocent," roared Cailean. "We know about the mermaids!" He spat the word at him. "Ye took them down to the shore! We saw them an' meant to return them to their book, but the beasts were too quick an' swam off long before we could reach them."

"I rather think ye were too slow to catch the lassies. I hope they had a good laugh at ye?"

"Pah," said the second Macalister, Tevin, who up to this point had hung back from the fight. But now all of a sudden there was a dagger in his hand and he, too, was bearing down on Malcolm. "Mythical beasts in the outside world—how could ye?" he cried. "They could be anywhere by now! Folk'll see them! They'll think they're real."

"Well, they are real. In books." Malcolm grinned, despite the fact that he was now being attacked from both sides. He could only have been a few years older than his assailants, but he was a much more skillful fighter than either of them. He whirled around the room with ease, and his sword seemed to be everywhere at once. But the Macalisters did not give up. Their assaults on Malcolm grew ever more desperate.

"The Laird will surely be angry to find ye out of bed at this hour," teased Malcolm, sidestepping them elegantly.

Cailean and Tevin were fuming with rage—but then, all of a sudden, their eyes widened in fear and they abruptly dropped their weapons.

"Are ye afraid the Laird will scold ye?" Malcolm laughed. "He might even refuse to read ye a bedtime story, as punishment."

But the Macalisters simply pointed speechlessly to the hearth, where several books had gone up in flames. Malcolm must have kicked them into the fire when he'd dodged out of the way of his opponents.

Now he, too, dropped his sword. "Good God," he murmured, plunging his bare hands into the flames. The boys did the same. They fished out one burning book after another and stamped on them frantically to try to put out the fire. I wanted to rush over and help them, but Betsy held me back with an iron grip. "You really don't get it, do you? We don't intervene," she hissed as our panic-stricken ancestors fought to extinguish the blazing books.

At last there was only one book left in the fire.

Malcolm cursed and thrust his burned hands back into the fireplace one last time. The majority of the book had crumbled away to ash by this time—only a few scraps of its pages remained. As he pulled it out and his eyes fell on the title, he began to curse loudly. "It's the only copy!" he shouted. "It's a manuscript!"

"What?" yelled Cailean Macalister.

Tevin Macalister, meanwhile, had discovered that his coat was on fire. He ripped it off and flung it away from him and it landed on the armchair, where the animal skin that served as a cushion immediately started to smolder. A few glowing logs had also rolled out of the fireplace and set fire to some tapestries and a wooden footstool.

But neither Malcolm nor the Macalisters were paying any attention to the blaze. All three were staring in shock at the remains of the still-smoldering manuscript.

"We have to get to the *Porta Litterae*!" thundered Malcolm at last. "Come on! It's our only chance of saving whatever's left to save."

The two boys nodded. The next moment, all three went running out of the room.

I looked around frantically. "We need something to put the fire out with!" I cried. Why was there never a bucket of water around when you needed one?

"It's a story, you idiot!" shouted Betsy. "It's not real, okay?"

I sniffed. It felt pretty fricking real to me. So real it was starting to scare me.

The blaze had spread rapidly—even the wooden beams that jutted out of the walls were on fire now. The whole room was filled with thick black smoke that stung our eyes. Every breath was torture. I blinked, unable to see a thing, and felt Betsy push me roughly forward. Coughing and gasping, we stumbled the few paces back to the spot where we'd landed.

A few seconds later we rolled back onto the woven mat in the stone circle on Stormsay, where it took me a little while to get my breath back. Greedily I drank in the fresh air and waited for the tears in my eyes to subside. My lungs were burning.

At last, Glenn helped me and Betsy to our feet.

"Could you not have told us to put on some old clothes before we went?" huffed Betsy, pointing to her soot-stained dress. Her face and hair were also coated with a layer of black dust, and I guessed I didn't look much better. But I didn't particularly care about that right now.

"Was that the fire that burned down my clan's castle?" I asked.

Glenn nodded. "But that is not why I sent you there. The loss of a castle is trivial compared to what was lost forever that night," he explained. "The manuscript that fell in the fire was the only written record of a story that, when the manuscript was burned, was erased forever. The disaster hit the families very hard. They had dedicated their lives to the protection of the book world, yet their enmity had ended up destroying a part of that world."

I dimly remembered Glenn mentioning something about that burned book on my first day of lessons. "Since then the families have observed a truce," I said.

"That's right, Amy." Glenn smiled.

But Betsy snorted. "We've heard that a hundred times before. You didn't need to make me ruin my hair just for that." She tweaked her ponytail. "I'm not stupid enough to go chucking manuscripts on the fire."

"I wanted you to see how quickly things can get out of hand. And nobody was 'stupid enough' to do it that night either. Neither the Macalisters nor the Lennoxes would ever have dreamed of destroying a story. But it happened nonetheless—through carelessness. Just as carelessness allowed Sherlock Holmes to fall victim to that terrible accident," said Glenn.

"I get it," said Betsy brusquely. "I'm going to go and have a shower now. Unless you're planning to make us jump into a chronicle about the Great Fire of London?"

"No. Lessons are over for today."

Betsy stalked off without another word. I stayed to help Glenn roll up the mat.

"What was the story that fell in the fire? Does anyone know?" I asked.

A sad smile flitted across Glenn's face. "It was a fairy tale," he said. "An age-old fairy tale."

*The monster rampaged across the land.
It knew no mercy. It brought death and
destruction wherever it appeared. Soon
the princess was no longer alone in her terror.
Now everybody else in the kingdom
feared for their lives too.*

DISCOVERIES

Over the next few days, although he continued to show up for lessons in the Secret Library, Will refused to jump into the book world. He just sat there and stared down at his desk while Glenn bored us with speeches about the history of Stormsay and the feud between our families.

When the theoretical part of our training was over, Will would disappear so fast that I didn't even get chance to ask him how he was, and in the afternoons I couldn't find him anywhere on the island—but something had changed between us since that evening in his cottage. Sometimes, when nobody was watching, he looked up from his desk and shot me a glance as if to say that we understood each other.

I was worried about him, of course, as was everybody else on the island. But I also realized that he needed some time. Will had barricaded himself away in his shell of guilt and self-doubt, and it would take a while for him to emerge again. I knew what it felt like to lose a friend. For that reason I'd decided to give him some space for a while and focus my energies on the book world instead.

I was still so intrigued by the book world that I just couldn't get enough of it. The brief jumps we did in our morning lessons weren't nearly enough to satisfy my curiosity. I usually jumped again in the afternoon, from my bedroom—in secret, of course, so that it wouldn't occur to anybody to ban my unsupervised excursions.

Since Sherlock's death, however, these excursions had not been quite as carefree as before. Everybody seemed by now to think that he had fallen off the cliffs during the storm. But I had a strange feeling about the whole thing—especially when I thought about the hole in his chest. Something about it wasn't right and I got the impression, although we never spoke about it, that Will felt the same way. But I was even more puzzled by what I found out in the book world that Sunday morning. Werther and I had just been admiring Dorothy's silver shoes in *The Wizard of Oz* and were sitting together in a little nook of the Inkpot, when a swarm of fairies came buzzing in through an open window. The little creatures were barely as long as my thumb; their leathery blue skin was stretched tightly over their bony faces and their wings were like dragonflies' wings.

The swarm flew over to the bar, and the fairies' tiny voices came together in a buzzing chorus as they ordered a glass of flower nectar. The cloud of blue bodies then arranged itself into the shape of a hand, which closed around the goblet of golden liquid and picked it up. They set the drink down on the table next to ours and began to dive into it headfirst, one after the other, smacking their lips loudly.

Werther shook himself. "Ugh," he said. "Fairies have no manners." He leaned forward to sip from the straw in his bottle of cola. This was his new favorite drink, having—unlike ink cocktails—no disagreeable side effects. In his hand he held a stately quill pen with which he was scratching something on a sheet of handmade paper. Werther loved writing letters to other characters. This one was addressed to a good friend of his named Wilhelm and in it Werther described, in florid language, how he had recently got drunk out of sheer existential despair. The way he told it, it had been an almost heroic act.

From across the table I read, in Werther's ornate handwriting, something about an *unquiet soul* and *afflictions of the heart*. You had to hand it to him: the man was good with words. But the lip-smacking fairies at the next table seemed to be stifling his creativity. The quill hovered in the air for a moment above the half-finished letter; then he set it aside and sighed. "Vexatious creatures," he murmured. "They stick their pointed noses into everything imaginable and go flying about in stories where they have no business to be, for the sheer amusement of it."

"Well—we do that, too," I reminded him gently as the fairies at the next table began a competition to see who could perform the best dive-bomb into the flower nectar.

Werther massaged the bridge of his nose. "Indeed," he said. "But we, unlike them, know how to behave." He rolled up his letter to keep it dry, since we were now getting splashed with nectar.

I brushed a glistening droplet from my cheek and felt as though I'd put my hand in superglue. My index finger immediately stuck fast to my chin. "Maybe so," I said, trying discreetly to free myself.

"Inquisitive beasts," grumbled Werther.

My index finger wouldn't budge.

The fairies, meanwhile, had emptied their goblet and were now lolling around on the table with full bellies. A couple of them belched heartily.

I thought for a moment. "So they go flying around all over the place, did you say?"

Werther nodded. "A veritable plague. Nobody in the book world with an ounce of self-respect will have anything to do with them."

"I will," I resolved, standing up. "Excuse me—may I sit with you for a moment?" I asked one of the belching fairies.

The fairy opened its bright green eyes wide with surprise and squeaked something I couldn't understand.

"Pardon?" I asked. I used my non-glued hand to pull up a chair.

The fairy sat up straight, and the rest of the swarm perked up, too, and started buzzing. "Why," the fairy in front of me repeated (and her fellow fairies hissed an echo of her words), "are you holding your chin?"

"My finger's stuck." I tugged at the finger again. To no avail.

"Ah," sighed the fairy chorus.

"I . . . um . . . wanted to ask whether you . . . um," I stammered, distracted by one of the fairies as it flew close to my face, wings whirring. A moment later I felt its needle-sharp teeth sink into my fingertip. "Ow!" I shook the fairy off and it landed with a bump on the tabletop.

"Sorry," it mumbled, rubbing its head. "Just trying to help."

I frowned. "By biting my finger off?"

"Only the nectar," chirruped another fairy, landing on my wrist.

Its wings tickled my cheek as it bent down and started gnawing at the gluey droplet.

The other fairies looked on sulkily.

"So—what I was wondering was—have you happened to notice anything strange recently on your travels around the book world?" I said in a rush.

"Mhmpf," grunted the fairy on my wrist. The rest of the swarm shot up into the air in front of me. A myriad of glowing green eyes fixed themselves on my face. "Yes," they buzzed in chorus. "Bad things are happening. Terrible things. Somebody is on the prowl. Somebody is stealing them. Somebody wicked."

I thought of the White Rabbit in *Alice in Wonderland* who had lost his watch, his waistcoat, and his ability to talk. "You mean more ideas have been stolen?"

The fairies nodded vehemently, and the hum of their wings swelled to a drone as they flew closer to me. I felt an icy draft on my face. "Sleeping Beauty has woken up halfway through her hundred years' sleep and refuses to wait for the prince," they whispered. "Dorian Gray has lost his picture. The Elf-King has vanished. It gets worse by the day. More and more ideas are disappearing. And not just any ideas."

At last the fairy had nibbled my finger free of my face. "Thanks." I waggled my hand about a bit. "But what do you mean, 'not just any ideas'?"

"The *fundamental* ideas," whispered the fairies even more softly. Their words hissed in my ears. "The core ingredients. The author's initial ideas, without which a story simply breaks down. Somebody is sneaking around the book world stealing them."

Werther and I sat talking in our nook for a long time after the fairies had left the Inkpot. What did the thief want with all these ideas? How was he or she managing to steal them? Who *was* the thief—and could whoever it was be stopped? But our reflections on the subject went round and round in circles and we couldn't find a satisfactory answer to any of our questions. After a while we gave up. Werther headed back to the plot of his story to commit suicide, and I returned to the outside world, where the weather soon took my mind off the thief.

The afternoon had brought blazing sunshine to the island and the temperature had reached almost summery heights. I spread out a blanket on the grounds of Lennox House and lay down on my back, gazing up at the blue sky above me and marveling at how high and clear it was. My skin drank in every sunbeam and I was reveling in the warmth on my shoulders and feet when suddenly I heard footsteps. At first I thought it was one of the sheep wandering over in search of fresher and juicier grass. But then a mop of dark hair appeared in the cloudless sky. It was followed by Will's face. There were dark shadows under his eyes.

"Hi," he said uncertainly.

I sat up. "Hi!"

"I was going to go down to the beach and have another look at the place where he got washed up. I thought I might find some kind of trace—some clue as to what happened." He swallowed and held out his hand to me. "Will you come with me?"

So this was it—the first timid feeler to emerge from Will's shell. I knew it! I smiled tentatively so as not to frighten him straight back in, and let him help me up. As he did so, Will's hand held mine a touch longer than was strictly necessary, and suddenly Stormsay seemed even more radiant than before. The sunshine painted bright patterns on the sleeves of my shirt and made the colors of the wild-flowers on the moor even more vivid. Only Will still looked gray and gloomy, as if he were standing under his own personal rain cloud.

We headed down the path that led to the beach.

"Have you searched the cliffs too? If he did fall into the sea from there, then there might be other—" I began.

"Yes, I have," said Will. His eyes were glued to the shipwreck in the distance.

To our right the waves washed gently over shingle and broken seashells. We tramped along the beach until we were approaching the remains of the submarine fleet. All of a sudden there was a sharp intake of breath from Will beside me.

"Are you okay?" I asked.

He pointed mutely to a shadow in between the metal ribs that looked horribly like a human body. I gasped. Though it wasn't cold, I started shivering and my legs felt funny, as if they didn't belong to me. They carried me toward the wreckage as if of their own accord. As if I was being pulled by an invisible string, inexorably, toward something horrific. Like in a dream when you want to run away but can't.

The closer we got, the more clearly we could see the human shoulders jutting out of the water. They were draped in a flowery tunic. And above the tunic was a mop of dripping, dark red hair.

My stomach lurched. All of a sudden there was complete silence inside my head. I ran into the waves.

"Alexis!" I tried to scream, but all that came out of my mouth was a hoarse croak.

I tripped over a sharp piece of metal and fell headfirst into the water. When I resurfaced, I found myself looking straight into Alexis's astonished face.

She wasn't dead. Of course she wasn't. Relief flooded through me—until I realized my mum wasn't alone. There were two arms around her waist, hugging her tightly. Alexis was nestled against the chest of a man with a scarred face. It was a very young face. And it belonged to Desmond.

I stared from one to the other, openmouthed. They were both dripping wet and their cheeks were flushed. Their clothes clung to their bodies. It looked like they'd come out here into the shallow water to swim and . . . *make out?*

"Hello, Amy," mumbled Alexis, hastily trying to button up her blouse.

I made a gurgling noise.

Grinning, Desmond plucked a shell out of Alexis's hair. His eyes shone when he looked at her. How old was the guy? Twenty? Nineteen? Eighteen? My mouth opened and closed again.

"Amy—I can explain," said Alexis. She was still nestled in close to this . . . *boy!*

At last I regained control of my legs. I turned and ran. Water flew up around me and splashed into my eyes. I stumbled ashore, slipped on the shingle and fell forward onto my hands and knees. I picked myself straight back up and lurched onward. I had to get away from here. Far away!

Alexis shouted something after me. Will's voice drifted over to me too. Then Desmond's. But I didn't hear a word. The blood was roaring in my ears, drowning out every other sound. I was startled, therefore, to suddenly feel a hand on my shoulder. Will was jogging along beside me.

"I think you misunderstood," he panted.

"Oh really?" I spat. There wasn't much to misunderstand, after all. "I can put two and two together. Alexis has obviously got over her broken heart. I'm very happy for her!" I broke free of his grasp and scrambled up a sand dune.

Will didn't follow me.

I ran blindly onto the moor, wishing I could retreat into my own shell now.

For a long time I roamed across the wild moorland. Thorns clawed at the legs of my jeans and a crust of mud formed around the soles of my Chucks. My thoughts had knotted themselves together into a kind of fireball inside my head, and all the stories I'd ever read hung like deadweights from my feet. Stories about heroes, stories about people who were exactly the opposite. Stories about love. Stories about war. Exciting stories. Comforting stories. Sad stories. They clung to me and whispered to me how life should and shouldn't be.

To me, Alexis had always been one of the heroes. She was my role model, the mum who looked after me, the best friend who I could talk to about absolutely anything. But now dark blotches marred my bright, shining image of her. Today I'd seen a different Alexis—an Alexis who had feelings for a boy not much older than me. An Alexis who seemed to have completely forgotten her love for Dominik in the space of a few days. This was an Alexis I didn't know.

I was starting to get a stitch, but still I ran on. Sweat trickled down my temples. I was completely out of breath, but still I ran. At first it was anger that drove me. Then shame at the thought of this incongruous romance.

But I wasn't really ashamed of Alexis and I wasn't angry either. More than anything the feeling that weighed heavy on my chest, threatening to suffocate me, was disappointment. It was the realization that Alexis had drifted away from me. That she didn't understand me anymore. A few days on Stormsay had been enough to create a rift between us.

I arrived back at Lennox House just in time for dinner. I sat down, mud and all, at the table where Lady Mairead and Alexis were already seated. Alexis had a dry dress on and a big felt flower in her hair. My grandmother raised her eyebrows at the sight of me.

"I fell over," I muttered with a shrug.

Alexis quickly steered the conversation around to the flower arrangement in the middle of the table. After a while Mr. Stevens came in with a large silver platter and, with the air of a man taking his life in his hands, presented us with a joint of tofu he had marinated in the oven with onions and carrots. It was accompanied by vegan mashed potatoes and green beans, and tasted amazing. Without saying a word I wolfed down as much as I possibly could and disappeared upstairs, where I showered and got into bed.

A little while later, when the door creaked open and I felt Alexis sit down on the edge of my bed, I pretended to be asleep.

The next morning Glenn came into the classroom looking grave. "I must remind you," he said, "that it is forbidden for book jumpers to jump into the book world outside of lessons until their training is complete. That is one of the most important rules of all. Have you learned nothing from what happened to Holmes?" The usually friendly twinkle in his eye had vanished. He looked hard at each of us in turn.

I gnawed at my lower lip. Had Werther and I messed something up in the book world? I cast my mind back to our last couple of expeditions. We'd been in *The Wizard of Oz*, and before that in *Twenty Thousand Leagues Under the Sea*. But both times we'd been very careful and restrained in our explorations. Had we made a stupid mistake?

Glenn pursed his lips. He seemed to take the fact that somebody had broken the rules again as a personal insult.

Part of me felt bad because of course I knew the rule and yet I persisted in breaking it. But another part of me felt that it was impossible only to visit the book world for half an hour a day under Glenn's supervision. The temptation was just too strong. "So what's . . . um . . . what's gone wrong?" I asked.

"Nothing, yet," he said sharply. "But the mere fact that Desmond saw one of you up at the *Porta Litterae* last night is worrying. A careless jump could lead to goodness knows what—potentially something even worse than the death of a protagonist."

Had I heard right? "Um—there was somebody at the stone circle?" I mumbled. Was Glenn not referring to my little escapades from the four-poster bed after all?

He nodded sternly. "Where else? This *somebody* had their hood up and was sneaking about on the hilltop. Desmond was coming back from a . . . a nighttime walk, and he spotted the glimmer of a book from which a book jumper must just have emerged. But by the time he reached the portal, whoever it was had disappeared. So, which of you was it?"

I swallowed hard—mainly because I had a pretty good idea who Desmond had been visiting on his "nighttime walk."

Glenn was waiting for an answer. His gaze bored into mine, then slid to Will and then to Betsy, who gave an indignant sniff. "Jumping in secret is so irresponsible," she said. "Obviously after so many years training I know I *could* do it without causing chaos in the book world at the first opportunity—but I would never take such a risk. And I think you know that."

The corners of Glenn's mouth twitched.

Betsy took this as agreement and went on: "And anyway it's pretty obvious who it must have been. Given that Will isn't jumping at all anymore, there's only one other person it *could* have been—someone inexperienced and naïve enough to go sneaking into books at night."

I turned to face her.

"Someone who doesn't give a crap about Stormsay and our family traditions. Someone who doesn't have the true book-jumper blood of the Macalisters running through their veins," Betsy went on.

"What do you mean? I'd never go to the stone circle at night to jump," I said, and in my head I added: *because I don't need the stone circle to get to the book world.*

"Are you and Desmond sure this person was using the portal?" Will put in.

"We are," said Glenn.

"Perhaps there's another book jumper that we don't know about. A distant relative or something," I mused aloud. "Perhaps that person is the thief as well."

"Thief?" inquired Glenn. "What thief?"

I told him about the strange goings-on in the book world and the fairies' theory that somebody was stealing the core ingredients of stories. To be on the safe side—not wanting to arouse Glenn's wrath by telling him about my unauthorized excursions—I made out that the fairies had just popped up in *The Jungle Book* recently. But by the time I'd finished, Glenn, Betsy, and even Will looked more amused than alarmed.

"You do know you can't trust fairies, don't you? They probably just made it up as a prank," said Will.

"But we—er—they saw it with their own eyes! The White Rabbit from *Alice in Wonderland* can't talk anymore and—"

"And it's not as if *Alice in Wonderland* is full of crazies that like to play tricks on people," Betsy interrupted with an affected little laugh.

"At any rate, you do not seem to be doing what you are supposed to be doing, which is concentrating on *The Jungle Book*," Glenn remarked. "I cannot condone that. Do you not think you need any training?"

I looked down at my desk. "It's not that. But the book world and what the other characters have to say is so exciting."

"I think we can all understand that sentiment. But from now on you must do as you are told and focus on the characters from your own story, do you understand?" Glenn looked a little friendlier now.

"Yes," I said. "So is it not even a possibility that there might be other book jumpers out there we just don't know about yet?"

Glenn shook his head. "Who else could there be? This island is tiny. We would know if somebody new arrived, wouldn't we?"

An hour later, Glenn issued us detailed instructions for our jumps and sent us off to the portal. But no sooner had we left the class-room than I almost collided with Desmond, who came careering around a corner with a pile of heavy books. He managed to pull up just in time, but the tower of books he was carrying started swaying dangerously and he had to weave to and fro for a few seconds to steady them.

"Amy!" he exclaimed. "Er . . . could I talk to you for a moment?"

I looked at his scarred cheeks and the freckles on his nose. His gray eyes shone through the haze of dancing dust motes that filled every corner of these underground passageways. For all intents and purposes he seemed like a nice guy. But under the present cir-cumstances . . . "I don't see what we could have to talk about," I said, lifting my chin.

"See—he thinks it was Amy too," Betsy whispered to Will. The two of them were walking behind me.

I left Desmond standing there with his pile of books, his shoul-ders sagging as he threw a helpless glance at Will, and marched on toward the exit. Just as I was wondering whether Betsy was tell-ing the truth about never having jumped in secret when she seemed to think she was by far the best of the three of us, Will dragged me without warning into a gap between two shelves.

"You go on ahead," he called to Betsy, drawing me deeper into the dusty thicket of the library. He finally came to a stop in a corner between some frayed rolls of parchment and a weird painted globe.

"Look, Amy—I know this sounds weird, but Desmond is older than he looks, okay?" he whispered, suddenly so close to me that the smell of moorland and soap filled my nostrils. Will spoke quickly, as if that would make what he had to say less implausible. "He's not a real person—he's a book character. So are Glenn and Clyde. All three of them have been living here in the library for nearly three hundred years. Our clans rescued them from the burning manuscript."

"They're *book characters?*" I stammered. "They seem so . . . real and everything."

Will pulled one of the scrolls from the shelf behind me and unrolled it carefully. "Where do you think they got those burn scars from?"

I remembered how sad Glenn had looked when he'd told me about the fairy tale that had caught fire. So that had been his home. No wonder he found it difficult to talk about. "Can't they go back?"

Will's fingertips glided over the text. "No. Because their story was destroyed, they're trapped forever in the outside world."

"Oh," I said, and now I, too, ran my fingers over the porous parchment. It was weird how valuable a scrap of paper like this with a few symbols on it could be. "I didn't think book characters could live in the outside world permanently."

"They don't, normally. But they can. Though they never feel properly at home outside the book world because they're different, and always will be. You don't notice it at first glance. But they're stronger than us, for example, and they don't sleep. Every hundred years or so they have a kind of nap for a few years, and then they're ready to go again. Oh yeah—and they don't age." Will looked me straight in the eye. His thumb brushed the back of my hand and a shiver ran through me. A lovely shiver. I looked down, embarrassed. "Desmond only *looks* young, on the outside. So if your mum does want to be with him, there's no—"

I let go of the parchment and pushed past Will. "That's no

excuse!" I said. "She went behind my back and basically threw herself at the nearest guy she could find, okay? The whole reason we came here was because she got her heart broken. Dominik literally just broke up with her. And she was devastated by it, but now she seems to have completely forgotten about that all of a sudden and I really don't understand what's going on with her." I couldn't help it—tears welled up in my eyes. I blinked furiously at the ceiling.

"*That's* why you came back to Stormsay?" asked Will.

I nodded. "Alexis was so down about Dominik and I . . ." My mouth went dry. "I needed to get away from it all too. Have a change of scene."

"That's easy to do when you're a book jumper." Will rolled the ancient parchment up again and placed it back on the shelf. He gazed at it a moment longer, then took a deep breath. "Don't get me wrong, I think book jumping is a very good way to distract yourself when you're feeling sad," he began, and it sounded as though he'd been planning for days what he was going to say. "But do me a favor and be careful. It's easy to underestimate how much damage you can do. I learned that the hard way."

"Mhmm," I said. "I'll be careful."

"That's what *I* thought. And now Sherlock's dead."

"I won't bring any characters to the outside world, don't worry," I reassured him. "All I want is to have a look around their stories." I couldn't suppress a grin. "To be honest, I've been to a few other stories as well as *The Jungle Book* and *Oliver Twist*. This really is the best thing that's ever happened to me."

Will's face remained solemn. "And what if you do end up

disrupting something?" he asked. "What if the White Rabbit has lost his voice because of you?"

"So you do believe me? That there's something going on in the book world—that somebody's stealing the ideas?"

"No, I don't. But I do worry that you're not taking your gift seriously enough."

"Rubbish," I said. "I'm just doing a bit of exploring. I know exactly what I'm doing."

"You mean sneaking into books at night."

He suspected me! I folded my arms. "And what if I was?" I sniffed. "Just because you made a mistake, that doesn't give you the right to judge me. And just because you suddenly think it's wrong doesn't mean we all have to stop jumping." I glared at him. "That's what you want, isn't it? You'd prefer it if me and Betsy stayed out of the book world too."

Will shrugged. "At least that way we could be sure nobody else would die."

"Sure," I said. "But I'm not going to give up the book world just because you're feeling guilty. It's too amazing. I won't give it up. Ever."

Will nodded jerkily. "I get it," he snapped. "Just wait till you do something stupid and destroy a story, then. I won't warn you again."

"Is that a promise?"

He turned and stomped off without another word.

The dagger's blade was cold and silver.
And it was sharp. It seemed to slice even
through the moonlight that glanced off its surface.
The knight reached for the jewel-studded hilt.
It molded itself to his hand, as if this dagger
had been forged especially for him. As if it were part
of him—a part of his body, long believed lost, and
now returned to him. "I thank you," said the knight.
His eyes still rested upon the weapon.
The princess closed the velvet-lined casket
and replaced it on her dainty little dresser.
"Kill it," she whispered.

8

A CHANGE IN THE WEATHER

"Now how the winds soar, and they rush, and they whirl," sighed Werther, looking out at the wet fields and the swaying trees at the edge of the wood. Rain came pelting down on us. It was dark, and we were standing somewhere in the fictional version of a nineteenth-century British shire. The downpour had left me and Werther soaked to the skin. Within seconds my sweater had been completely saturated with rainwater and now hung heavy on my shoulders. Werther's linen shirt had turned see-through and was sticking to his chest, and his stockings and velvet knee breeches were spattered with mud. We shivered as the water continued to trickle inside our clothes. But I wasn't ready to go and warm up in another, drier story just yet.

I couldn't take my eyes off the dark-haired young woman lying on the doorstep of a small house nearby, crying. Her dress was filthy from days of wandering across country, and her shawl looked just as sodden as my sweater. But none of that seemed to bother her. Her eyes were closed and she was waiting for death. Luckily, however, I knew that she was about to be rescued. Because this was Jane Eyre, who had recently fled from Thornfield Hall and her beloved Mr. Rochester after discovering a dark secret from his past. Soon the clergyman St. John Rivers would appear and he and his sisters would take Jane into their home. I was determined to wait and see it happen. Luckily, the rain was finally starting to die down.

"Such weather always brings to my mind the poem 'Spring Celebration,'" Werther declared. "Is not Nature wonderful after such a downpour?"

"Yes," I said. But more wonderful, in my opinion, was the fact that St. John Rivers had just appeared and taken poor Jane inside the house. Yet again I had to remind myself that this wasn't a dream—I really was inside one of my favorite stories.

"Do you know it? It is by Klopstock," said Werther, suddenly giving me a strange sideways glance.

"What? Oh, the poem. No, I'm afraid not," I murmured. Werther seemed *very* disappointed by this, so I added hastily: "But it sounds nice."

"Yes?" he asked hopefully. "Then you love Nature just as I do?"

"Er—of course," I said. "Nature and literature."

Werther smiled and was about to launch into another speech about poetry when something very small and very blue came plummeting out of the sky toward us and landed on Werther's nose.

"The thief has struck again," piped the fairy. "We saw him. He's wearing a cloak, and sneaking through *The Wizard of Oz*!"

"We're on our way!" I called.

The fairy went zooming off and we followed her at a run.

We arrived a few minutes later at the gray farm where Dorothy lived with her uncle, her aunt, and her dog, Toto, and all four of them came running out to meet us in great agitation.

"He was here!" cried Dorothy's uncle, a man with gray hair and a gray face to match.

"The thief was in our story—he stole the cyclone that's supposed to carry off Dorothy and our house," explained Dorothy's aunt, who looked just as colorless as the farmland around her.

"Who was it?" I asked. "How did he do it?" How on earth did somebody *steal* a cyclone?

"We couldn't tell—all we saw was a shadow!" sobbed Dorothy. "He was so far away. He came sneaking though our pages, right at the edges, and then over there on the horizon he broke something out of the story. Something that lit up. He tucked it inside his cloak. Then all of a sudden he was gone." She sniffed hard, and Toto howled. "Since then the cyclone's been missing."

"What would anybody want with a stolen cyclone?" I asked.

Dorothy shrugged.

"It is a mystery to me," murmured Werther.

We looked out at the horizon. Not so much as a breath of wind was stirring.

Will lay on his threadbare sofa and tried to imagine what it must be like to be dead. Had Holmes stopped existing completely or had he just passed on to another place? What was it like there? Was he angry with Will for bringing him to the outside world and putting him in danger? Question after question whirled through his head as if there were a storm raging inside his skull. He couldn't concentrate.

He'd thought it would get easier if only he didn't have to look at those words anymore. He'd painted over the writing on the wall above the stove with white paint to stop it intruding on his thoughts. But he'd found he could still read it. And in any case, the words were already etched into his memory. He could see them even when he closed his eyes, blazing red before him:

I HAVE AWOKEN

Who the hell had left him that message? And what did it mean? He would have liked to tip another bucket of white paint over his own thoughts.

Will hadn't been to the Secret Library for two days. Not since the argument with Amy. And why should he? He wasn't a book jumper anymore, and nobody would pay any attention to his warnings. Instead he lay on the sofa, lost in thought, as the sun's brief guest appearance came to an end and the air grew colder and damper.

Betsy had come to the cottage yesterday. She'd stood outside and knocked at the door and said the Laird would not allow this and that Will had to come to lessons. In the afternoon Glenn had come by and asked Will was he still alive, or had he drowned in self-pity? He hadn't replied.

But he had to admit that he was starting to go a bit stir-crazy in here. He sat up and put on his boots. Perhaps fresh air and a little exercise would make him feel like himself again.

He didn't realize how dark it was until he opened the door. It was nighttime already. The starry sky arched high and clear over the ghostly expanse of the moor. Wisps of fog hung in the air above the slippery paths that snaked through heather, peat moss, and sundew. He breathed in and then out again. On the wind was the tang of moist earth. Will stepped out into the darkness.

He'd been roaming this moorland since childhood, and it greeted him tonight with the same sucking, gurgling noises he'd come to know well. It covered most of Stormsay, and Will knew it concealed some treacherous depths. People even said there were lost graves from Celtic times hidden somewhere on the island. But Will wasn't afraid—not even when the fog patches thickened and wrapped themselves around his shoulders like a clammy shawl. It soon grew so misty that the light of the stars was barely visible, and he switched on the little flashlight he always wore at his belt.

Immediately a beam of light sliced through the darkness around him. He could just about make out something darting away from him at the edge of his field of vision. Something big. Something that couldn't possibly be an animal. He stood still and swung the flashlight around in a circle, trying to see what it was that had fled from him. Or had he just been scared by his own shadow?

He was about to conclude that this must have been the case when the flashlight fell on a human form. It slipped into a gap between two bushes a few yards away from him and stopped dead. In the fog, all Will could distinguish was its outline.

But it was definitely a human being.

"Who's there?"

No answer.

"Hello?"

The figure hovered motionless in the fog.

Then Will took a step toward it. It retreated before him, farther into the darkness.

"What's going on?" called Will. "Betsy? Glenn? Amy, is that you?" He quickened his pace.

There was a rustling laugh and then, all at once, the shadow was gone. Will ran to the spot where he'd last seen it. He shone the flashlight over the bushes and berries that grew on this part of the moor. Some of them looked as though they had been trodden flat.

Suddenly there was a whisper from behind him. "She knew," breathed a voice, "that he would stop the monster." The words ensnared him, enticed him, echoed strangely in his head. Will felt someone's breath on the back of his neck. He turned around.

But there was nobody there.

In the pool of flashlight were a few pillows of moss and a mound of rotting vegetation, nothing more. Whoever had been standing behind him seemed to have vanished, in a matter of seconds, into thin air. What was going on here? Was someone trying to freak him out?

She knew, said the echo in Will's head, *that he would stop the monster*. What kind of bizarre phrase was that? Had he read it somewhere?

Ever since I'd found out who Alexis was visiting when she went off on one of her long walks or snuck out of bed at night, evenings at Lennox House had gotten a whole lot quieter. Having pretended to be asleep the day before, I'd managed to avoid Alexis yesterday by locking myself in the bathroom and spending hours in the bath. But this evening at dinner Lady Mairead had announced that she wanted us all to have a game of Monopoly after dessert, which was why Alexis and I had been sitting at the table for what felt like an eternity staring down at a brightly colored Monopoly board. It was late, past midnight, and I was tired from my trips to *Jane Eyre* and *The Wizard of Oz*. But my grandmother couldn't seem to get enough.

"Your go, Amy," Lady Mairead prompted me from the head of the table. She'd just bought Park Lane and was busy counting a substantial heap of Monopoly money.

I rolled the dice and got sent to Jail. Great.

Alexis bought a railroad.

Lady Mairead was still counting her money. When she'd finally finished, she looked first at Alexis and then at me. Both of us were stone-faced. Then she slammed her wad of cash down on the table. "Fine," she said. "Fine, fine, fine. There doesn't seem to be much point in this. I thought playing a game might take your minds off things, but it seems I was wrong. So, what's the matter with the two of you?"

"Nothing," I said, scratching at a little blob of sauce on the tablecloth.

Alexis was silent.

I folded my arms.

Alexis put her head in her hands and closed her eyes.

Lady Mairead sighed. "You haven't so much as looked at each other for days. Where are we, nursery school?"

I laughed out loud. *Nursery school* was very apt.

Alexis looked at me incredulously. "Amy, I told you—I can explain. Why won't you at least listen to what I've got to say?"

I pressed my lips together.

"Would you rather carry on sulking like a five-year-old? Let's clear this thing up."

"What is there to clear up?" I snorted. "You've managed to get over Dominik at the speed of light? Great. You've fallen in love again? Great."

"You know what—it *is* great!" cried Alexis.

"In love? What's all this, Alexis?" asked Lady Mairead. "Here on Stormsay? With whom?"

Neither of us paid any attention to my grandmother.

"You could at least have told me," I hissed. "I thought you trusted me. I thought we told each other everything." There was bitterness in my voice. "But I guess I was wrong." First my so-called friends in Bochum had betrayed me, and now my own mother! Was everyone I cared about conspiring against me?

Alexis blinked. "I . . . I wanted to tell you, but . . ."

"But you were too busy snogging, right?"

"Does this mean you're going to stay?" inquired Lady Mairead. "Once the holidays are over? Are you going to get married, Alexis?" She looked as though all her dreams were coming true. "You could live here at Lennox House, of course," she mused aloud. "Is it Henk? Or the ferryman?"

Alexis stood up. "I don't know how to make you see, Amy. What I have with him is something special." She walked around the table and laid a hand on my wrist.

"Oh yes," I sighed theatrically. Even I could see how mean I was being to her, but I couldn't help myself. "Young love," I hissed. "*Very* young love."

"Stop it," said Alexis, angry now. "Stop embarrassing yourself." She pulled me out into the hallway, away from Lady Mairead and her wedding plans. "Let's talk about this properly, okay?" She put her hands on my shoulders, but I shook them off.

"I'd say *you're* the one who's embarrassing yourself," I said. "Do you know what it looks like when you kiss him? He's barely a day older than me!"

Alexis sighed and lowered her voice as if she were afraid my grandmother might be listening at the door. "He only *looks* young, Amy. Desmond isn't a real person, he's—"

"A book character, yes, I know. Will already told me. Blah blah blah! But even if he was a thousand years old, what about Dominik? I mean—how could you forget him so quickly? Do you even remember how upset you were two weeks ago?"

"Of course I do," murmured Alexis. "And part of me is still upset, but on the other hand—"

"You found a passable replacement."

"Would you stop interrupting me all the time?" cried Alexis. "I'm trying to explain."

"Well, fine—please do. Because I really don't understand." My whole body was shaking now and I was finding it hard to breathe normally.

Alexis nodded, thought for a moment and then took my hand. "Come with me," she said quietly. "It's time you knew the whole story."

"What whole story?" I stumbled after her.

"Come with me," Alexis said again.

We climbed the stairs to the top floor of the house, but when we reached the corridor where our bedrooms were, Alexis led me straight past them and down to the end of the hallway, to a door hidden behind a wall hanging (which explained why I'd never noticed it before). Behind the door was a steep staircase whose boards creaked beneath our feet as we climbed higher and higher. We soon found ourselves peering into the dusty darkness of an enormous attic. Chests and assorted bits of junk were piled almost to the roof beams. But we still hadn't reached our destination. Alexis now made for a rickety old chest of drawers from which she pulled several blankets, before directing me toward a narrow ladder that led up to a skylight.

Dust rained down on us as she opened the hatch. We pushed through a veil of cobwebs and out onto the roof, where we were met by the icy chill of the night air. I shivered. Alexis went ahead, wobbling across the ancient roof tiles toward a dormer window and spreading out one of the blankets on its flat, narrow surface. I slithered after her, trying not to look down. When I reached Alexis she draped a second blanket around both of our shoulders. Then we sat down and laid the third blanket over our legs. We were both out of breath from the climb, and for a while neither of us said a word.

Overhead, millions of stars glittered like diamonds in the black velvet of a jewelry box. Below us lay the moor, swathed in thick fog. In the distance loomed the silhouette of Macalister Castle. There were still lights on in some of its windows.

"This was my favorite place when I was your age," said Alexis at last.

I nodded. "Because you can see the whole island from here?"

"Because your grandmother never thought to come looking for me here."

"Mmm," I said, wrapping the blanket more tightly round my shoulders. Something glimmered out on the moor, a little light. Or was I mistaken?

Alexis took a lock of my hair between her fingers, twiddled it for a moment and tucked it gently back behind my ear. "I didn't mean to hurt you, little giraffe," she whispered.

"But you did." I kept my eyes on the moor, where the tiny point of light now appeared to be moving.

"The thing about Desmond is . . . I didn't just throw myself at the nearest man I could find. And I did want to tell you about it, but I couldn't. Desmond and I have known each other a very long time. In fact, he's one of the reasons I left Stormsay in the first place."

I turned to look at her. My mum suddenly seemed older. Nothing about her was lively or colorful now. Even her hair looked dull all of a sudden. I spotted little wrinkles in the skin around her eyes. "You and him—back then, were you . . . ?"

Alexis's eyes bored into mine. "Desmond . . ." she said slowly, as if it cost her great effort, "Desmond is your father."

I looked out across the moor again. The little dot of light had vanished. I stared at the fog patches without really seeing them.

"Amy?" murmured Alexis.

I shut my eyes for a moment as what she had just told me sank slowly into my brain. Desmond was my father. It sounded absurd. I saw him in my mind's eye. To all appearances he was barely older than me. A book character with burns on his face who'd been living in the Secret Library for generations. I was used to not having a father. The very idea of it felt wrong. I, Amy Lennox, did not have a father. That was how it had always been. Alexis couldn't just come along and—

"Amy?"

I blinked. Alexis lifted her hand as if to stroke my cheek, but when it was halfway there she let it drop again.

"We never told anyone," said Alexis. "Desmond and I always met in secret. We knew it was forbidden. A book jumper and a book character—the clans would've flipped. They would never have allowed it. If they'd caught us . . . Desmond and I loved each other very much, but we knew we would always have to hide. And then there was the fact that Desmond doesn't age—even at seventeen I knew our love couldn't last. We meant the world to each other, but at the same time there was this constant fear. The fear that we'd be found out. And I was afraid I'd get old and Desmond would lose interest in me. And then when I realized I was pregnant . . ."

"I . . ." I stammered. "I thought you went away because of something that happened in the book world?"

Alexis smiled sadly. "Yes—that too. My practice book in those days was *Anna Karenina* and I found it difficult to watch as Anna's love destroyed her and she threw herself under the train at the end. Anna and I were friends." She cleared her throat. "And that was how I knew I had to do something about my own situation, if I didn't want to end up like her. Sooner or later my love for Desmond would have destroyed me, too, I was sure of it. I realized I had to go away. I told my family I couldn't bear to carry on jumping anymore."

"But really you were leaving because you wanted to get away from Desmond?"

"I didn't *want* to get away from him, but I had to. Mainly because

I was afraid of how the clans would react to a baby that was . . . well, that was only half human."

Only half human? It felt as though the roof had given way beneath me. My stomach lurched, and a thick fog filled my head. *Only half human. Only half human.*

Alexis was still talking, but all I could hear were those three words: *only half human.*

I'd always known I was different. But *this* different?

". . . thought that if I left straightaway everyone would think your father was someone from the mainland."

I looked at my hands, turning them this way and that in front of my face. They were human hands! There was no way I could be half fictional, was there?

". . . have to keep it a secret, okay? Amy? AMY?" She shook me.

I let my hands drop. Out of my mouth came an unintelligible croak.

"Are you okay?"

"N-no." I was shivering again.

Alexis put her arms around me and drew my face into the crook of her neck. She stroked my back. "Of course you're not," she said. "This must be a shock for you. I didn't even want to have to tell you about all this, really—that's why Desmond and I tried to keep it a secret that we were seeing each other again, but . . ."

I hung heavy in her arms as if turned to stone.

"I don't think you've inherited all that much 'literary-ness' from him, you know," Alexis went on. "Before your first jump I was very nervous—about how your body would react, about whether you'd even be able to use the portal, about whether you'd be able to get back on your own. But it looks like the only thing you've inherited from Desmond is the fact that you're quite a talented book jumper, and other than that—"

"I can jump from anywhere," I whispered into her hair. "I don't need a portal to get to the book world."

Alexis's hand on my back stopped moving for a moment. I felt her breath catch in her throat, but then she seemed to force herself to carry on breathing normally. "That," she began after a while, "seems pretty logical actually. After all, book characters don't need a portal to get from the outside world back into their own stories. And since you don't come from or belong to any specific story, you can probably just jump into any story you choose."

I said nothing. I breathed in the scent of her organic shampoo, which reminded me of my childhood, and tried to make sense of the bombshell my mum had just dropped. Eventually, however, Alexis let go of me. "It's getting a bit cold," she said. "Let's go to bed, shall we?"

I nodded. As Alexis bundled up the blankets, I looked again for the light on the moor. It had vanished. There was movement, however, on the grounds of Lennox House. There—wasn't that a shadow flitting between the hedges? Something dark. Definitely not a stray sheep. It looked as though somebody was creeping along between the flowerbeds. Somebody with their hood up.

I squinted, but couldn't make out anything distinct. So I clambered back across the roof after Alexis, lowered myself through the skylight, and climbed back down the ladder. Alexis put the blankets away in the chest of drawers, and we said good night outside her bedroom door. Then I muttered something about wanting to get a glass of water from the kitchen and rushed down the stairs, through the dark corridors of the mansion, across the entrance hall and out, at last, into the grounds.

The figure had been a little way away from the house. Somewhere over there, by the rosebushes . . .

Gravel crunched under my feet. I tried to move more quietly, intending to creep up on whoever it was . . . and stubbed my toe on a birdbath. Crap! I bit my lip to keep myself from yelping as I hopped around on one leg clutching my throbbing toe, spraying gravel in all directions. I fervently hoped it would sound like nothing more than one of the sheep having a nightmare.

Crouched low, I pressed myself against one of the neatly trimmed hedges and inched along it toward the next turning in the path. But the hedge seemed to go on forever. It felt like an eternity before I finally reached a break in the foliage and peered around the corner.

But there was nobody there. Roses twined, solitary and peaceful, around a metal archway. The lawn beyond glistened with dew.

"Thirty-three," mumbled a voice behind me, so suddenly that it made me jump. When I turned around I found myself face-to-face with Brock, still wearing his blue dungarees and muttering numbers to himself. His eyes were trained on the path and his hair and beard were unkempt and dirty. There was no sign of a hood.

"Oh, hello," I said, backing away a little. "Are . . . are you counting again?"

"Yes," he grunted without looking up. "Brock likes counting at night."

"Oh, okay—I'll just let you get on with it, th—"

"Black pebbles," he barked, pointing to a few isolated dark

nuggets in among the light gray gravel on the path. "Pretty. Thirty-four, thirty-five, thirty-six, thirty-seven." He carried on walking.

"Right, then. Enjoy," I murmured as I headed back to the house.

I was dog-tired when I finally got back to my room and snuggled down under the quilt on my four-poster bed. But sleep was out of the question. My toe hurt and my head was buzzing. Desmond was my father! I was half fictional! And the thief was sneaking around somewhere on Stormsay under cover of night!

According to my phone it was already half past one. I had to be up for lessons in a few hours. But still I reached for the e-reader on my bedside table and scrolled through my library. I wouldn't be able to sleep now anyway, that was for sure. And the prospect of spending hours tossing and turning and going over and over everything in my mind wasn't particularly inviting. What I needed was an escape from reality. A little rest and relaxation in a benevolent world.

That ruled out thrillers and fantasy adventure stories for starters. I scrolled on past some soppy romances. I really was not in the mood for lovers slobbering all over each other. The children's book section looked more promising. I browsed through some fairy tales and children's classics and eventually clicked on *Heidi*. Yes—just the thing! A trip to an Alpine pasture, a carefree afternoon with Heidi and Peter: that sounded like the perfect distraction.

I selected a sunny, cheerful scene and laid the e-reader over my face. A moment later I landed in a brightly blooming mountain pasture.

A little girl was running toward me, barefoot, with an armful of flowers. She was laughing.

*The knight mounted his horse. Tucked inside his boot was
the princess's dagger, and his saddle bags held provender,
a map, and a thick, strong rope.
Thus accoutered, he rode out into the kingdom.
The princess waved farewell to him from
the highest battlements of her castle.
She knew that he would stop the monster.
He would do as she had bidden him.*

THE CHASE

I FELT AS THOUGH I'D BARELY had time to blink and already it was morning. The ringing of the alarm clock on my phone jolted me from sleep after what had been little more than a two-hour nap and I dragged myself, head pounding, downstairs to breakfast. Alexis greeted me with a smile, no longer avoiding my eyes. Suddenly everything she'd told me yesterday came flooding back. The fact that Desmond was my father still felt hard to believe—especially when he appeared a little while later at the entrance to the Secret Library, just as lessons were about to begin, and told us Glenn had gone to Mainland to pick up a delivery of new books and had asked Desmond to stand in for him.

He was dressed, as always, in his monk's habit. The web of thin scars on his face spread from the left-hand corner of his mouth across his cheek and up to his temple, where it disappeared into his blond hair. But in spite of everything he must have lived through, his gray eyes were still those of a young man. And so were the long slim hands emerging from the sleeves of his robe, with which he beckoned to us to follow him.

Desmond glided smoothly down the spiral staircase. My eyes were glued to the back of his head as I slithered—much less elegantly—down the steps. My neck ached as if every shelf in the library had collapsed on top of me, and my eyes were swollen from lack of sleep. I was limping a bit, too. Behind me, Betsy and Will (he had unexpectedly turned up to lessons this morning) were muttering something about the Laird, who had apparently flown into a rage the day before and made all sorts of wild threats to Will because he wasn't jumping anymore.

I was longing to flop down on my chair, lay my head on the desk, and have a little snooze. But Desmond wasn't taking us to the classroom. Instead, he led us deeper inside the library than I'd ever been before. He grabbed a cast-iron lantern, lit it, and strode on down ever dustier aisles of shelves, as if he'd been this way a hundred times before. He probably had, I reflected, over the course of many, many decades—perhaps even centuries. The shelves around us were so crammed with (increasingly moldy) books that they had started to sag. There was a smell of very old paper and our route took us continually downhill. The library seemed to be carving its way deeper and deeper into the bedrock of the island. At the same time it grew steadily darker all around us, with the passageways lit only by the odd lamp here and there. Eventually the lamps stopped altogether. The yellow light of Desmond's lantern danced ahead of us and threw shadow patterns onto the rows of books and scrolls as we passed.

We entered a circular room somewhere deep beneath the island. It had walls of roughly hewn rock and was completely empty apart from a claw-foot table in the middle.

"This is the end of the Secret Library," Desmond explained. "There are no more books here. Apart from this one." He pointed to the table.

We moved closer and now I saw that there was a pane of glass built into the carved wooden tabletop, and that beneath the glass lay a few scraps of charred paper. I read the words *monster* and *knight*. Written on one of the larger fragments was the phrase: *"I choose you," said the princess. "Kneel."*

"This is all that remains of the manuscript," said Desmond. "It is all that your ancestors were able to rescue from the flames. Just these scraps of paper and . . . us." His hands trembled on the glass. He looked me straight in the eye and a look of pain that was much older than his outward appearance flickered across his face. "Glenn, Clyde, and I—we can never go back. We have been living in the outside world ever since, getting by as best we can on Stormsay." *Please don't condemn me*, his eyes seemed to say.

I nodded almost imperceptibly. Since my conversation with Alexis I no longer blamed either of them for having fallen in love. When people lived so close together on such a tiny island they were going to fall in love sometimes, like it or not. . . . The whole thing was still weird, obviously. Finding out that Desmond was my father had been a shock. But I would get used to it in time.

"I didn't know there was so much of it left," said Betsy, leaning over the pane of glass with evident interest. "It's a shame none of it seems to be connected. Have you ever tried to fit the pieces together?"

"We have tried everything, believe me. But it is difficult," said Desmond. "Too many memories."

Will, too, seemed fascinated by the remnants of the manuscript. He pored over the scraps of paper, dotted with burn holes and soot marks. "He would stop the monster," he murmured under his breath.

I, on the other hand, was still staring at Desmond. He was studiously avoiding looking at the manuscript.

"Who . . ." I began at last, gnawing at my bottom lip. I hardly dared ask the question. But I felt that I had to know, if I was to understand who and what my father was. "Glenn said the manuscript was a fairy tale," I whispered at last, too quietly for Betsy and Will to hear. "Who were you in the story? What was it about?"

Desmond lowered his eyes. "I was a knight," he said. "And the story was about the pursuit of a terrible monster." Then he handed me the lantern. "You three go back. Glenn wants you to spend some time in your practice books today."

"But don't you need light for the way back?" I asked. The lantern was heavier than I'd expected.

"No. I know the way." He looked as if he wanted to be alone for a while in the darkness. Alone with his memories. We left him.

Half an hour later Betsy jumped from the stone circle into her book of fairy tales and I jumped into the jungle, while Will sat on one of the boulders watching us. He was still refusing to return to the book world.

I landed, as usual, among the roots of the giant jungle tree. By now I'd mastered the art of landing without falling over. As soon as the greenery of the forest unfolded around me I picked my way out of the tangle of tree roots and went over to join Werther and Shere Khan the tiger, who were discussing the strange thefts and debating whether or not the fairies could be trusted.

"Hello," I greeted them.

"Ah, how wonderful! There you are!" Werther beamed at me.

The tiger gave me a nod.

"So—any news?" I asked.

"Dracula's on the warpath. Says somebody's raided his treasure chamber," rumbled Shere Khan.

"Perhaps we should go there first, then, and have a scout around," I said to Werther.

But he immediately turned a shade paler and shook his head.

"If the fellow really has been robbed, it might be best to give his story a wide berth," Shere Khan chipped in. "He can be rather irascible at times, and when he gets like that he'll bite you as soon as look at you."

"And besides, I already had, er—an alternative plan," added Werther, straightening his ponytail, which had got tangled up in a creeper. "If you will permit me, Miss Amy, I should like to show you a flower."

"A flower?"

"It is a very special flower—the only one of its kind in all the universe. It is beautiful, just like y—"

"If there really is a criminal going around destroying stories, I wouldn't have thought this was the best time to be looking at ridiculous flowers," Shere Khan cut in.

Werther pursed his lips, offended. "Botanical study is *not* ridiculous," he said. "Don't you agree, Miss Amy? Do you not wish to see this extraordinary flower?" He gazed hopefully at me. "It really is wonderfully, wonderfully pretty!"

"Well," I began hesitantly. "Where is it? Is it far from here?"

"Not at all. A stone's throw, so to speak."

The tiger sighed. "At least wait for me to finish my next scene, then, and I'll come with you. Who knows what the thief is up to? You need somebody to protect you, Book Jumper."

Werther squared his shoulders beneath his embroidered frock coat. "I am perfectly capable of protecting a young lady under my—"

"Wait for me," repeated Shere Khan, and slunk off through the undergrowth.

Werther was evidently affronted, and barely said a word as the three of us set out a little while later along the roads of the book world. Lips still pursed, he led us along a series of winding paths to another crossroads. This one also had a signpost at its center, and we followed the sign for *The Little Prince*. Soon afterward the road petered out in the middle of a sand dune. It was suddenly so stiflingly hot that I took off my sweater and tied it round my waist. In a T-shirt I padded out across the fine golden-yellow Sahara sand that stretched in billowing waves to the horizon. The air shimmered above the smooth hills, and it was a while before we could make out what the dark blob in the middle of the desert actually was.

It turned out to be an airplane, with somebody sitting in the sand beside it.

"It doesn't look to me as though there are many flowers around here," grumbled Shere Khan.

"Ha—just you wait," said Werther, strutting on ahead with his head held high.

I followed them, trying to think what I knew about the story we were in. I'd heard of *The Little Prince*, of course. When I was at primary school there'd been a poster on the wall showing a boy perched on the surface of a tiny planet. But as for the plot . . . I seemed to recall something about a fox asking to be tamed. But what else? I couldn't remember what the desert had to do with the story.

We marched for a long time over the hot sand before reaching the aircraft, which turned out to be a little propeller plane. Various tools lay scattered on the ground beside it. A man with an old-fashioned flying cap on his head was sitting with his back to the landing gear. He seemed to have given up on repairing his plane for the time being and was scribbling something on a piece of paper. A small boy with white-blond hair, dressed in a long blue coat, was looking over his shoulder. "No, that sheep is too old," said the little prince. "Draw me another one."

The man screwed up the piece of paper and started again.

Not until we were standing right in front of them did the man and the boy look up.

"Good day," said Werther. "Please do not let us disturb you— I merely wished to show this young lady—"

"Can any of you draw me a sheep?" asked the Little Prince. "I would so love to take a sheep back with me to my planet."

"Well," I said, "I could try. But wouldn't that be interfering in the plot?"

The Little Prince shook his head. "I'd hide your drawing in my pocket. Then I'd have two sheep, yours and the one he's drawing."

He pointed to the man. "There'd be just enough space on my asteroid for both of them. But we'll still tell the readers there's only one sheep."

"Fair enough," I said, and I, too, sat down in the sand. The pilot gave me a pencil and a sheet of paper from his notepad. I started drawing, and the Little Prince turned to Shere Khan. "Would it put you off eating a flower if it had four thorns?" he asked.

"Tigers don't eat flowers," said Shere Khan.

"But if they did?" inquired the prince, and told us about his home planet where there were three knee-high volcanoes and a rose with four thorns. He told us that if you didn't watch out, the surface of the planet became overrun with baobab trees.

Bit by bit the story came back to me: of the Little Prince who left his asteroid to find a friend and ended up visiting a whole series of other planets, finishing with the Earth, where he tamed a fox and realized that he loved the rose he had left behind in spite of her capricious nature. I drew the prince a woolly little lamb and handed it to him.

"Thank you," he said, putting the piece of paper in his coat pocket. "So you've come to see my flower?"

Werther nodded. "There is no other flower like her in the universe, after all."

"Yes," sighed the Little Prince. "And she's all the way up there, so far away from me. But when I look up at the stars I'm happy, because I know she's waiting for me."

"Um . . ." said Shere Khan, who had been studying the sky for a while now with his head tipped back. "What did you say the thief was doing, Werther? Stealing the core ingredients?"

We looked up. At the same moment, the little prince began to sob loudly.

"No!" he cried. "Not my flower!"

In the sky was a whole row of little planets. And on one of the asteroids, where I could also make out the silhouettes of three knee-high volcanoes, a shadow was plucking the most beautiful rose I had ever seen.

The Little Prince screamed when the stem finally broke. The rose glowed brightly for a moment and then disappeared. The prince threw himself down on the sand and beat it with his fists.

Werther and I exchanged a glance, then set off at a run. Shere Khan overtook us in huge bounds. He struck out with his paw at an insignificant-looking stone lying in the sand and the desert snapped shut on top of us. We flicked through the pages of the story as fast as we could until we found ourselves out in space.

But by the time we reached the Little Prince's asteroid, the thief was gone. Where once the rose had stood, all that remained were the first few shoots of a baobab tree poking up out of the ground.

There was something moving, however, on one of the neighboring planets, which was very small and inhabited by a king in a voluminous ermine robe. "Ah, a subject! What a pleasant surprise!" cried the king. We skipped hastily forward a few pages, jumping from planet to planet.

"We mustn't let him escape!" panted Werther. Beads of sweat stood out on his pale forehead.

The tiger growled in agreement. "I've a good mind to rip somebody to shreds." He bared his teeth.

But the thief was fast. We followed his shadow past a lonely

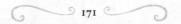

lamplighter, a garden full of roses, and a fox who begged us to tame him. But we couldn't catch up with the thief, so deftly did he skip back and forth between the pages. At last we came to the end of the story and found ourselves on a road that stretched across a tract of English countryside. We saw the shadow go scurrying off into the distance. Shere Khan was about to set off in pursuit when Werther came to a halt and stood bent double with his hands on his knees, huffing and puffing. I was out of breath, too.

"We must go on," urged the tiger. He closed his yellow cat's eyes for a moment and sighed. "Climb onto my back if you must. I will carry you."

"A gentleman does not ride on a tiger," said Werther. "And a lady most certainly does not."

But I had already swung myself up onto the tiger's muscular back. "Come on—we don't have time for this!" I called.

Werther dabbed at his face with his embroidered handkerchief for a moment before finally relenting and clambering laboriously onto the tiger's back behind me.

Shere Khan shot off toward the horizon. He bounded over the hills so fast that the countryside around us soon became a blur. I held tightly to his fur while Werther clung to my shoulders, yelping. Soon we were whizzing past mansions, balls and fine ladies sitting in drawing rooms and at pianos, but Shere Khan was flicking us through the story far too quickly for me to make out any details. The tiger's back rocked back and forth so violently with every bound that I had to focus all my energies on not falling off. The whole thing reminded me of my first and only ever ride on a roller coaster a few years before. In the end I just shut my eyes and prayed it would soon be over. Behind me, Werther was yelling something about having a delicate stomach.

Our wild ride through the novel ended as suddenly as it had begun. Shere Khan came to such an abrupt halt that Werther and I were flung forward and fell head over heels into the grass. We were greeted by the sound of voices and quickly got to our feet. Feeling slightly wobbly, we made our way toward the source of the sounds.

Dusk had fallen over the English countryside, and there was somebody sitting in a ditch by the roadside nearby. But it wasn't the thief in his hooded cloak. It was a girl a few years older than me with dark hair and dark eyes. She was wearing a ball gown, its skirts stained with blood, and cradling her right leg, which was sticking out sideways at a funny angle. Her face was contorted with pain. Four other girls in frilly dresses, all bearing a strong resemblance to the injured girl, were clustered around talking to her along with a middle-aged married couple who looked like their parents. Behind the family lay an overturned carriage with a broken wheel axle. Two horses pawed the dusty ground nervously.

"Have you had an accident?" I asked.

The father of the family nodded. "Somebody appeared in the road all of a sudden," he said, stroking his whiskers in puzzlement. "A hooded figure, just like that, in the middle of the plot. We weren't able to stop in time. It's a mystery to me where this person suddenly appeared from. A mystery!"

Shere Khan, having prowled all the way around the scene of the accident, was now sniffing at the sand on the road. "From the outside world, I should say, judging by the smell around here," he growled.

"Oh—we shall be late to Netherfield!" cried one of the younger girls. "It is too horrid! We may miss a whole dance!"

"And there will be so many officers there!" cried another.

I approached the injured girl. "Lizzy?" I asked—for I had realized by now which story we'd stumbled into. I'd read *Pride and Prejudice* so often that I was almost ashamed not to have recognized the family earlier.

The girl nodded. "Elizabeth Bennet," she introduced herself and added, turning to her sisters, "I believe we will have to miss the ball entirely. I am afraid I have broken my leg."

Now Mrs. Bennet, the girls' mother, chimed in too. "We cannot miss the ball!" she cried. "Your sister Jane must dance with Mr. Bingley! They are as good as engaged!"

"It does not matter, Mamma," said Jane, the eldest of the five daughters.

"What are you thinking of, child? Do you not want to be mistress of Netherfield Hall? Do you want your sisters reduced to poverty when your father dies? Come, Lizzy, try to stand, at least. You may be able to dance after all. Make haste, child!"

"My dear," Mr. Bennet said with a sigh, "Lizzy is hurt. We need a doctor, not a dance." He led his wife gently over to the upturned carriage. "The coachman must have reached the village by now. Sit down here while we wait."

"Oh!" groaned Mrs. Bennet, burying her head in her arms. "My poor nerves! Why must she break her leg today of all days!"

"Indeed, that was most tactless of Lizzy," said Mr. Bennet. "How could she be so selfish as to injure herself, and compromise all your matchmaking schemes?"

"Oh!" wailed Mrs. Bennet again.

The sisters were whispering together.

"Might we be of service to you?" Werther asked Lizzy meanwhile. "We happen to have a tiger with us, and he makes an excellent mount. We would be delighted to lend hi—"

Shere Khan let out a hiss that clearly indicated he considered it beneath his dignity to be described as a *mount*.

"No, thank you. We will manage. The doctor will be here soon," said Lizzy quickly. "I will probably have to forgo balls for a while, but I do not mind that. I did not care to dance with that conceited Mr. Darcy anyway."

"Lizzy!" cried Mrs. Bennet.

I turned to the tiger. "Someone from the outside world, you say?" I felt a knot of rage form in my stomach. Now even *Pride and Prejudice*, one of my favorite books in the world, was coming apart at the seams! I had to find out who was responsible.

Shere Khan nodded his massive predator's head. "The scent is weak and not entirely clear—but unless I'm very much mistaken, it smells rather like your island, Amy."

When I got back to the stone circle I realized it was already five o'clock in the afternoon. There was no sign of Betsy—she'd probably gone home long ago. But Will was still there. I glimpsed his tall, thin figure in the shadow of one of the stone arches where he lay sleeping in the grass.

My stomach was rumbling. I hurriedly stuffed the red leatherbound copy of *The Jungle Book* into my bag and was about to walk past Will and down the hill, but something held me back. Perhaps it was the smile on his face. I'd only seen him looking serious and sad recently, and it was amazing how different he looked when the corners of his mouth quirked just a few millimeters upward. A dimple formed in his cheek. What was he dreaming about?

Will's tousled hair was sticking up all over the place. His eyelashes formed two dark half-moons on his pale skin and his cheekbones seemed to have grown even more angular over the past few days. Only his lips looked soft and relaxed and gave his face a friendly sort of—

I must have bent over him, because my bag suddenly slipped off my shoulder and landed with a bump on Will's chest.

He opened his eyes.

"Um, hi," I said, snatching up my bag again. "Sorry, I dropped it."

Will blinked at me, too drowsy to understand what had jolted him out of the pleasant dream he'd been having. "What time is it?" he mumbled.

"Five o'clock. I just got back, and my bag—"

Will sat up. "Five o'clock? Man, I really could have done with a few more hours' sleep last night."

"Tell me about it," I said, yawning. It was a wonder I'd been able to stay awake this long.

All at once Will's eyes narrowed to slits, and the last traces of his dream smile faded. "Lessons finished hours ago. What have you been doing in the book world all this time?"

He gave me a piercing glance. I remembered I was supposed to be angry with him for not wanting me to jump anymore. I swallowed hard. "Nothing that would interest you. I know you prefer to just bury your head in the sand."

Will raised his eyebrows. "Is everything okay? Are you okay?" He seemed genuinely concerned.

I bit my lip. "There's . . . been . . . a few problems. But given that you've turned your back on the book world now, I'm sure you don't ca—"

"Problems with the Sherlock Holmes books?"

"No idea. *I'm* not responsible for them. But it might be happening there too." I pushed past him to get to the path. "The thief is pretty diligent, at any rate. Today he ruined two stories in one go."

He followed me. "Do you still think somebody's stealing ideas on purpose?"

"I don't think it. I know it. We've seen it, okay?"

"Okay," he said quietly.

"So you've changed your mind? You don't think I'm being naïve and that the characters are just playing pranks on me? Or that I'm the one messing everything up?"

He shook his head. "I've been reading *Alice in Wonderland*. The whole story is basically kaput. It does look really bad—and not like an accident."

"No shit!"

"I'm sorry I didn't believe you at first."

"It's okay."

As we made our way slowly down the hill, I told him about the latest thefts and about Elizabeth Bennet's carriage accident.

"How exactly does somebody steal a cyclone?" asked Will the moment I'd finished.

"No idea—I've been wondering the same thing myself. But," I said, looking straight into his blue-gray eyes, "did you happen to see Betsy when she landed back here? Did she have a . . . a rose with her?"

Will stopped dead. "You think Betsy's the thief? Why would she do something like that?"

I blew a stray lock of hair out of my face. "It was just a thought. Shere Khan reckons it might be somebody from Stormsay, and since I'm not sure what to make of Bet—"

I fell silent.

From somewhere overhead came a crunching, rumbling sound.

Suddenly, several things happened at once: something very large and very heavy broke free of its moorings above our heads and came half rolling down the hill, half hurtling through the air toward us. Will grabbed me by the shoulders and flung himself against me with such force that we both fell to the ground. I landed roughly on my hip bone and jabbed myself in the ribs with my own elbow, and Will landed on top of me. And there, onto the very spot where I'd just been standing, one of the gigantic boulders that made up the stone circle came crashing down to earth.

The stone slammed into the grass so hard we felt the ground shake. I clung to Will in terror, digging my fingers into his back, while he shielded my head with his arms. The tips of our noses touched. At last everything went quiet again.

We looked at each other for a moment, and then Will rolled off me, stood up, and offered me his hand. I let him help me up.

"What was that?" I asked once I'd got to my feet. My knees felt like jelly, and I was pretty sure it wasn't just the shock.

Will pointed up to the brow of the hill where one of the stone gateways was now, unmistakably, missing its horizontal stone lintel. How many hundreds of years had those things up there been standing? I massaged my rib cage. "Something like that doesn't just fall apart by itself, does it?" I muttered.

Will rubbed his face and eyes, then squinted back up at the now broken archway. "No," he said at last. "Especially not at the precise moment you're standing underneath it, I would've thought."

It was very difficult to recognize the monster,
for it was cunning and disguised itself well.
Unless you looked closely, you might almost
have taken it for a human being.
Almost.

VISITORS TO LENNOX HOUSE

OVER THE NEXT FEW DAYS Shere Khan, Werther, and I trawled the book world for clues as to the identity of the thief. After the incident in the stone circle, Will finally believed my theory that there was somebody with evil intentions causing havoc in the book world, and he asked for regular updates on our progress. But he still wasn't willing to jump again himself, no matter how much I urged him. And unfortunately, none of the fictional characters we questioned had seen the thief's face or indeed anything other than that damn hooded cloak. We were still groping in the dark. More ideas were stolen, but we didn't manage to catch so much as a glimpse of the hooded figure. Whoever it was seemed to have learned from the chase through *The Little Prince* and *Pride and Prejudice* and had now adopted a more circumspect and, above all, slower approach.

By this time I was almost certain Betsy had something to do with the thefts. I'd been watching her closely during lessons and I'd seen how nervously she'd glanced at us one break time when the subject of Dracula's stolen gold had come up. At the first mention of the vampire (who was still incandescent with rage), Betsy had been so startled that she'd accidentally poked herself in the eye—and a sloppily mascaraed eye at that—with the rubber on the end of her pencil. To me that was a clear indication of her guilt. But Will assured me time and again that Betsy saw the protection of the book world as her sole purpose in life and that he really couldn't imagine her ever doing anything to harm literature.

So, as July gave way to August, we still didn't have any new information. And one day a great commotion broke out at Lennox House. It turned out that the anniversary of the clans' truce was just around the corner and that this year it fell to our family to organize the celebrations.

All of a sudden I noticed that Mr. Stevens was never to be found without a mop or some other cleaning utensil in his hand, and that the house sparkled and shone more brightly with every passing day. One afternoon I saw him perched on a ladder, his smart suit twinned with yellow rubber gloves, polishing each individual curlicue of the chandelier in the entrance hall. And Alexis squealed like a stuck pig when she staggered into the bathroom early one morning to find Mr. Stevens in our bathtub, whistling merrily as he descaled the showerhead. As if the guests were ever going to set foot in our little attic bathroom! But Mr. Stevens, who seemed to harbor a secret passion for cleaning, scrubbed and polished everything in his path, and my grandmother left him to it. She was really very glad, she said, that our butler showed such enthusiasm for such disagreeable tasks. The family had had to forgo the luxury of employing a cleaner years ago.

Lady Mairead herself, meanwhile, wrote endless shopping lists and mused aloud about table decorations and menus and the intolerable tastes of the intolerable Laird, and generally became increasingly grouchy. One evening she inquired crossly of Alexis whether we'd brought *any* suitable clothes with us: we were barely presentable, apparently, in our usual attire. The next day we found ourselves drowning in a sea of fabric as we battled with the puffed sleeves of the cocktail dresses Mr. Stevens had bought for us on Mainland.

As I stood in front of the mirror on the evening of the party, my mood plunged as low as my grandmother's. My dress was bottle green like the stag on our family's coat of arms, with a puffy tulle skirt that ended just above the knee. It looked like an excessively generous tutu. But what the dress lacked in skimpiness at the bottom, it made up for at the top. True, I didn't miss the enormous puffy sleeves which Alexis (thank goodness) had unpicked for me, but the neckline could have done with being somewhat less low-cut, and the narrow straps drew unflattering attention to my bony shoulders. Alexis was wearing an identical dress in wine red, and it made her look like a princess. Lady Mairead, at any rate, was delighted with her daughter when we stepped into the banqueting hall on the ground floor around seven o'clock. But she seemed to resent the fact that I had slung on one of my baggiest cardigans over the top of my dress. Only a narrow strip of tulle could be seen poking out at the bottom.

"I get cold easily," I muttered.

Lady Mairead, who was wearing a wine-red-and-green checked shawl over her shiny black dress, did not reply. Perhaps it was not my outfit but the imminent arrival of our guests that had made her expression turn sour, I thought.

And at that moment: "Reed Macalister, Laird of Stormsay," announced Mr. Stevens from the other end of the hall.

Lady Mairead sighed as the Laird, dressed from head to toe in tartan, rolled into the hall in his wheelchair. He was followed by Betsy and Will. Will was wearing a jacket that matched his dark hair beautifully. And a kilt. I'd always found the idea of men in skirts faintly ridiculous. But seeing Will in his dark-green-and-grayish-blue-checked kilt, which sat so perfectly on his hips and showed off his well-muscled calves in their traditional knee-high socks, I promptly changed my mind. Will looked so different without his scuffed boots and old sweater! He seemed even taller than usual and the check pattern on his kilt was the same color as his eyes. Stormy-blue eyes.

I gulped.

Even though Will and I had seen each other pretty much every day for weeks now and were getting on really well together, a strange feeling constricted my throat. An old fear I'd almost forgotten over the past few weeks, but which was now threatening to suffocate me. The fear of being laughed at, being mocked. Why did he have to look so perfect all of a sudden?

On Will's arm, looking no less perfect, was Betsy. She floated across the parquet floor in an ice-blue dress with a cowl neck and a train. As they came closer I did up the top buttons on my cardigan just to be on the safe side, and took half a step behind Alexis. I was trying to make myself invisible, but somehow I managed to do just the opposite. As I stepped backward I collided with a chest-high marble pillar on top of which Mr. Stevens had placed a vase full of roses from the grounds. The vase began to wobble and, though I lunged to catch it as it fell, shattered with a loud crash on the floor. Water and roses sprayed in all directions. Every head in the room turned to look at me.

The old Laird let out a dry laugh. Betsy tittered.

My face turned scarlet, and Alexis hurried off to fetch something to mop up the mess. I crouched down and started gathering up flowers and shards of broken glass, dunking my skirt in the spilled water in the process.

"Please do sit down," urged Lady Mairead, hoping to distract everybody. She moved to the head of the banqueting table, which Mr. Stevens had set with crystal glasses, weighty silver cutlery, and the good porcelain emblazoned with the family crest. The guests followed her.

The Great Hall of Lennox House, just like its magnificent entrance hall, had a vaulted ceiling covered in paintings and with chandeliers fashioned from golden letters. It was about the size of a sports hall and must originally have been used for hosting lavish balls. For the handful of clan members left on Stormsay, however, it was far too big. The table looked lost in the middle of the enormous hall. In fact, with a few extra folding chairs we'd have been able to fit everybody here into our tiny kitchen back home in Bochum.

"The families feel the need to show off their wealth," Alexis whispered to me a few minutes later as Mr. Stevens wheeled in a hog roast on a trolley.

It was a strange assortment of people. On my grandmother's right sat the Laird in his wheelchair, wearing an old-fashioned suit with a waistcoat and a scarf around his neck instead of a tie. His head was bald and shone with a grayish tinge; his eyebrows met in the middle and lowered like a black beam over his eyes. He stared down at his plate, lips pursed.

To Lady Mairead's left was my uncle Finley, languidly unfolding his napkin. (I'd given up on trying to get to know him by this time: I'd been to visit him twice in his shop and both times he'd managed to evade every single one of my questions about our family. Instead he'd talked about the weather and tried to palm me off with some tinned sweet corn that was on special offer.)

Opposite us sat Betsy and Will, and at the foot of the table Glenn, Clyde, and Desmond in their usual gray robes. It was customary for the clans to invite the book characters who had survived the great fire to the anniversary feast.

Mr. Stevens served up enough dishes to feed a small army: glistening joints of roast meat, bowls of mashed potatoes and steamed carrots, croquettes, salmon in cream sauce, beans with bacon, various soups and salads, skewers of grilled vegetables, rice with spicy sauce, tofu cutlets . . . There was so much that I seriously started to wonder when and how he'd managed to prepare it all.

We watched in near silence as the table filled up. Despite the posh clothes and the mountains of food, most of the guests were in a distinctly unfestive mood. Wasn't it a bit ridiculous, after all, for two families who'd hated each other for generations to insist on a gathering like this?

At last, once all the dishes had been served up and there was not so much as an egg cup's worth of space left on the pristine tablecloth, Lady Mairead cleared her throat. "Welcome, dear guests," she began, forcing a smile. "Welcome to the celebration of the two-hundred-and-ninety-third anniversary of our truce! Let us raise our glasses to the end of our feud and to eternal friendship between the honorable clans of Lennox and Macalister. May both families always strive as one to protect the things we hold dear: the island of Stormsay and the world of literature that has been entrusted to our care!"

"Hear, hear," growled the Laird.

Everyone raised their crystal glasses and drank.

"And now all that remains is for me to wish you *bon appétit*," said Lady Mairead.

The food was delicious. Unlike Betsy, who nibbled daintily on a few microscopic morsels, I chomped my way through as many dishes as I possibly could in quick succession. But the mood didn't lighten much as the evening went on. The Laird and the Lady made a little stilted small talk; Desmond sprayed half the table with sauce after accidentally sticking his elbow in his bowl because he couldn't take his eyes off Alexis; Betsy eyed me and my still-damp garments with disdain; and Glenn and Clyde discussed the fact that some unknown person had apparently been helping themselves to Finley's food stocks. The evening finally hit rock bottom when we were eating dessert. It all started with a perfectly innocuous question from Will as he turned to Alexis over a vat of tiramisu. "So, have you settled in well?" he asked, breaking the uncomfortable silence that had descended on the room between the main course and the cheeseboard.

Alexis nodded. Her eyes darted almost imperceptibly to Desmond. "Yes, thank you. We feel almost at home."

"Probably because this *is* your home," said Lady Mairead, spooning lemon cream into a little glass bowl.

"Mmm," said Alexis, and I thought that was the end of it, but after a moment she put down her spoon and added, with a look of determination, "For another two weeks, at least."

Desmond knocked over his glass.

"I beg your pardon?" exclaimed Lady Mairead.

"Well—you know we're just visiting. Amy's summer holidays are nearly over and we have to go back to Germany soon."

I shot a sideways glance at Alexis. She looked almost relieved about what she'd just said. Did she really want to leave the island? Leave Desmond? "But . . ." I stammered. The longer we'd spent here, the more difficult it had become to imagine ever having to leave, and I'd assumed Alexis felt the same way. But it seemed I'd been wrong.

"That was always the plan." Alexis lowered her eyelids. "You have to go back to school."

"She can do that here," said my grandmother. "The book world needs her."

The Laird snorted. "The book world would be a great deal safer without her." He crumpled the corner of the tablecloth in his hands. "Betsy tells me they're saying in the Margin that Amy goes roaming around the book world as if it were a playground! They even say she's been keeping young Werther from his story, and—"

"Amy knows she has to stay inside *The Jungle Book*," said Glenn. I sank lower in my chair.

"But she *doesn't* stay there." Betsy jabbed a finger in my direction. "Everything's a joke to her! She goes around wreaking havoc in stories and she doesn't even care—just look what she's done to *Alice in Wonderland*!"

I tried to protest, but the words wouldn't come.

"No, no—the characters are just playing the fool again," said Glenn. But Betsy was adamant.

"In the book world they're saying Amy jumps wherever she likes. And *when*ever she likes," she cried.

The whole table fell silent.

"What is the meaning of this?" asked Lady Mairead.

I felt the blood rush to my cheeks again. "N-nothing," I mumbled. "I didn't . . . I wasn't . . . I haven't been sneaking up to the portal."

"Nonsense. She's the one who's been using the stone circle at night," declared the Laird, pounding the table with his fist so hard it set the crockery clinking. "Amy is a danger to everything we Macalisters have fought for for hundreds of years!"

"There's a thief stealing ideas," I cried. "Werther and I are trying to catch him but he keeps getting away from us." I'd had just about enough of this. *I* was certainly not the biggest threat to the book world right now.

The Laird drew himself up to his full height in his wheelchair and glared at me. "So you admit it?"

"What?"

"That you've been meeting with young Werther. That the two of you go wandering through the book world from story to story, somewhere different every day!" For a moment he rose unsteadily to his feet, but his legs could not support his weight.

I let out a breath. "Yes," I said. "But I haven't been sneaking—"

"You never should have been allowed to attend lessons. I knew it the moment I heard of your arrival. You ought not to have sent her to the Secret Library, Mairead!" The Laird's eyes were almost popping out of their sockets.

"She is a Lennox. She has a right to jump," hissed my grandmother. "And a duty."

The Laird let out an unpleasant laugh. "She is further testament to the fact that your family is the worst thing that could possibly have happened to the world of literature. All she wants to do is throw her weight around, the naïve little brat—she has no respect for—"

"Hey!" Alexis broke in indignantly.

"I—" I tried again.

"She brings shame on all book jumpers," said Betsy, helping her father back into his wheelchair.

"Yes, great shame," the Laird agreed, and as he did so I was suddenly possessed by another, braver Amy I hadn't known existed until now.

"STOP IT!" I yelled, jumping up from my seat. Alexis put a hand on my arm to hold me back but I shook her off. I looked furiously at each of them in turn. "It's true—I never stayed inside *The Jungle Book* like I was supposed to, not even once. Ever since the first time I jumped I've been going into different stories, and often Werther does come with me. But the reason we're doing it is to look for the thief! Don't you get it? There's something going on in the book world. Something dangerous, something we have to put a stop to! Just look at a few books and you'll see: *Alice in Wonderland*, *The Wizard of Oz*, *The Little Prince*. . . . There are ideas missing all over the place. The stories don't work anymore! You can't just pretend that's not happening!"

"But . . ." murmured Glenn.

I'd talked myself into a rage. My voice echoed through the over-sized hall as I continued: "Everyone on this island is always talking about how it's our duty to protect literature. But you obviously don't really mean it, because that's exactly what I'm trying to do! Protect it!" I turned to Alexis. "I'm sorry, but I'm not leaving. Not till we've caught the thief."

"A thief in the book world? A thief who steals ideas? That's ridiculous!" bellowed the Laird. His head had gone bright red, like a tomato with eyebrows.

"Oh really?" asked Will. "Do you still think Sherlock's death was an accident? Amy's right—there is something going on in the book world . . . and here on Stormsay. We have to do something."

"You're taking her side?" hissed the Laird. "A Lennox?" He uttered our surname as if the word was something slimy and disgusting in his mouth.

Will sighed. "This is not about the childish hostility between our two families. It's about literature," he said. "When are you going to realize?! The days of the clans and their feuds are over. Bloody hell—there are so few of us left!"

"Childish?" The Laird grimaced. My grandmother had turned pale. Betsy was looking at Will as if she was seeing him for the first time. Suddenly everybody started shouting at once.

I left the hall as quickly as I could. I hurried across the entrance hall and up the stairs and stumbled into my bedroom, where I switched on the bedside lamp and flopped down onto my bed. I could still hear Lady Mairead and the Laird yelling at each other from here.

It was a long time before the voices fell silent. But at last, after several doors (including the front door) had been slammed, the house was quiet once more. So quiet that I jumped when I heard a knock at my bedroom door.

"Come in," I said, without sitting up or opening my eyes. I wasn't sure I was ready to listen to Alexis's account of how the family party had ended just yet.

The door opened and closed. I heard footsteps approach the bed and come to a stop a few feet away from me.

"I hate family parties," I grunted.

"Me too," said a male voice.

I sat up. Will was standing in the middle of my room. He gazed for a moment at the books on my bedside table and the clothes I'd left lying around. "These anniversary dinners always end up with everyone shouting at one another. Don't worry," he said at last, crossing his arms. "I'm afraid when people live on Stormsay too long they lose sight of the important things."

I rubbed my cheeks and eyes. They felt wet. "It's really not like me to get angry and—well, to shout at people I barely know."

"I know," he said. "Still, I am starting to think you're the only sane person on this crazy island. You're right—we have to catch the thief before he destroys even more stories."

"Does that mean you're going to start jumping again?"

He blinked. "That . . . I don't know if that would be right."

"It would." I got off the bed and started to gather up some of the clothes and kick the rest out of sight. "The Laird seems pretty angry with you," I remarked.

"You're telling me." Will shrugged. "But he really surpassed himself today. He went so red I thought his head was going to explode. And everyone else carried on screaming at one another too until your mum mumbled something about a book she wanted to borrow and ran off with Desmond. Betsy, Clyde, and Glenn are taking the Laird home, and I . . ."

He faltered.

When I looked up I found his eyes fixed on me—they seemed to have got stuck at a point somewhere a little way below my chin, and there was an unexpected softness in them. I looked down at myself and got a bit of a shock. The buttons of my cardigan must have come undone in all the commotion and my dress was visible in all its skimpy glory. I hastily pulled the cardigan tight again.

Will cleared his throat. ". . . And I . . . I just came to tell you they've all gone and . . . I'm going to help you look for the thief," he stammered.

I nodded and tucked a lock of hair behind my ears. "Thanks."

We looked at each other.

The light from the bedside lamp cast a warm glow over Will's features and I suddenly felt a little dizzy. Slowly, Will moved closer to me and I took a small, unsteady step toward him. He smiled at me, and . . .

Somewhere downstairs, a door slammed. We both jumped. We heard the click of stiletto heels on the stairs.

"Um—is Betsy still here?" I asked, my mouth dry.

Will raised his eyebrows. "I thought she'd gone with the others."

We went out into the corridor. Although I could still feel Will's eyes on me, I didn't dare look at him. We could still hear the footsteps, and now we heard voices too.

"What was all that about?" hissed Lady Mairead from somewhere below us. "What on earth were you thinking?"

"I just wanted to . . ." Betsy muttered something.

Will and I tiptoed down the stairs. After one and a half flights, Betsy and Lady Mairead came into view. They were standing outside my grandmother's bedroom door. Now I did venture a glance at Will. "What?" I mouthed. Will shrugged, perplexed. Trying not to make a sound, we crouched on the stairs and peered down at them through the banister posts.

"You wanted to shout it from the rooftops?" hissed Lady Mairead. She had drawn herself up to her full height in front of Betsy and was glaring at her.

Betsy, who was standing with her back to us, shook her head vehemently. "No! I thought that if everyone thought—"

"Nonsense. We'd agreed, had we not? Besides, I don't like the way you talk about my granddaughter."

"She's reckless," Betsy retorted.

"She is a book jumper, like you. And she's talented."

"She's sticking her nose in where it's not wanted."

"Enough."

Betsy snorted. "It's not as if I enjoy doing favors for a Lennox," she said sharply. I gasped in surprise as she continued, "And we're not out of the woods yet. What if she finds ou—"

Lady Mairead suddenly lifted her hand and signaled to Betsy to be quiet. She looked up.

Will and I pressed deeper into the shadows.

"I thought I heard something. Come." My grandmother pushed Betsy into her room and disappeared after her. The door closed behind them and we heard the sound of a key being turned.

"It's almost as if the two of them had something to hide," I whispered. "I told you—we need to keep an eye on Betsy."

Will grimaced.

And perhaps on Lady Mairead too, I thought.

That night, Will had a strange dream.

He was back in Baker Street, in Sherlock's study, and the darkness was thick outside the window. But Will took up the magnifying glass from the desk anyway, the way he often had as a child. His hand fastened around the smooth, familiar handle. He turned the lens this way and that and although there was no sunlight, a fairy fleck appeared on the white stucco ceiling. It was a big, bright fleck, green and red and glowing. It was Amy.

Amy in her green fairy dress. Her long hair fell shining over her shoulders and down her back and her eyes sparkled. She floated just below the ceiling as if it were the most natural thing in the world. She smiled, and at the same time she looked afraid.

"What's wrong?" asked Will. "What are you afraid of? I won't let you fall."

The fairy-Amy didn't answer. Her tulle skirt brushed the chandelier.

"She wants to be invisible," said Betsy.

Will turned around and saw Betsy in one of the two armchairs by the fireplace. She was wearing a long hooded cloak and stroking the Hound of the Baskervilles's head. "It is a great honor to belong to the Macalister clan," she declared. "A great honor. You must forget Amy."

Will sniffed. "She needs my help."

He carried on turning the magnifying glass this way and that, and now Amy went floating along the walls. She paddled with her arms like a swimmer to propel herself forward.

"Amy and the book world. Both of them," said Will.

Betsy drew her hood over her face so that shadows fell across her features. "Now I'm invisible too."

Will was about to tell her he could still see her, but at that moment the door opened and Holmes came in. He was wearing his checked suit and had his pipe in his mouth. "What's that?" He cocked his chin in Amy's direction. She was currently gliding up one of the heavy curtains.

Will raised the magnifying glass. "Nothing, just a fairy fleck," he said. "Like before."

"Like before?" asked Holmes, dropping into the second armchair.

Suddenly his suit was wet and there was seaweed in his hair.

"Nothing is like it was before," said Holmes, his voice a hoarse rattle. He looked pale. And bloated. "Nothing at all."

"What's happened?" asked Will. "Don't you feel well?"

But at that moment, without a sound, the great detective's eyes grew sightless. They stopped moving, stared blankly into space.

Then Will saw the blood.

The carpet was soaked with it. Thick and heavy and red. The blood was everywhere. It flowed from Holmes's chest, for there was a hole there where no hole should have been. It flowed over Holmes's stomach and thighs and dripped from his knees.

And in the hole in his chest was a dagger. Cold and silver with jewels glittering at its hilt.

Will dropped the magnifying glass and it landed with a squelching sound on the wet carpet. Blood splattered up Will's ankles.

"The monster," somebody whispered. "The monster!"

Will spun round. But he didn't know where the words were coming from. Betsy's face was still in shadow. And Amy?

The fairy fleck by the ceiling had disappeared.

The knight crept closer to the monster.
Softly, softly.

11

THE CHILD ON THE MOOR

"I WAS GOING TO GET YOU TO COUNT the monkeys in *The Jungle Book* today. To check they're all still there and in good health," Glenn informed me at the beginning of our lesson the next morning. "But I suppose I may as well save myself the trouble. You wouldn't do as you were told anyway."

It sounded like more of an observation than a reproach. Glenn's scarred face was completely deadpan and the expression in his good eye was impossible to read. It was hard to tell whether he now approved of my hunt for the thief or whether he still thought I was just imagining things. "Off you go, then, and jump," he said at last to Betsy and me, and we did.

As Will examined the broken archway in the stone circle, Betsy disappeared as usual into her collection of fairy tales. I landed shortly afterward in *The Jungle Book*, where Shere Khan told me that, unfortunately, Werther would be unable to accompany me today. Apparently he'd been neglecting some of his duties in the book world and needed to spend the day attending to them. Falling in unrequited love, for example. And committing suicide. That sort of thing.

So the tiger and I set off alone. We spent the whole morning trawling *Don Quixote*, in the afternoon I jumped from my bedroom and we investigated one of Shakespeare's sonnets, and between times we went to the Margin to see if there were any more rumors doing the rounds about missing ideas. But to no avail. Either the thief had got a lot cannier recently, or he or she was taking a break from stealing. . . .

It wasn't until late in the evening that I crawled into bed back in the outside world, feeling very frustrated. I had planned to jump once more before going to sleep. But I suddenly got the feeling that it probably wouldn't do any good. Even if the thief did strike again, it was pretty unlikely that I'd be in exactly the right story at exactly the right time. Since the previous day, however, I'd been more determined than ever to stop the thief. Once Will had said he'd help me I'd even thought it would be easy, for some reason. But of course there wasn't actually a lot Will could do if he kept refusing to jump. Was there?

I tossed and turned for some time. It was already midnight when it occurred to me at last that there *was* something I could do. I groaned aloud with frustration and clapped a hand to my forehead. The solution was so simple I couldn't believe I hadn't thought of it before.

I slipped on my jacket and shoes and tiptoed through the corridors of Lennox House. The front door creaked softly as I opened it a crack and squeezed out. But inside the house, all remained quiet. I hurried across the grounds, the square-trimmed hedges observing me silently. Then I stepped out onto the moor.

The moon was a thin crescent in the sky, casting a ghostly gleam over the grass and bushes. The night air blew cold through my thoughts; its scent was a mixture of damp musty earth and sea salt. From far away came the rumble of the waves as they broke on the cliffs. Beneath my feet the moor made sucking sounds with every step I took. They sounded like little sighs—as if the ground was disappointed at having to let me go again. But nothing was going to stand in my way tonight, because I had a plan. And the more I thought about it, the more brilliant this plan seemed. Simple, but brilliant.

By the time I arrived at Will's cottage half an hour later, I'd almost forgotten my frustration. I had to knock several times before I heard movement inside the cottage, and I shifted impatiently from one foot to the other. There was a clatter on the other side of the door, as if a chair had been knocked over. At last light appeared in the dirty windows.

Will opened the door.

He had a T-shirt and boxer shorts on and his hair was sticking up even more wildly than usual. He was wearing one old sock and holding the other in his hand. He blinked groggily at me. "Amy!" he whispered. "What's going on?"

"I've had an idea," I explained. This time I was the one who couldn't take my eyes off him.

"Could it not have waited till tomorrow?" asked Will, pulling on his other sock.

I shook my head. "You wanted to help me, didn't you? Then come with me—we're going to catch Betsy in the act."

Will frowned. "Look, if you think I'm—"

"You don't have to jump," I said quickly. "But you do need to put on something a bit warmer." I pointed to his bare legs and felt my face turn red.

Will grinned and looked for a moment as though he wanted to say something back, but in the end he just nodded and disappeared back into the cottage. I waited outside gnawing at my lower lip until Will—fully clothed now—eventually reappeared in the doorway. "Will I do?" he asked, giving me a twirl.

We set out for the stone circle, which towered silent and deserted on the hilltop above us as we approached. We hunkered down between two bushes from which we had a good view of the portal to the book world but couldn't be seen ourselves. And then we waited. We waited a long time.

At first we didn't say a word, and looked warily in all directions at the slightest sound. But as time went on the night grew colder and darker and eerier. My feet went numb and I started shivering. Will gave me his sweater and we huddled a little closer together.

"I'm s . . . sure she'll be h . . . here soon," I said through chattering teeth.

Will put his head in his hands. "I still can't imagine Betsy jumping in secret. And certainly not stealing ideas. I mean—why would she do that?"

"Why would *anyone* steal ideas from books?" I shot back.

"Yes, okay, the whole idea is absurd—but Betsy? We grew up together—I've known her practically my whole life. It's true she can be a bit abrasive sometimes, and she's not particularly fond of you.

But she loves literature. She's a book jumper through and through. Why do you suspect her of all people?"

I sighed. "It's just that there aren't very many book jumpers. And if it is somebody from Stormsay—"

"Perhaps it's some megalomaniac book character."

"Shere Khan says the thief smells of our island. And besides, we know there's somebody using the portal at night. And the thing with Lady Mairead last night on the staircase . . . That was pretty weird, no?"

Will sighed. "Betsy has no motive."

I wrinkled my nose grudgingly, because on that point at least I had to admit he was right. Betsy didn't have a motive—none that I could think of, at least.

"There were tracks around the broken archway, by the way," said Will. "I think someone used some kind of lever to roll that rock down the hill."

I eyed the archway's two remaining stone slabs. They looked incredibly heavy. These boulders had resisted centuries of wind and weather. "Do you think Betsy would be strong enough to move one of those things?"

Will snorted.

"Okay, okay." I decided to drop the subject for the time being and snuggled deeper into Will's sweater, which smelled lovely—of salty sea air and Will's laundry shop.

We gazed at the starry sky overhead. Millions upon millions of little dots, glittering up there in the darkness. I tried not to think about how close together Will and I were sitting. Our shoulders touched; my knee rested on his thigh. And I noticed Will looking at my hair from time to time when he thought I wasn't looking. . . .

"I saw somebody creeping around the grounds of Lennox House the other night, by the way," I said at last. The silence was making me nervous all of a sudden.

Will looked at me. "Somebody in a hooded cloak?"

I shrugged. "I went down to have a look, but it was just Brock."

"Brock?"

"Counting the gravel stones on our path."

"Brock is definitely strong enough to have moved one of these boulders."

"And Brock is a foundling." I frowned. What if he hadn't come from very far away at all? What if his mother or father belonged to one of the clans, and had abandoned him? Was that too far-fetched? "Might he have—" I began, but Will put a finger to his lips. With the other hand he pointed to one of the bushes on the opposite edge of the stone circle.

There was something moving there.

Something human.

A figure slipped out of the shadows and between two of the stone archways. She was wearing a long robe and her hair fell like a curtain across her face. She was small. She was not Betsy.

Facing away from us now, she crouched beneath one of the gateways. In her hands she held something barely any longer than a finger. It looked like part of the spine of an ancient book.

Will and I stood up. We moved silently toward the figure. Not until we were standing directly behind her did Will clear his throat. She turned around.

Her face was narrow, her nose pointed. And her long, dirty hair came down to her hips. There were leaves and bits of moss tangled in it. As she hastily stuffed the object she had been holding into a bag, I saw that her hands weren't even half the size of mine.

It was a little girl.

A little girl, staring at us, eyes wide.

For the length of a heartbeat we looked at one another. Bewildered. Who was this girl? Where had she come from? What was she doing here in the middle of the night? But before I could ask even one of these questions the child recovered from her shocked paralysis, turned on her heel and bolted.

Ducking and diving like a fleeing rabbit, she sped down the hill and out onto the moor.

We sprinted after her. The girl was nimble, zigzagging this way and that. But we kept her in our sights. I ran as fast as I could, so fast I could hear my own heartbeat hammering in my ears. Eventually, though, I fell behind Will and the child.

The moor was vast, but the farther I ran the more familiar the bushes and pathways became. Will's cottage soon emerged from the darkness. As I approached I could see that Will had managed to grab hold of the child by the upper arm and was attempting to maneuver her through the door.

The three of us stumbled inside the cottage. Will shut the door behind us. I switched on the light and was shocked by what I saw.

The child was standing in the middle of the room, looking around as if hoping to find an open window to escape through. Outside in the moonlight I'd hardly been able to see a thing, but now I saw that the child was skin and bone, and much dirtier than I'd first imagined. Her skin was covered with dried mud and stretched tight over her sharp cheekbones. Her blue eyes were set deep in their sockets, and the color of her dress was faded beyond recognition. It was threadbare and stained and so full of holes that the child's skinny body showed through the fabric. Her ribs stuck out far too much. The hem of the dress was soaked with mud, which was dripping off onto the floor.

The child seemed to sense that she was trapped, and after a while she stopped looking around for an escape route. Instead she turned her eyes on us and pursed her lips defiantly.

"Don't be scared," I said. "We won't hurt you. Who are you?"

"What's your name?" asked Will.

She didn't answer. She dug her bare, blackened toes into the rug without a word.

"How did you get to Stormsay?"

"How old are you?"

"What happened to you?"

The little girl turned away and started wandering around the room. She ran her tiny hand over the sofa upholstery, then spotted a loaf of bread and a jar of jam on a shelf by the window and reached out to grab them.

"Are you hungry?" I asked.

The child fished out a slice of bread and tried to open the jam jar, but the lid was on too tight. Will took the jam and the loaf from her and started making a sandwich. The child stood on tiptoe and rocked forward and backward, spellbound, watching his every move. No sooner had he spread the first slice than she snatched it out of his hands and bit into it. She wolfed it down in a matter of seconds.

"I'll take that as a yes," said Will, spreading jam on another slice of bread.

"Perhaps she can't understand us," I mused.

Will shrugged.

"Hallo, mein Name ist Amy. Wie heißt du?" I tried in German as the little girl polished off her second slice. But to no avail. We tried again in French, Spanish, and Gaelic respectively, but none of them drew any response from the child. She gobbled up half the loaf in record time, then curled up on the sofa and instantly fell asleep. Will draped a woolen blanket over the tiny body, and then we sat down by the stove and pondered.

For a while the only sound was the crackle of the flames and the quiet bubbling of the stove at our backs, mingling with the child's snores. At last, however, we began to speak in whispers.

"Who is she? Where does she come from?" I asked. "Do you think she got washed ashore too?"

Will put his head to one side. "Maybe. But look at her clothes. She must have been living out here on the moor for quite a while. Perhaps in one of the caves to the north of the island."

I looked at the child's gaunt face. "But who is she? I . . . she's a kid, she can't be more than about nine. How did she get here? Why would she hide?"

"No idea."

The snores grew louder. The little girl rolled onto her stomach in her sleep, leaving one of her little arms dangling off the sofa. I gnawed at my lower lip.

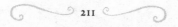

"Might she—" I ventured at last, "might she . . . have come from the book world? Perhaps Betsy brought her here and now she doesn't want to go back and—"

"If she was a book character don't you think she'd prefer to jump back to her story rather than starve to death here?"

"Hmm," I said. "She seems frightened of something, anyway."

Will put more wood on the stove. I rested my chin on my knees, which were drawn up close to my chest, and let the fire warm the back of my neck. I was lulled by the child's steady snores. Will's voice washed over me, saying something about a figure on the moor and a monster. Had he really just said monster? I was about to ask him what he meant when my eyes fell shut.

I was woken by my own shivering. The first thing I saw when I opened my eyes, blinking in the gray morning light, was the underside of the coffee table. My back hurt: I'd fallen asleep in my chair and must have slid down onto the floor during the night and slept at a funny angle. Groaning, I struggled to my feet and realized the reason I was so cold was not only that the stove had gone out, but that a chill wind was blowing through the cottage.

The door Will had locked the night before was wide open.

The sofa was empty.

I turned and saw Will lying close by. He too had spent the night on the floor, and was still fast asleep. The child, however, had vanished.

I was by the door in a flash. The key was in the lock. The child must have pilfered it from Will's trouser pocket.

"What's the matter?" asked Will drowsily.

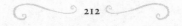

"She's gone!" I called, rushing outside. But the child was nowhere to be seen.

"Gone?" said Will, stepping outside to join me.

I nodded.

The sky was blue and wisps of fog hung over the moor, gradually dispersing as the sun rose higher. Dewdrops glistened wherever a ray of sunlight had managed to pierce the mist. The summer morning smelled so fresh and new and peaceful that the memory of the darkness and the mute child suddenly felt unreal. Had there really ever been a dirty little girl roaming the island? Or had the thin form on the sofa been a dream all along?

I would have liked to believe that, but the footprints in the damp earth, leading away from the cottage, told a different story.

The child on the moor continued to haunt my thoughts as I tiptoed along the corridors of Lennox House. Who was the little girl? What had she been doing at the stone circle? I could almost hear my questions reverberating through the silent mansion. But I was being ridiculous, of course. Nobody could hear me. It was Saturday morning, after all, and only seven o'clock. Everyone would still be asleep—which was a good thing, too, since I didn't really feel like explaining where I'd been all night.

I crept hurriedly up the stairs to my room, looking forward to my soft, warm bed. I would close the curtains and pull the covers up over my head and treat myself to a nice long lie-in. My plan was to have breakfast about midday, after I'd had a nap. Then later I might go and see Will, and we could look for the child together. Something inside me rejoiced at this thought and a kind of warmth spread through my chest—a warmth that fascinated and scared me at the same time. Or was it just tiredness?

I reached my bedroom door and had just laid a hand on the doorknob when I heard footsteps behind me.

"Ah, excellent—you're already up," cried Alexis, climbing the stairs toward me with a jam sandwich in her hand. "I was just coming to wake you up."

"What?" I said. "Why? It's Saturday, isn't it?"

"Exactly." Alexis beamed at me.

I raised my eyebrows. Was I missing something?

Alexis looked at her watch and murmured, "Perfect, perfect—this means we can get going straightaway. Go grab your jacket and I'll wait for you here, okay? What *is* that baggy old sweater you've got on?"

"Er," I said. I realized I was still wearing Will's sweater.

"I know you like baggy clothes. But you couldn't have found anything more shapeless if you tried, could you?!"

I shook my head. Alexis, seemingly unable to wait any longer, charged past me into my room without any further ado and fetched my jacket herself. Five seconds later she was already hustling me down the stairs.

"Um—so—where are we going?" I suppressed a yawn.

"We're having a day out!" Alexis explained. "We're going to Lerwick. I've already arranged the whole thing, as a surprise. Are you excited?"

"Lerwick?" I asked. "Isn't that on Mainland? How are we going to get there?"

"By boat, of course." Alexis laughed. What was she so chirpy about all of a sudden?

She practically dragged me down the stairs I'd climbed just minutes earlier, bundled me through the huge front door, and ushered me across the grounds. We arrived in the village at a run and hurried past Finley's shop. Brock was sitting on the steps outside his house again. He was counting princesses today; he told us as we wished him good morning. Alexis was number one and I was number two.

"He'll probably count us again on the way back," said Alexis with amusement.

"What time *will* we be back?" I asked, thinking longingly of my four-poster bed.

Alexis didn't answer. The jetty was in sight now and she was waving to somebody in a little motorboat. At first I thought it was the ferryman who'd brought us to the island when we'd first arrived, but then I noticed the blond hair and youthful physique.

It was Desmond.

He'd swapped his monk's robes for jeans and a checked shirt, and grinned as we clambered into the bobbing boat beside him. I swallowed hard. It had just dawned on me that I was going to be spending the day with two lovebirds who—however unbelievable it still seemed to me—also happened to be my parents.

Alexis and Desmond greeted each other with a kiss, while I pretended to be picking a bit of fluff off my sleeve. Then Desmond started the motor and Alexis burbled something about our first-ever family outing together. The boat glided out onto the open sea, which was far more kindly disposed toward us today than it had been last time. The water was clearer than I would have expected in these latitudes, and sparkled in the sunlight. If it hadn't been for the cool breeze that played around our faces and tugged at our hair, we could've been forgiven for thinking we were somewhere in the tropics.

The journey to Mainland took almost two hours and the farther we got from our island, the less I thought about the child on the moor. The memory of her skinny, dirty body faded with every mile we put between ourselves and Stormsay.

Lerwick Harbor, where we eventually moored the boat, was small, as was the town itself. But after weeks on Stormsay it felt like a buzzing metropolis. There were people everywhere, and shops and supermarkets and cafés and a bank. Lerwick was tiny in comparison to Bochum, but it felt almost hectic to us now. I hadn't realized how much I'd missed this hectic pace of life. Alexis and I plunged into the colorful hustle and bustle, browsing the shop windows and watching the passersby. Only Desmond looked uncertain, surrounded by all these people. He held Alexis's hand and jumped whenever somebody went by on a motorbike or a baby started crying. "I haven't been here for nearly a hundred years," he said quietly, his eyes glued to a shop window full of plasma TVs.

"Well then, it's about time," said Alexis, with a sideways smile at him.

Ten minutes later we were standing in a clothes shop, with Alexis pulling one brightly colored sweater after another off a pile and holding them up against me. "This one is Scottish lambswool," she told me. "That'll keep you warm." I sighed and nodded, having already realized that she would not rest until she had purchased me a particularly flamboyant specimen. I resolved simply never to wear it. Desmond seemed to have opted for the same strategy; when she thrust a plastic bag containing a bright yellow raincoat at him he merely muttered something about his monk's robes, which were apparently very waterproof, and took the bag from her anyway.

Around noon we went into a bookshop in which perfectly ordinary people were buying perfectly ordinary books to read in a perfectly ordinary way. In the children's section I spotted an illustrated edition of *The Jungle Book* and suddenly Stormsay and the book world felt like a dream. A lovely dream, from which it would hurt to wake up.

I turned away from the children's books. Alexis was buying a new vegan cookbook; Desmond had stopped by a shelf full of volumes of medieval poetry and was gazing at them wistfully. An elderly lady, meanwhile, was waving a copy of *Pride and Prejudice* around under one of the shop assistants' noses. She declared furiously that the story was not as she remembered it and that Elizabeth Bennet's broken leg was an outrage. I gulped.

"Okay," said Alexis, returning from the till and pulling out a shopping list, "now the health food shop?"

Desmond was still looking at the poetry books and didn't seem to have heard her. I yawned. "Or a coffee?" I suggested—I was so tired by now that I reckoned a sizable dose of caffeine was the only thing that was going to stop me falling asleep on the spot.

Alexis nodded. "Let's split up, then."

So while Alexis set off in search of biodegradable shampoo and vegan sandwich paste, Desmond and I sat down outside a tiny red building with a stepped gable at a tiny round table. I ordered us two cups of coffee and a double espresso, which I downed straightaway.

There was a busker standing outside the building opposite, playing a jazz piece on the saxophone. It was the music that finally brought Desmond out of his reverie. He smiled suddenly. "Your mother and I danced to this song on her sixteenth birthday," he said.

"Really?" In my mind's eye, a younger version of Alexis whirled around and around in Desmond's arms. Her red hair flew out behind her. They were both laughing.

Desmond nodded and looked as though the same film reel was playing in his head. But his smile quickly gave way to a bitter expression. Was it really the age difference that had kept him and Alexis apart, or something else? I remembered the look on his face just now in the bookshop. "Do you find it very difficult, being here?"

He cleared his throat. "Well—I'm not used to so many people."

"That's not what I meant."

Desmond cupped his chin in his hands and hesitated for a moment. "I don't belong in the outside world," he said slowly. "I don't fit in here, and that will never change. But I still . . ."

"You still like being here?"

"No. But I have come to terms with what's happened." He stared down at his coffee. "And I am thankful for having had the chance to meet Alexis. She is the love of my life. You're very like her, by the way."

I snorted. "As if."

"Yes, really." He looked at me. The corners of his mouth twitched once or twice before he spoke again. As if he was wondering whether to say what he was thinking. "In the book world, I never would have had the chance to be a father," he murmured at last. "I honestly can't believe I have a wonderful daughter like you."

I looked down, but felt something swell in my chest. However strange the circumstances, it felt good to have a father.

The jazz musician went around with a hat, and Desmond dropped in a few coins as he came past our table.

"Some characters in the book world have children, though," I said, thinking of Mr. and Mrs. Bennet and their five daughters.

"Of course," said Desmond, "if the story dictates it."

"And your story didn't?"

"No."

"You were a knight."

"Yes."

"Were you happy?"

He sighed. "Yes and no. I managed to defeat the monster, but . . . the way it happened was . . ." He closed his eyes for a moment. "In the story, the knight had to die at the end and it was . . . it was not a good death," he explained haltingly.

My cup clinked as I set it down a little too violently in its saucer. "Did you get killed?" I whispered.

Desmond didn't answer. Instead he drained the last of his coffee, sprang to his feet, and beckoned to Alexis, who was crossing the road toward us with two large shopping bags. She was a bit out of breath when she arrived, but she beamed and flopped down on the chair between us.

"Do you remember?" she asked Desmond, nodding in the direction of the busker, who appeared to have a rather limited repertoire and was playing the same song over again.

Desmond nodded. "How could I forget?"

*When he finally came face-to-face
with the monster, he did not realize it at first.
What he saw made no sense.
Or did it?
A pearl of recognition formed in his mind.
He was afraid.
Then he reached for his weapon.*

A MIDWINTER NIGHT'S DREAM

IN THE NIGHTS THAT FOLLOWED Will and I kept watch at the stone circle again several times but nobody—not even the child—materialized. This gave us plenty of time to talk. We discussed our favorite books in whispers, and the more time went on, the more often our hands touched—as if by accident. Or was I just imagining things?

But then, a few days later, the thief struck again. In broad daylight this time. Werther and I heard the news in the Margin one day during one of my jumping lessons. We'd just been in Heroes Direct talking to Hercules (who was being fitted for a new pair of sandals) about how things were going in the Classical dramas, and he'd assured us that everything was fine: there was still no shortage of tragic demises, so all was as it should be. As we stepped out into the street, however, a large, translucent *thing* came whooshing through the air toward us. We managed to jump aside just in time, narrowly avoiding being flattened by the creature as it went hurtling past us in the direction of the Inkpot. It was as tall as a house, and its lower body consisted not of legs but of a weird plume of smoke. At the end of this plume of smoke hung a dented oil lamp which clattered along the ground behind it.

"The thief!" thundered the genie in an Arabian accent. "He has robbed the Sultan! Gold and jewels from his treasure chamber! An outrage!"

My heart beat faster.

"Excuse me—to which Sultan are you referring?" asked Werther. But the genie had already gone sailing past us. Luckily, I knew which story he came from. " 'Aladdin,' " I said tersely to Werther, tugging at his arm. At last, we had a clue! We had to get to *The Arabian Nights*, ASAP!

Unfortunately, however, Werther wouldn't budge, no matter how much I tugged at the sleeve of his frilled shirt. Instead he stood with his back pressed against the window of Heroes Direct and closed his eyes. All the color drained from his face. "Not again," he breathed.

"What's wrong?" I asked, still trying to drag him along the road. "Come on, we have to hurry—we might still catch the thief."

Werther didn't move an inch. He was trembling now. *"Something wicked this way comes,"* he croaked.

"Pardon?" I exclaimed. "What do you mean, *something wicked*?"

Then I, too, noticed the flapping sound that filled the air. It was the flap of ragged hooded cloaks. A dark, restless sound, the kind that signals an impending thunderstorm. A moment later, the three old women I'd found tormenting Werther on my first ever visit to the book world came swooping down out of the sky. I knew by now that they were the witches from *Macbeth*. They whirled through the street, shrieking, leaving the stench of decay in their wake. "Alas!" they wailed. "Alas, it doth snow in *A Midsummer Night's Dream*!"

"What's that supposed to mean?" I cried.

The witches turned to look at me.

"Sisters, 'tis the impudent Reader!" said the first witch, jabbing a long fingernail in my direction.

"And young Werther!" leered the second. Her warty nose quivered with pleasure at the sight of her favorite victim.

"Hail to thee, young Werther!" screeched the third, grinning. "Thou shalt wed her by and by!"

Werther slumped to the ground and hid his head in his hands. "Begone," he muttered, almost inaudibly.

"Thou shalt find happiness with A—" the first witch began, but I cut her off.

"What's happened? Is there a problem in *A Midsummer Night's Dream*?" I called.

The unnatural fluttering of the witches' cloaks fell silent.

" 'Twas the base thief," explained the third witch, and her shoulders drooped. The grin faded from her face. "Nothing is sacred to him; not even the works of the great Shakespeare! Now he hath stolen summer itself!"

"Alas!" wailed the other two witches. "Alas, it doth snow in *A Midsummer Night's Dream*!"

"But I thought Betsy had only just stolen from the Sultan in 'Aladdin and the Magic Lamp,'" I murmured. "How can that be? She can't have been in two places at once, can she?"

"Alas! Then this is like to be the blackest magic," screeched the witches, rolling their eyes in fear. "Blacker even than our own."

"Black magic?" I raised my eyebrows. I believed in many things by this point, but magic certainly wasn't one of them. "Well, I don't know . . . what do you think?" I said, turning to Werther.

But Werther didn't answer, because he'd fainted.

This seemed to cheer the witches enormously. Leering, they dangled their witchy hair into his face and scraped their fingernails down the windowpane beside his ear before flying away.

Even after I'd shaken Werther awake, dragged him inside the Inkpot, and pepped him up with a glass of cola, I still couldn't make any sense of it all. At first I'd wondered whether Betsy might have gone on a kind of thieving spree, stealing from several stories in quick succession. But both the genie and the witches, when they'd arrived at the pub, had repeatedly assured everyone at the bar that they'd come straight there after the robberies to raise the alarm. And all the book characters present agreed that nobody could flick through literature that fast. Not from *The Arabian Nights* to Shakespeare, at any rate.

By the time I finally jumped back to the outside world, I still didn't know who was behind the thefts or how to stop them, but I was very conscious of the fact that I was going to need more help in the book world. Help that was less prone to fainting fits than Werther.

Will was sitting in the grass beside one of the boulders in the stone circle, reading (in the traditional sense) *Peter Pan*. He was so absorbed in the story that he didn't even look up until I was standing right in front of him.

"I'm back," I announced superfluously, nodding at the book of fairy tales lying on a mat under one of the archways. "I take it Betsy's still inside her book."

Will nodded absentmindedly. His mind, it seemed, was still whirring with thoughts of Neverland.

"Good," I murmured, pacing up and down the stone circle. It was eleven o'clock; we still had an hour till Glenn came to fetch us back to the library for a lesson on literary history. Now that clues had started appearing again as to the identity of the thief—who might be wreaking havoc in the book world even now—it was obvious what we had to do!

Without stopping to think I marched back over to Will, grabbed him by the elbow, and pulled him to his feet. "Come on," I said brusquely.

He blinked. "What? Where?"

"It's snowing in *A Midsummer Night's Dream*," I said. "The thief has struck twice already today." I opened up *The Jungle Book* and tried to maneuver Will toward one of the gateways.

But he stayed rooted to the spot. "What?"

"What do you think? We have to try, and we have to go now."

Will folded his arms. "I'm not jumping again, Amy," he said quietly.

"But you have to. I need your help." I lay down under the portal.

He sighed. "Not like this, though. I don't want to do any more damage. Holmes—"

"Enough about Holmes. Come on," I said, patting the mat beside me. "Please. It's for the book world, after all."

"I'm not jumping again," Will repeated. "I've made my decision."

"You can't stop jumping, Will. We have to stop Betsy. We *have* to." How could he not understand that? A knot of anger tightened in my stomach.

"But I still don't think Betsy—"

"Fricking hell!" I shouted. "Then it's somebody else, Will! Whoever the thief is and for whatever reason he or she is stealing ideas, it's destroying literature! Doesn't the book world mean anything to you? All the stories we love? What if *Peter Pan* is next?"

Will's jaw tightened. He gripped his favorite book so hard his knuckles went white.

"You can't just stand by and watch, Will. That's not what Holmes would have wanted, is it?" I looked him straight in the eye.

He was silent.

Three seagulls were circling overhead. Their screeches were not unlike those of the witches, only quieter and less piercing. As if the three old women were calling to us for help, from far away. Will tipped his head back and looked at the flying gulls without really seeing them. His eyes were fixed on a point somewhere beyond the clouds. I could see him searching his soul, wrestling with himself. The roar of the waves that drifted up to us from the shoreline sounded like the storm of thoughts inside his head. Then, after what felt like an eternity, Will took a very deep breath and sighed.

"No," he said at last, his voice firm. "You're right. Holmes would have wanted us to catch the thief. Holmes never lets a criminal get away." He sighed. "But I'll only jump until we've caught him. After that . . ."

I nodded and moved over a little to make space for Will beside me. For a moment the sky looked higher and wider than it ever had before, as we lay there shoulder to shoulder. Then I slid *The Jungle Book* over our faces.

We found Werther exactly where I'd left him: at the bar of the Inkpot. In front of him were several empty cola bottles, and he was rocking restlessly back and forth on his bar stool. Possibly because there was now more caffeine and sugar running through his veins than actual blood. How had he managed to drink so much in the short time I'd been away?

"Helloo-oo, Miss Amy!" he greeted me chirpily. His eyes lit up. But when he saw Will standing beside me his smile stiffened a little.

"Will Macalister," said Will, holding out his hand. "Pleased to meet you."

"Likewise," said Werther, clearing his throat. "Yes, indeed, very pleased."

"I've decided to go and look for clues in *A Midsummer Night's Dream*," I explained.

Werther nodded. "I shall accompany you, of course. As long as our route does not take us through *Macbeth*. That play does not seem to agree with me, as you know." He tried to sound nonchalant, but his fear of the witches was written all over his face.

"Good—let's go, then, shall we?" asked Will. "I know a short-cut, by the way. We won't even have to go near a certain witches' cave."

Werther studied Will with a mixture of relief and disappointment. "I take it the young gentleman is to accompany us?" he inquired.

I nodded. "He's a book jumper, like me. He'll be helping us from now on."

"Aha," said Werther, straightening the ribbon in his hair. "Well then."

Will led us out of the pub, straight down the Margin and then, with the precision of a sleepwalker, through an astounding number of Shakespeare plays. At first I marveled at Will's purposefulness, but it shouldn't really have surprised me. Will was a much more experienced book jumper than I was—he had years of training behind him. Of course he knew his way around the book world. And now that he'd decided to jump again—now that he'd realized he had no choice, if we were to save the book world—he was showing the same fierce determination as when he'd refused to set foot in it ever again.

So Werther and I followed Will through Italian city-states and British fields until we came to a mountain range, at the foot of which lay a Mediterranean-looking city. The sun was setting on the horizon, bloodred, bathing olive groves and ancient temples in a warm glow. Unfortunately, nothing else about the place was warm. It was snowing, in fact. The roofs of the houses and towers looked as though they had been coated with white icing, and frost glittered on the ancient marble columns.

"Is this Athens?" asked Werther, pulling his velvet waistcoat more tightly around him.

"Yes," said Will. "This is it." He flicked us through the pages, through the snowflakes that fell thicker and faster every minute, to one of the gates in the city wall. At that moment a pair of lovers slipped out into the night and ran off into a nearby wood. They were both far too scantily clad for the wintry conditions.

"What—um—what's *A Midsummer Night's Dream* about?" I asked.

Will shrugged. "It's about love and fairy magic," he said. "Lysander and Hermia are in love but they can't be together because Hermia's dad wants her to marry Demetrius. So she runs away from Athens with Lysander. Then there's a character called Helena, who's in love with Demetrius and wants him for herself. She tells Demetrius about Hermia and Lysander's plan to run away together, and Demetrius goes after them. And then Helena follows Demetrius, and they all end up in the woods. The fairies cast spells on them and make both the men temporarily fall in love with Helena, so they suddenly forget about Hermia. Oh yeah, and there's a weaver whose head gets turned into a donkey's head. The whole thing is pretty confusing," he explained as another young man came running out of the city and into the woods, followed by a young woman.

"Hermia is promised to another? It is about unrequited love?" stammered Werther.

"It's about fairies?" I asked.

Will nodded. "But the story usually takes place on a warm summer's night. So someone must have stolen the idea of it being summer." He folded his arms for a moment and pondered. I half expected him to pull a magnifying glass out of his pocket. Or at least a pipe to chew on. But he didn't, of course. He just pointed to the edge of the wood and murmured, "Let's see if there were any witnesses. Perhaps someone will be able to identify the thief, or at least give us something to go on."

We left the city behind and trudged off after the four lovesick characters. This was no easy task, however, since we were now ankle-deep in snow. We made slow progress. My sneakers were soon soaked through and my toes were numb with cold. Will lent me his sweater again, while Werther's teeth chattered so loudly that the whole of the forest must have heard them.

There was no sign of the lovers. Instead, the trees began to thin out and eventually gave way to a clearing full of dancing fairies with butterfly wings sprouting from their backs, dressed in clothes made of flower petals. It would probably have looked quite magical if the delicate little creatures hadn't been shivering so violently. They weren't so much dancing, in fact, as hopping about rubbing one another's wings to warm them up. Their bare feet had turned completely blue, and they were crying ice crystals instead of tears. Icicles of snot hung from their noses. "Our poor Queen!" they cried. "If we could but light a fire for her!"

At the center of the clearing hung a sort of hammock lined with moss, and in it lay a fairy wearing a dress of shimmering cobwebs and a crown of pinecones. Her long golden hair was draped over her shoulders like a cloak. She too was shivering. Beside her perched a fairy with an impish face, twirling a flower between his fingers.

"Titania," Will greeted the fairy queen.

Titania's eyes fluttered open reluctantly. "Who are you?" she breathed.

"My name is Werther," said Werther with a bow.

"Amy and I are Readers. We're looking for the thief who has stolen the summer from you. Have you noticed anything out of the ordinary today?"

The fairy queen rose from her bed of moss and floated over to us. Frozen dewdrops glittered on her eyelashes. Her eyes were far too large and far too blue to be human. "No," she said, her voice as clear as a bell. "No. All was as it should be. Peaseblossom and Mustardseed did dress my hair, when all of a sudden it turned cold. Terribly cold. Then at last the frozen water fell from the heavens and now we can no longer sleep for shivering, and the story cannot go on." She floated very close to Will, circled around him, and brushed his cheek with her delicate fairy fingers. "So thou art a Reader?" she murmured.

I cleared my throat. "Why can't the story go on?"

The fairy queen shot a glance at me. "My husband, Oberon, must anoint my eyelids with the juice of this flower, fetched here by Puck," she explained, pointing to the fairy with the impish face. "The flower's liquor must enchant me so that when I wake, I fall in love with the ass-headed weaver who will be here anon. But if I do not fall asleep, the magic cannot work."

"Lysander and Demetrius do likewise fear to lay them down to sleep," said Puck. "They fear to freeze to death. But I must drop the juice of the flower into their eyes, too, that they may fall in love with Helena."

"But if you lot can do magic, can't you just make it a bit warmer?" I asked.

Puck shook his head. "The only spells we have the power to cast are the spells we use in our play."

"And aren't there any of those that might help?" I asked. Puck and the fairy queen looked at each other. "Well," said Titania. "Perchance—the fog."

"The fog?" asked Puck.

"Fog is warmer than snow, at least." She batted her glittering eyelashes.

Puck furrowed his brow, then nodded and started murmuring something about dark fogs, covered stars, and a veil of night. It stopped snowing instantly. The sky grew darker, and then darker still. Swathes of murky cloud descended on the clearing and swallowed up the figures of the fairy queen and her subjects.

"Can't you conjure—like—a see-through fog or something?" I asked Puck, but he too had vanished. I heard Werther's teeth chattering somewhere close by, but I couldn't see him anymore. "Werther?" I asked.

"Miss Amy?" he replied, from a completely different direction to the one I'd been expecting. It also sounded as though he was no longer standing right beside me but a few yards away, in the trees somewhere. I put out my hands and felt about for Will, who had been standing to my left, but my fingers found nothing but empty air. "Will?" I called. "Will? Werther? Titania? Puck?"

Nobody answered.

"M . . . Mustardseed?" I stammered. What was the name of the other fairy Titania had mentioned? "Pea . . ." I swallowed. ". . . Pea-soup?"

Off to my right, somebody giggled.

I spun around and stumbled blindly a few paces toward the sound, but it didn't seem to come any closer. The giggling grew fainter and fainter and eventually fell silent. I stood still and listened in the darkness. Perhaps, I thought, the fog swallowed up any sound you made and released it again in a completely different place. Or perhaps I'd just lost my bearings? Still, at least the fog had thawed the wood out a bit. The temperature was more like autumn than winter now. Wasn't this pitch blackness going to make it difficult for the story to carry on as normal, though? Or was there an end to the darkness somewhere? Was I the only one left behind in Puck's fog?

Wait—what was that?

There was something rustling in the bushes behind me. And a snapping noise, like somebody stepping on a twig.

I groped my way cautiously deeper into the wood. There was somebody breathing in the trees, and I moved slowly toward the sound.

"Will?" I whispered. "Is that you?"

"I love thee not, Helena," said a man's voice. "Follow me no more, or I shall end by killing thee."

"Better to die by the hand I love than to go back. Now come, Demetrius, make not such a fuss. Lay thee down to sleep, that Puck may cast his spell upon you. 'Tis warmer now," a woman's voice replied.

"Never," Demetrius retorted. "My heart belongs to Hermia alone. I do not wish to forget her nor to freeze to death this night."

"Here—take thou my kerchief," Helena said with a sigh.

From somewhere nearby came the sound of sobbing—somebody was obviously overcome with emotion at this touching little scene. It sounded suspiciously like Werther. I stumbled onward, trying to get to him; but now the sobs turned into giggles, produced—unless I was very much mistaken—by Puck. I changed direction, angrily and a little too hastily, and walked slap bang into a tree. I hit my head on the trunk so hard it sent me staggering backward.

"Ouch!" I gasped, landing on my bum on a particularly solid tree root. I rubbed my forehead and felt a lump swelling rapidly beneath my fingers. Great. And to think I was actually *less* clumsy in the book world than the outside world! Although I'd probably been tempting fate a bit by running through a forest in the pitch dark, to be fair.

When I got to my feet again I felt slightly dizzy. My forehead throbbed, and I groped my way through the darkness even more gingerly now. I couldn't hear Demetrius and Helena anymore and Puck's giggles had receded too. For a while I walked deeper and deeper into the thicket without hearing a sound. There didn't even seem to be any animals stirring. I felt almost like the only living creature in the whole wood. I wouldn't even have been sure there were trees either side of me if I hadn't been running my fingers over their trunks and branches.

I almost tripped a few times after catching my foot on a vine or a tree root, and several times I had to stop to untangle my hair from low-hanging twigs and brambles.

But the darkness persisted.

I was completely enveloped by Puck's fog. The blackness was thick and impenetrable and showed no sign of lifting as I went on. I'd long since lost all sense of where I was. Was I getting closer to the city? Was I going around in circles? Or was there no longer an end and a beginning—had the darkness become all-encompassing, omnipresent? I started to feel afraid.

Where was I?

Where were Will and Werther? Where were all the characters from the play?

I tugged frantically at anything I could lay my hands on: ferns, stones, tree branches. If I could only turn the page! Take myself somewhere a bit lighter! But no matter how much I tugged and strained, it was no use—the pages would not turn, and the darkness persisted. Why could I not find the corners of any of these pages? Had I really come so far from any sort of plot? Shouldn't I at least have come to the edge of the play eventually, and crossed over into another story? Was there no way out?

Panic welled up inside me.

A little voice in my head whispered spiteful things: *You're lost. You're never going to find your way out of this wood. You're going to die in this fog.*

No, I thought, standing still and forcing myself to breathe deeply. The darkness wouldn't last forever. Eventually I'd run into one of the others and together we'd find our way back. I would get out of this book—I just had to stay calm. Damp, cold forest air filled my lungs. But my heart was still racing. Panic clutched at my throat with a grip like iron, and I couldn't shake it off.

And then I saw it. All of a sudden, in the darkness.

It was a blade.

The silver blade of a dagger flashed before me; its bright gleam hurt my eyes. I gasped. The antique weapon was jewel-encrusted and gripped by a pale hand—I couldn't see who it belonged to. Perhaps the wrist disappeared into a black sleeve, or perhaps it was a hand without a body, floating through the night.

One thing was certain: the hand was preparing to strike.

The blade glinted in the blackness of the fog as the dagger hummed through the air. Somebody was driving it toward my chest. Somebody was aiming for my heart. I realized all this within a fraction of a second. I heard myself scream. At the same time I took a step backward, tripped over a stone, fell. The blade missed me by millimeters. The back of my head cracked against a tree.

I blacked out for a moment.

When I came to, the dagger and the pale hand that held it had vanished. I blinked. The blackness was total once more. It surrounded me, heavy and unbroken. I sat there with my back to the tree trunk. My whole body trembled.

I listened intently to the darkness.

Was I alone again?

You're going to die in this wood, whispered the cruel voice in my head. *You see—you're going to die, just like I said. It's only a matter of time.* Tears welled from the corners of my eyes and trickled down my cheeks. I didn't wipe them away. Perhaps it was only a matter of time until the attacker found me and tried again, I thought. Then I heard the footsteps. I knew I had to run. But my body was paralyzed. I couldn't move.

A rustling noise nearby. There was somebody there. Far too close.

I held my breath.

"Amy? Amy, where are you? Was that you screaming?"

It was Will's voice, unmistakable. "Amy, is everything okay?"

Will! Relief flooded through me and I let out my breath. "I'm here," I whispered.

"Amy?"

"Will?"

The rustling came closer. Will bumped into my shoulder, and his fingers moved tentatively along my hairline, over my ear, and down to my chin.

"Why are you crying?" asked Will. I felt him lower himself to the ground beside me.

"I . . . somebody attacked me," I faltered. "With a dagger."

"What? With a *dagger*? Are you hurt?"

"No, I . . . I managed to get out of the way and then . . . then all of a sudden he was gone."

"Thank God," said Will. "Did you see who it was? Or where he went?"

"No. I'm just so glad he's gone. Do you know where Werther is?"

"No."

I sighed. "I hate this fog. I wish Puck would make it stop."

"That might take a while," said Will. "Puck is having way too much fun confusing everybody."

"Oh, great!" I shuddered at the thought of being stuck in this darkness a moment longer.

"Are you cold?" Will put his arm round me. In daylight I'd never have dared but now I leaned gratefully against him. The darkness seemed to wrap itself more tightly around us, pushing us closer together, as if it were trying to shackle us to the tree behind our backs. My breathing gradually slowed as I listened to Will's heartbeat. His T-shirt gave off a smell of moorland and soap. It smelled of Stormsay—a kind of proof that the island did still exist beyond this darkness. And it smelled of Will.

"I'm so glad not to be stranded here on my own anymore," I murmured into the thin fabric.

"Me too," said Will. "Thank you for opening my eyes."

"What do you mean?"

"Coming here was the right thing to do. The chaos in this story is unbelievable—we have to do something about it. You were right: I can't keep hiding in the outside world." He shifted his weight a little. "Amy?" His face was suddenly very close to mine. So close that I felt his breath on my cheek.

I felt a flutter in my chest. "Yes?"

"I . . . I'm glad you and your mum came to Stormsay," he murmured.

"Really?"

Will's reply was soft and warm. It brushed my lips as gently as a butterfly's wing.

"Miss Amy!"

Will's reply ended abruptly.

"Werther," said Will, letting go of me.

It was only then that I realized I'd had my eyes closed, because when I opened them again the darkness had given way to a dusky light; the fog still clung to the grass and ferns in places, but it was starting to recede. I must have gone around in a circle after all, because we were back in the fairy queen's clearing (if indeed we had ever left it). There was no sign of the dancing fairies or of Titania herself, but the hammock with the bed of moss was still there, swinging gently to and fro.

In it sat Werther.

Loose strands of hair hung down around his face, leaves and twigs tangled up in them. One of the sleeves had come off his frilled shirt and his silk stockings were in tatters. He scrutinized us, lips pursed, his eyes moving from me to Will and back again. Then he nodded slowly, looking as if he'd just bitten into a lemon.

"Good to see you again," said Will.

Werther's nostrils flared. "Well," he said, without looking at Will, "I have been looking everywhere for you, Miss Amy, anxious to ensure your safety. Are you quite well? Are you wounded?"

"Just a scratch." I prodded the lump on my forehead, which had already started to go down. "Um—where are the fairies?"

Werther shrugged.

"No idea," said Will, tipping his head back. It had started snowing again. Thick flakes rained down on us from the sky. The temperature was dropping with every breath we took. "Let's get back to the city before Puck conjures up the fog again. Perhaps the summer was stolen right at the beginning of the story, and the characters there can help us."

"Hmm," I said, unconvinced. "Oh well—if that's the case at least we won't freeze to death trying to find out."

Will stood up and put out a hand to help me to my feet. Werther climbed down from the fairy hammock, and we left the enchanted wood. Soon we were passing through the gates of the city of Athens.

The princess waited
for the knight to return.
For days on end she waited.
Had he forgotten her?

SHAKESPEARE'S SEAT

I T WAS ALREADY LATE AFTERNOON by the time Will and I decided to jump back to Stormsay. We'd spent hours questioning the characters in *A Midsummer Night's Dream*, but our efforts had met with little success. Only one character—the weaver who'd ended up with a donkey's head partway through the story—had reported seeing a hooded figure scurrying through the woods just before the summer had been stolen. Though he wasn't entirely sure whether it had been the thief he'd seen, or just a fairy.

I was frustrated by our lack of progress. We urgently needed a more effective plan of action: far from making things clearer, our foray into *A Midsummer Night's Dream* had just confused matters. Instead of catching the thief, I'd nearly got myself stabbed. And then there was the thing with Will, whose eye I'd been avoiding ever since the fog had lifted.

Had he really kissed me, out there in the dark? Our lips had

touched so briefly . . . or had it just been my imagination? Just a prod-
uct of the fairy magic that had given rise to such unlikely pairs of
lovers, and had even made a fairy queen fall for a donkey? I felt
another flutter in my chest when I remembered how close I'd been
to Will. But at the same time a horrible memory popped into my
head, a memory that had been fighting its way to the surface with
increasing persistence for the past few hours. The memory of a school
trip. The others had been playing Truth or Dare one evening and—

"You're jumping again!" squealed Betsy the moment we landed
on the mat in the stone circle. A second later she was rushing over
to Will, hugging him fiercely. "I knew it!" she cried, ruffling his hair.
"You've seen sense! At last!"

I stood up and took a few unsteady steps away from them.

"You've been in *The Jungle Book* together, have you?" Glenn
inquired.

I gave a start—I hadn't seen him standing there. A gray monk's
habit in a circle of gray stones was the perfect camouflage. "Yes . . .
Um, actually we were in *A Midsummer Night's Dream* and—"

"Not to worry," said Glenn, who was sitting on one of the boulders with a thermos flask between his knees. Beside him were two
used teacups. He and Betsy had clearly been waiting for us for quite
some time. He smiled. "If Shakespeare is what it takes to get Will
jumping again, that's fine by me."

"You're jumping again, you're jumping again!" sang Betsy. She'd
taken both Will's hands and was trying to spin him around in a circle.
He went along with it reluctantly but stared over her shoulder the
whole time, exhausted. I kept looking at his lips.

On that school trip Paul had asked for a dare and Tamara had given him a simple task: kiss Amy. It was pretty easy as dares go. Especially considering that his best friend Tom had just been made to eat half a lipstick. I hadn't exactly been mad keen to kiss Paul either, but the fact that he hadn't even been able to bring himself to do it. . . . He'd shuddered in disgust and flatly refused. "Ew! Not her!" he'd shouted. "I'd rather eat the other half of the lipstick! Please!" The others had laughed and come up with a new dare for him. I'd gone to bed.

At last Betsy released her hold on Will. She was out of breath, but still beaming. "It's all sorted now, but you have to come up to the castle," she panted. "Your parents have been going mental at us on the phone for hours."

"What?" Will exclaimed. All at once he was wide awake.

"Apparently they heard about what happened to Holmes and they want you to go and live with them on Mainland," Glenn explained. "They're saying that if you're not jumping anymore anyway—"

"Really?" Will's face darkened.

"Don't worry—my dad is fuming. He's already given them a piece of his mind," Betsy assured him, but this only seemed to make Will angrier.

"Let's go," he growled. "I'll talk to them." He stomped down the hill, Betsy following behind.

Glenn, meanwhile, tucked the cups and the flask away in the folds of his robe and set off back to the Secret Library.

At last I stood alone in the middle of the stone circle, pressing the soft red leather of *The Jungle Book* against my chest. On the moor the shapes of Betsy and Will grew smaller and smaller the closer they got to Macalister Castle. The wind blew in my face and brushed my lips, so much harsher and colder than Will's kiss. Assuming he had actually kissed me, and it hadn't just been one of Puck's pranks. In my imagination, a gawky girl with a donkey's head and a red pony-tail ran through a dark wood and the boy she met did not realize, because he had been enchanted by the juice of a magic flower.

The Macalisters had always been proud of their warlike past—hence the suits of armor, helmets, and chain-mail shirts lined up along the walls of the knights' hall. Behind them hung swords and flails and paintings of various battle scenes. The Macalister Dragon stared out from every corner of the hall, keeping a watchful eye on proceedings. There was something menacing in its look. The family had once been famed for its bloodthirstiness and the Laird, regally ensconced in a huge armchair at one end of the room, still liked to remind people of this fact when he wished to intimidate them. Unfortunately for him, however, his brother and sister-in-law Arran and Liza Macalister could not see him, and therefore had no idea how majestically he was holding the telephone.

Will strode hurriedly across the hall and snatched the handset from the Laird without a word. "Mum? Dad? What's up?" he asked.

"Will!" sobbed his mother on the other end of the phone. "How are you?"

"Fine. Everything's fine."

"Really?"

"Your mother is very worried about you," his father chimed in. They'd obviously put the phone on loudspeaker. "We heard what happened." Was it just Will's imagination or did his father's voice sound older than when they'd last spoken a few weeks earlier? He was reminded once again of how long it had been since he'd last seen them both. Will only visited his parents once a year, at Christmas, and that was a while ago now. He only ever stayed for two days. He couldn't bear to stay longer; it hurt to spend too much time with the family he had lost.

"Will, are you still there?" asked his father.

His mother was crying quietly in the background.

Will sighed. "I really am okay," he protested. "What's wrong with you two all of a sudden?"

His father cleared his throat. "Well—we want you to come and live with us on Mainland, of course, as we always have. And now Sherlock's dead, we're very worried about you. Who knows what'll happen next? Come back to us—back to reality."

Will sighed. His parents had been trying for years to persuade him to leave Stormsay. But he wouldn't. Not ever. "The book world *is* my reality. I can't just abandon it. How many times do I have to tell you that? And what happened with Holmes was an—"

"It wasn't an accident," his father broke in.

No, thought Will. He had never for one moment believed Holmes's death to be an accident, but he was surprised to find that his parents were of the same opinion.

"How do you know?" he asked.

"Brock wrote to me. He does that sometimes, when he's feeling lonely," explained Will's mum.

"Brock doesn't know how to write."

"No, but . . . I sent you a copy of his letter. Over a week ago, now. Didn't you get it?"

"Oh, right," stammered Will. "No, I . . . er . . . the post gets mixed up here sometimes." He turned to the Laird and held out his hand.

His uncle tried to play the innocent, but it was clear from his face that he knew exactly what Will's mother was talking about. Will glared at the Laird. "Oh yes, it's here. The letter was given to Reed by mistake," he said into the phone, still waving his open hand around under the Laird's nose. The Laird sniffed, but proceeded to rummage through the papers on the little table to his right and eventually handed Will a crumpled sheet of paper. As he did so he growled something about the clan's affairs and his right as head of the family to manage its correspondence.

Will ignored him. He unfolded the sheet of paper and suddenly understood what his mother had meant. Brock had indeed written to her. It was just that the letter was in the form of a picture—little more than a child's drawing, really. Bright colors, wax crayons. As he looked at it, however, Will felt a chill run through him. He stared at the picture. For a moment he forgot that his parents were still on the line. He forgot the Laird on his armchair throne. He even forgot Amy and their encounter in *A Midsummer Night's Dream*.

In the middle of the paper was a picture of Holmes. He was lying in a pool of blood that flowed from a hole in his chest down to the bottom edge of the paper. A dagger floated in the air above him, and behind him stood the inhabitants of the island. Will recognized himself in the middle, kneeling on the ground, tears dripping from his face onto the corpse. To his left stood Amy and her mother, hand in hand, and behind them Glenn, Desmond, and Clyde in their monk's habits. They'd pulled their hoods up over their heads and stood huddled together as if in fear. Desmond looked the bravest of the three: he was stretching out his hand toward the dagger as if to take hold of it.

To Will's right, Lady Mairead and Betsy could be seen whispering to each other. Behind them sat the Laird in his wheelchair, grim-faced, and along the horizon danced a thin figure with a jam sandwich in its hand. The jam was the same color as the blood. And there, right in the foreground in the corner of the picture, was another person, seen from behind. The person was wearing blue dungarees, their hems stained red, and was pointing a finger at the cluster of people as if to count them.

Will swallowed hard.

That wasn't how it had been. He and Amy had discovered the body on their own—none of the others had been there. Had they? What had Brock seen?

"Will?" asked his mother,

Will swallowed hard.

"There's something dangerous going on on Stormsay. You have to get away from there, do you hear? Come and live with us."

Will's eyes were still riveted to the drawing in his hand. "No," he said quietly.

"Please! Please think about it."

Will closed his eyes. He'd made this decision a long time ago. He'd been a child back then and had only guessed at what he now knew for certain: he belonged here. The world of stories needed him. "I'm sorry."

He hung up before his parents could say another word.

"Very good," murmured the Laird as Will handed back the phone. "You are a true Macalister."

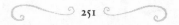

Will shrugged, folded up Brock's drawing, tucked it in his trouser pocket, and left the castle. He strode swiftly out onto the moor.

It was already dusk, and as his cottage came into view Will could see it only in outline. It sat crouched in its hollow, waiting for him. This was his real home, he could feel it. Why couldn't his parents understand that? It was then, as he approached the cottage, that he spotted the shadow slipping through the bushes nearby. The pony-tail looked familiar. "Amy?"

I spun around and saw Will standing just a few feet away from me. I put a hasty finger to my lips.

Will raised his eyebrows. *What's going on?* said his eyes.

I pointed to the open door of his cottage. Something was moving about inside. It was the half-starved child, helping herself— so it seemed—to Will's supplies. I'd seen the little girl roaming around the grounds of Lennox House, and had followed her here.

Will crouched down in the bushes beside me. "What's she up to?" he whispered.

"I think she's making herself another sandwich."

He shook his head. "There's nothing left to eat in there."

"What else could she be doing?"

"No idea. But I sure am curious to find out," murmured Will.

Together we crept toward the cottage and edged across the threshold. The child didn't seem to notice us. She was hunched over the chest beside the sofa, scrabbling about inside it. Her matted hair was spread out across her back like the fur of a wild animal.

"Are you looking for anything in particular?" asked Will.

The little girl spun round. Fear glinted in her eyes. She stared at us for a moment with the terror of a cornered rabbit. Then she took a deep breath, and ran. Her bare feet thwacked against the floorboards as she dodged around the coffee table and came flying toward us. A moment later she dived through the middle of us. It happened far too quickly to be able to stop her. Will did step out in front of her, but she immediately ducked between his legs. I tried to hold her back, too, and grabbed at her dress. But the material was fragile and it ripped when the little girl tugged at it. She'd soon fought her way past us and fled.

We gave chase. Straight across the moor, just like the last time. Only this time she was running in the opposite direction. The skinny little thing didn't make it easy for us—she was far more agile than we were and seemed to know her way around the island extremely well. Better than Will, even.

We followed the child up to Shakespeare's Seat. There, somewhere between the bushes and the edge of the cliff, we lost her. All of a sudden she was just gone, as if she'd vanished into thin air.

"What if she fell?" I panted, peering over the precipice. The wind tugged at my jacket. Many meters below us, the sea thundered against the rock face. These cliffs were pretty damn high and pretty damn lethal, that much was certain.

"Let's hope she's just found a good hiding place," Will replied. "What's that you've got there, anyway?" He pointed to my right hand, in which I was still clasping the scrap of fabric from the child's dress. Now that I looked more closely at it, however, I saw it wasn't fabric at all, but paper. I crouched down and smoothed it out across my knee. The paper was old and dirty and charred at the edges. On the back was a curved line that looked as though it might be part of a letter.

"I was trying to grab hold of the little girl. I thought this was her dress."

"May I?" I flinched as his hands touched mine. He picked up the scrap of paper and held it under the light of his flashlight. "Looks old."

"Mmm." I stood up again. "As old as the remains of the burned manuscript?"

We looked at each other.

"What does this mean?" I whispered.

"I don't know," said Will, rubbing the bridge of his nose. "It's all so . . . confusing. The thefts in the book world, Holmes's death, this child. Brock sent a letter to my parents. He saw Sherlock's body too. He thinks somebody stabbed him."

"Who?"

Will shrugged and suddenly looked absolutely exhausted. A lock of hair had fallen into his face and it took all my willpower not to tuck it to one side. I moved a little farther away from him just to be on the safe side. Will's eyes widened almost imperceptibly.

"And then—that thing this afternoon in *A Midsummer Night's Dream*," he began, looking intently at me. A new kind of panic welled up inside me. Was he wondering what had come over him, what strange spell he'd been under? "We haven't even had a chance to talk about that yet . . ."

I prepared myself for the inevitable rejection to come, and stared down at my feet. I really couldn't face being snubbed again. Couldn't he just pretend nothing had happened?

"Oh," said Will. "I—er—I didn't mean to upset you, Amy. I really thought you—"

My face felt hot. "It's fine," I muttered. "Puck's fog must have stopped both of us from thinking straight."

"Yes," he said quietly, turning away. "Sorry."

He looked out to sea.

I tried to swallow the lump in my throat.

The waves roared.

It was almost dark by now, though nowhere near as dark as Puck's fog had been. Eventually, Will cleared his throat. "If you ever change your mind," he said, his gaze still firmly fixed on the horizon, "let me know, yeah?"

My heart skipped a beat. "What?" I stammered. Had I heard right? I felt dizzy. "But I . . . I thought . . . you know, because of the fog . . . I thought you kissed me by mistake—"

He was beside me in a heartbeat.

His lips tasted of words. Of hundreds, thousands, millions of words and the stories hidden inside them. And they tasted of salt, like the sea below us.

This time Will's kiss lasted longer. And it was different. This wasn't like in the fog in *A Midsummer Night's Dream*. It was more real. Perhaps because this was the real world?

The wind was still tugging at our clothes, but I didn't feel cold. I felt Will's body close to mine. Warm. One hand was on my waist, the other buried in my hair. I felt for his shoulders. The gentle flutter in my chest had swollen to a hurricane, and the blood roared in my ears. This wasn't fiction. It was really happening. With this realization, all my anxieties melted away.

"You thought I kissed you this afternoon by *mistake?*" asked Will when we moved apart. His voice was hoarse, but he was grinning.

"I thought Puck had put a spell on you. Isn't that what happens in the story—people fall in love with each other because the fairies have cast spells on them?"

Will put his head to one side. "Yes, that's true. But I liked you before that. Did you really not—" He broke off. Something behind me had attracted his attention. "There's somebody up at the stone circle!" he cried.

I whirled around. "The child?"

"Somebody's jumping. See that light?"

The stone archways at the top of the hill were silhouetted against the night sky. It was too dark to see who was up there. But there was indeed something glowing under one of the arches—something small and rectangular, that looked as though it might be a book.

Again we ran, along the path that led down from Shakespeare's Seat and across the fields. Luckily it wasn't far to the *Porta Litterae.* By the time we were close enough to have a clear view of it, however, the light from the book's pages had disappeared. Instead we saw somebody standing in the center of the stone circle. Somebody in a long coat with the hood pulled down.

It was Lady Mairead.

My mouth went dry. What was she doing here?

We ducked down behind one of the boulders. My grandmother didn't seem to have realized we were there. Pale-faced, shoulders quivering, she stood looking at the open book that lay just a few yards from her feet.

Was Lady Mairead the thief? I hesitated to believe it. It had to be a misunderstanding, didn't it? She was too old to jump, after all. And yet . . . what was she doing here? Rage sank its sharp claws into my stomach and burrowed into my guts. I wanted to run over to her, shake her, scream at her. But Will held me back. "It won't do any good," he mouthed.

I suspected he was right, so I contented myself with staring at my grandmother for the time being. A few strands of white hair had worked free of her usually so perfect hairdo, and she only had one earring on. Her lips were pressed tightly together in suspense. She appeared to be waiting for something. Or someone?

And at that very moment the book lit up again, and I recognized the cover. It was a book of fairy tales. Betsy's book of fairy tales.

A human body rose from the pages. A head of shiny blond hair was the first thing to emerge, followed by a high forehead with perfectly plucked eyebrows. I gulped as Betsy appeared. She was wearing a long dark coat over a gray shift dress. She climbed elegantly out of the book and picked it up.

"Right, that's all of it," she said, handing Lady Mairead an empty string bag.

Lady Mairead pocketed it nervously. "Did anybody see you?"

Betsy sighed. "No, of course not. I know what I'm doing."

"Good." My grandmother rubbed her upper arms to warm herself up. "It's taken care of, then. Thank you."

Betsy nodded and tucked the book into her coat pocket. They walked down the hill together, and Will and I followed them. When they finally parted without a word and hurried off in different directions, we split up too. Will went after Betsy, who seemed to be heading back to the castle. I tiptoed on after my grandmother. The whole way back, I wondered what on earth this could mean.

Was Betsy the thief? Was she the one destroying the literary world? On my grandmother's orders? It hadn't looked as though Betsy had stolen anything; the string bag had been empty, after all. But why had she been jumping at all tonight? Why was it so important to my grandmother that nobody should see her? What was it that the two of them were hiding from the rest of the island?

By the time we reached the grounds of Lennox House, I could stand it no longer. I had to know what was going on. I appeared at Lady Mairead's side so suddenly that she stumbled and very nearly ended up in one of the geometrically trimmed hedges.

"Why was Betsy jumping just now? What are the two of you up to?" I cried.

My grandmother regained her balance and smoothed the skirt of her dress. "Amy—you scared me half to death," she said.

I had neither the time nor the inclination to apologize. "Is it you, stealing the ideas?"

"Ideas?"

"What was that just now, at the stone circle? What's Betsy doing for you in the book world?"

"Nothing you need concern yourself with, Amy." She tried to move past me, but I wouldn't let her.

"I don't believe you!"

"I'm sorry, but I cannot explain it to you."

"I don't understand. The book world is in danger and you—"

"Amy!" said my grandmother, and there was an unaccustomed sharpness in her voice. The uncertainty she had shown just now up at the *Porta Litterae* had evaporated. "I am the mistress of Lennox House and the head of this family. Stormsay and the literary world are my life. If I say something is none of your business, then it is none of your business."

"But why is Betsy jumping in secret?" I persisted.

"That is between me and Betsy. She had my permission to jump tonight."

"But—"

"You can rest assured that everything in the book world is perfectly fine."

I laughed out loud. "I'm guessing you don't happen to have read *Pride and Prejudice* or *A Midsummer Night's Dream* recently, then?"

"Glenn told me about Elizabeth Bennet's accident. Such things do happen, Amy, even in the literary world. But her leg will heal, and the story will return to normal again."

"The carriage only went into the ditch because the thief ran out in front of the horse."

"Nonsense."

I snorted. "And what about the fact that it's snowing in Athens?"

"It's the first I've heard of it," said the Lady. "I shall ask Desmond what has been going on."

"The idea that the story is set in summer has been stolen! That's what's been going on!"

Lady Mairead frowned. "If that is the case, it is a very serious matter. One which I shall look into." With that, she seemed to consider our conversation at an end. She managed to push past me at last, and hurried up the front steps and into the entrance hall.

But she wasn't getting out of it that easily. "Which book was Betsy in just now? What was she doing there?"

"Nothing," said my grandmother, taking off her coat.

"What was that bag for? Why were you afraid somebody might have seen her? Seen her doing what?"

"You've been eavesdropping."

I shrugged. "Why won't you just answer my questions?"

"Because none of this is any of your business." She glared at me. "Listen: Betsy jumped with my permission, and she is not going to do it again. What she was doing for me, and why, is no concern of yours. And now, if you would please excuse me, it's late and I'm tired."

"Why—"

She sighed. "Go to bed, Amy! You've got to be up early tomorrow. And you'll wake the entire household at this rate." She turned and disappeared down one of the corridors, leaving me standing there alone.

The wound was fatal.

He knew it.

He had known it at once.

Blood oozed from the hole in his chest.

He watched the red river as if from afar.

Watched the bright drops well up as if

they did not concern him. As if the wound

had nothing to do with him. As if it was not he

who was dying, but somebody else.

Countless drops, one after another,

running together to form a stream.

Pulsing life, that turned the world

into a red sea.

It was beautiful.

It was the end.

IDEAS

WHEN WERTHER, WILL, AND I entered the Inkpot the next morning, we were prepared for the worst. We were fully expecting to hear that another theft had taken place overnight. But we heard nothing of the sort. Quite the opposite, in fact: an Arabian man, who came floating into the pub on a flying carpet, informed us that the Sultan's treasure chamber had been miraculously refilled. Were gold and jewels a renewable resource in the book world? We waited a little while longer for news, but apart from the landlord coming over to give Werther his post (a bulging envelope from his pen-friend Wilhelm), nothing happened.

Will and I returned to Stormsay around lunchtime. There was no sign of Glenn or Betsy in the stone circle, but the clamor of voices drifted up to us from the foot of the hill. From the sounds of it the Laird was down there, and was not at all happy. There was a heated debate going on between him and Lady Mairead. And there were other voices too.

What on earth was going on?

As fast as we could, we hurried down the path that led to the Secret Library. By the time we rounded the bend, the Laird's head had gone so red that it looked as though he was about to shoot up out of his wheelchair into the sky and explode like a firework. My grandmother was marching to and fro outside the entrance to the cave, Alexis was talking to Desmond and Clyde, and Betsy was arguing with Glenn—something about security measures—while Mr. Stevens attempted to pacify Lady Mairead. Sitting a little way away from them was Brock. He had his head cupped in his hands and was counting the blades of grass at his feet.

"What's happened?" asked Will and I together.

The Laird yelled something that sounded like *unbelievable* and *a catastrophe*, but he was in such a rage that we couldn't really hear what he was saying. Lady Mairead now began to pace up and down even more hurriedly than before, and I thought back to our encounter the previous day. Did all this commotion have anything to do with Betsy's secret jump?

It was Desmond who finally explained to us what had happened: "The manuscript," he said, "has disappeared. Clyde and I realized just a few minutes ago that it was gone. Somebody has smashed the glass and stolen the paper fragments." He sighed. "They were all we had left of our home."

"They were a monument to the fragile truce between our families," said Lady Mairead. "This must be a threat: whoever has taken them must be trying to provoke another war between the clans." She glared at the Laird, who took this as a personal insult and completely lost it. His inarticulate bellows showered everything and everyone within a two-meter radius with spit. I took a couple of steps backward.

So the remains of the manuscript had vanished. Will shot me a glance that told me he was thinking the same thing I was: the child had been carrying a charred scrap of paper. Might she have had more than one?

My grandmother in turn had started yelling at the Laird, who was still ranting incoherently. Though none of us could really understand a word he said, I was fairly sure he was accusing our family of being behind the crime. Alexis stepped hastily between him and my grandmother and tried to keep the peace. "It'll turn up," she said, but she didn't stand a chance against the Laird and Lady's expletive-ridden tirades.

Eventually the two adversaries must have decided to go and inspect the scene of the crime, because my grandmother disappeared suddenly into the library and the Laird ordered Desmond and Clyde to carry him down the stairs. Betsy, Alexis, and Mr. Stevens followed.

Will and I looked at each other.

"Should we go down too?" I asked.

Will shrugged. "Would there be any point?"

"Well," I said, pondering. Aside from the fact that we were pretty sure we already knew who the thief was, a few scraps of stolen paper were really the least of our worries right now. "No, I guess not."

All of a sudden, Will grinned. "Do you like pancakes?"

"What?" I blinked.

"Do you like pancakes?"

"Um, yes. Why?"

"I could make you some. I mean—it looks like lessons are over for the day and . . . pancakes are my specialty."

"Your specialty?"

He moved closer to me and took my hands in his. Our fingers intertwined. "Mainly because pasta and pancakes are the only two things I know how to make." He leaned forward so that our foreheads were touching. "But for you I'll learn how to make a third dish, obviously. Maybe even a fourth."

"Pancakes sound great."

"Good," said Will. We moved apart. "But first I've got a question for *him*."

Him? I looked around. Only then did I realize that Brock hadn't gone down to the library with the others. He was still sitting in the grass, counting. Will went over to him, pulled a piece of paper out of his trouser pocket and held it under his nose. "What's this all about?" he asked him. "Why did you write to my mum?"

Brock didn't even look up.

"Why did you draw all these people? What do you know about . . . about what happened? Did you find Sherlock's body before we did?" Will persisted.

Brock carried on counting. His lips moved silently as his large hands parted the blades of grass.

"Brock?" Will put the letter away and took him by the shoulders. "Please—it's important. Tell me what you saw." But even when Will shook him, Brock pretended not to know he was there. At last he stopped counting, stood up, and stomped off across the moor. The blue of his dungarees shone bright against the heather as he moved farther and farther away.

Half an hour later Will and I arrived at the cottage. We'd had to make a detour into the village to buy a few supplies from Finley's. Now we were laden with paper bags containing milk, flour, sugar, eggs, pasta, chocolate, and some fruit, as well as another loaf of bread and a jar of cherry jam. Together we unpacked it all. Then Will made the pancake batter while I curled up in the corner of his sofa and watched him.

"So the little girl stole what was left of the manuscript," I mused aloud as Will cracked the eggs into a bowl.

"She probably thought it was pretty," said Will. "I mean, I don't know what else anyone could want with those little scraps of paper. You can't even read the story anymore—there's not enough of it left."

"Hmm."

Will whisked the ingredients together. "Do you want apples in it?" he asked.

"Yes. And I want us to find out who the little girl is and where she comes from." I couldn't shake the feeling that it was crucial.

He nodded. "Let's go and check out the old caves on the north coast this weekend. I still reckon that's where she's hiding."

"Deal."

Will grinned at me and tossed the first pancake energetically into the air to flip it. I returned his smile and our eyes locked. At that moment, the half-finished pancake landed with a plop on the floor. Will gasped, embarrassed, and I couldn't suppress a giggle.

"I don't usually do that," he protested. "You distracted me."

What Will served up ten minutes later was hot and sweet, a little burned and somewhat splodgy round the edges. But it seemed to me the most delicious thing I'd ever eaten.

Will came and sat down next to me and we feasted on pancakes until we couldn't eat another bite. Then he stretched out his long legs contentedly and I rested my head on his shoulder. He ran his hand through my hair. I breathed in his smell and couldn't believe this was real, that it was actually happening. "Do you really mean me?" I whispered.

"Of course." Will stroked my cheek with his thumb. "You're the one that's stopping me from cooking properly and thinking straight," he murmured. "Even if I—well . . ." He swallowed hard. "I still have nightmares about Holmes—horrible nightmares. Luckily I can't usually remember them that well when I wake up. All I remember is that they were horrible and that my best friend is still dead." He cleared his throat. "But at least when it happens, all I have to do is picture your face and straightaway I feel better."

I smiled. Will turned his head to kiss me and I caught sight of the solitary lock of hair behind his left ear which, unlike the rest of his wild mane, was curly and usually lay hidden beneath the straight bits. A solitary curl on a head full of flyaway hair. I twiddled it around my finger and decided that this little curl was Will's cutest lock of hair. But I decided not to tell him that and lost myself in his gray-blue eyes instead as we kissed.

That afternoon on Will's sofa was like an island of light and warmth in the middle of a stormy sea. We both knew that these were stolen hours—that chaos still raged outside. But for a moment, all of that faded into the background. We were happy that afternoon, despite the fact that somebody was destroying the book world, that Holmes had been killed, that a mysterious child was haunting the island, and that somebody had tried to stab me. We couldn't help it—we were in love.

We kissed and read aloud to each other. We ate chocolate and talked about our childhoods. Will marveled at my descriptions of our high-rise block of flats and Alexis's vegan diet, and I laughed at the picture Will painted of a younger, less embittered Laird playing in the sandpit with him and Betsy. I found the very idea that there had once been a sandpit on Stormsay rather surprising. Will, lying down now with his head on my lap, asked me to grab his photo album from the chest beside the sofa so he could show me the photographic evidence. I leaned down over the armrest, because I was too lazy to stand up and because I didn't want to move even an inch away from Will. I stretched out my fingers, farther, a little farther, until they were almost touching the chest—and lost my balance.

I fell from our island of happiness and landed roughly on the wooden floorboards of reality. Will tumbled off the sofa, too—I'd pulled him down with me. But as he laughed and got to his feet again, I lay there on the floor staring openmouthed at what I had discovered.

They were under the sofa.

They shimmered and shone in every color of the rainbow, and they emitted an almost imperceptible hum as if they were vibrating very softly. Or were they breathing?

They appeared at first sight to be glass spheres. Seven in all, each about the size of a walnut, lying clustered together on the floor in the corner and glowing amid the dust and cobwebs. A beautiful flower bloomed inside one of the spheres; a cyclone stormed and swirled at the center of another. Inside a third sat a white rabbit wearing a waistcoat and looking nervously at a pocket watch every few seconds. I swallowed hard. Could these be . . . ? Were they . . . ?

"Amy!" Will was still laughing. He wound his arms around my waist and pulled me back onto the sofa. "Are you okay? Did you hurt yourself?"

I shook my head.

Will held the open photo album under my nose. "Allow me to introduce: Betsy and me, aged two. Yes, Betsy really did play in the mud with me and yes, we really did eat those sand cakes."

He put an arm around my shoulder and I pretended to look at his childhood photos. But I didn't really see a single one of them, because the seven glass spheres were still glinting in my mind's eye. Strange thoughts chased one another through my head.

Later that evening I lay on my bed in Lennox House and scrolled through the library on my e-reader. Once I'd got over my initial shock I'd left Will's cottage in a hurry. My plan had been to jump straight into the book world and look for evidence—evidence to disprove the terrible suspicion that was lurking at the edges of my consciousness. Ever since my discovery in the cottage that afternoon there was a thought at the back of my mind I'd been trying not to let myself think. Because I knew that if I did, it would tear me apart.

In the end, however, I hadn't jumped. Partly because I didn't even know where to start looking, but mainly because I was afraid I wouldn't find the evidence I needed. Instead those terrible thoughts had been going round and round in my head all evening and now I was utterly exhausted, in need of a story to distract myself with. I had to read a book, right this minute and in the traditional way, or I was going to go completely insane. Preferably something nice and peaceful.

I picked out a scene partway through *Heidi*. The sun was shining and Peter was driving his goats out to graze on the mountain pasture. Heidi lay in the grass picking bunches of wildflowers and stroking the baby goats. I read several pages, word by word, sentence by sentence, with my feet on the bed and the pillow at my back, and that in itself was wonderful.

I accompanied Heidi down the mountain into the city, where she met her friend Clara and the strict Fräulein Rottenmeier. And I rejoiced with her when she was finally allowed to return to the mountains and to her beloved grandfather. It was fun, reading like this. It felt familiar and comfortable and I would have carried on a lot longer if I hadn't suddenly come across a line of text that made me stop short.

Had I really just read a sentence about a young man in silk stockings and a velvet waistcoat?

I read on, and in the next paragraph I found something that definitely didn't belong there: *"Miss Amy!" came a whisper from the edge of the meadow. "It is important! Come quickly!"*

I cast my eyes several times over these lines that seemed to have absolutely nothing to do with the text around them—lines with my name in. There was only one person I knew who called me *Miss Amy*. When I realized who it was that was calling me I slid the e-reader over my face with a sigh. I'd have to jump after all, then. I still didn't really feel like it, but it didn't look as though I had much of a choice.

In the blink of an eye I found myself lying on the grass right in the middle of Peter's herd of goats. I was being snuffled at by a host of curious, twitching noses. A little billy goat butted my thigh cheekily with his horns, and a nanny goat proceeded to chomp away at my ponytail.

Werther pulled me to my feet. "At last!" he cried. "Did you not see me waving? Just now, behind Fräulein Rottenmeier's back?"

"Er—no," I stammered. "What's up? Why were you—"

"It is no matter," Werther cut in. "We must hurry, if we are to get there in time."

"Get where?"

Werther dragged me down the mountainside behind him, flicking us through the story's pages and down into the valley so fast it made my ears pop.

"The thief is on the prowl once more," he explained as we went. "The fairies spotted him and alerted me. It looks as though he is headed for *The Metamorphosis*."

"The thief is . . . metamorphosizing?"

"No. *Metamorphosis* appears to be his next target. Don't dawdle so."

I stumbled along behind him, still not understanding what he meant. "Eh?" I said, rather inelegantly.

"The thief is about to strike again—in *Metamorphosis*. By Kafka. Do you not know the book?"

In my head I went back over all the books I'd read in school the past few years. As Werther hustled me along a street and into what looked like an early twentieth-century city, I dimly remembered a story about a man who wakes up one morning to find he has turned into a giant beetle overnight. Ew. Insects were my least favorite creatures of all time. Especially when they were the size of people.

But the thought that we might just beat the thief to it this time trumped my misgivings.

Werther flicked hurriedly through the book until we came to a drab gray apartment—a small bedroom, to be precise. It was narrow and old-fashioned: on the wall hung a picture of a lady in a fur coat, and in the bed a man lay sleeping. This must be Gregor Samsa, the main character of the story. Though at the moment you couldn't really tell that he was a man—a man who usually spent his days journeying from place to place as part of his job as a traveling salesman. Because at the moment, Gregor Samsa had the body of a giant black beetle. But he hadn't woken up yet. He didn't know anything about his metamorphosis. The story hadn't even started.

I looked at the giant beetle under the covers. Its carapace shone blackly, its antennae rested on the pillow, and its little legs stuck up in the air. A shiver ran down my spine at the sight of this monster. Poor Gregor Samsa!

Werther, meanwhile, didn't even seem to see the beetle-man lying in his bed. He leaned against the window and peered down the street. "He will be here soon," he murmured. "Soon."

But I was no longer so sure I really wanted the thief to fall into our trap. It very much depended on who he or she was. . . . I took a few deep breaths and forced myself to focus on the here and now. "How do you know the thief wants to steal something from this particular point in the story?" I whispered, so as not to wake Gregor Samsa.

"Well—what would you take from *Metamorphosis*, if you were looking for initial ideas?" he asked, and answered his own question in the same breath. "Precisely. The metamorphosis itself."

"But he's already morphed into a beetle." I pointed to the monster.

Werther, who was now pacing up and down the room, nodded. "Because that is how the story starts. In truth, therefore, there *is* no un-morphed Gregor Samsa. But look." He ran a trembling fingertip over a spot on the beetle's head which glowed faintly as he touched it. "The idea of the insect body is just here. If we can prevent the thief from acquiring it—"

There was a rustling noise outside the bedroom door.

Werther fell silent and put a finger to his lips. We listened. There was complete silence. But now Gregor Samsa opened his beetle eyes. For a while he gazed at his domed belly and his delicate little legs. Then he tried to turn onto his side, but kept rolling onto his rounded beetle back again. Eventually he looked at the alarm clock beside his bed, which showed a quarter to seven, and gave a start—perhaps because he had just spotted me and Werther standing across the room from him. His antennae swiveled toward us in surprise.

"Gregor," called a woman's voice from outside the door. "It's a quarter to seven. Don't you need to be going?"

"Yes, Mother, yes, thank you—I'm getting up now," replied Gregor Samsa in a harsh beetle voice, trying and failing to get out of bed. He just couldn't quite manage to tip himself onto his belly.

The room had two other doors: Gregor's father could now be heard outside one of them, and his sister, Grete, at the other. Both wanted to know why Gregor had not gone to work yet, and whether he was unwell.

The little beetle legs paddled helplessly and ever more frantically through the air. There were knocks on all three of the bedroom doors. "Should we help him up?" I asked Werther.

Werther shook his head firmly. "No—we must not interfere with the plot," he said quietly, looking out of the window again. He seemed to think the thief was going to come marching down the street any second now. In fact, however, the thief must have come flicking through the pages of the story just as dexterously as we had, for a moment later there was a cry from outside the door where Gregor's mother was standing.

"What do you think you're doing? Who are you?" shrieked Gregor's mother.

"What's going on?" demanded Gregor's father.

"Has something happened?" called Grete.

"Pull down that ridiculous hood and show yourself!" ordered Gregor's mother. "Ow, you're hurting me!"

"What's the matter?" called Gregor's father.

"He pushed me out of the way!"

"Who?"

"The stranger!"

Werther and I held our breath as Gregor Samsa continued to rock laboriously to and fro on his back, trying to tip himself over the edge of the bed, and eventually landed with a dull thud on the carpet.

"Perhaps it's the chief clerk!" called Grete.

"I think I would recognize the chief clerk if he were standing right in front of me."

"I thought he had his hood up."

"And?" We heard Gregor's mother gasp. "That is my son's bedroom. Kindly stop tampering with the lock!"

And now, from our vantage point inside the room, we could see the key being pushed very slowly out of the lock by somebody outside the door. It fell to the floor and landed on a strip of paper that hadn't been there a moment before. The thief pulled the piece of paper with the key on it out from under the door. Then we heard the lock click. The door handle turned. The door opened, just a crack at first, then wider and wider, to reveal a black cloak.

Werther pounced on the hooded figure the moment it set foot inside the room.

At last! I had to help him, of course. I leaped forward too. This was the moment we'd been waiting for for so long. The thief had fallen into our trap! All we had to do now was grab hold of whoever it was and rip that stupid hood off their face. But what would we find underneath it? Did I really want to know the truth? By now I had begun to have grave misgivings about the thief's identity: I hesitated midleap and for a fraction of a second I forgot to think about what my feet were doing. I tripped over Gregor, who was lying on the floor with his legs waving in the air, then collided with Werther and sent him flying too.

We had lost the element of surprise.

Before we could get back up the thief had turned on his heel, shoved Gregor's mother aside once more, and flicked through the pages and away. It all happened so quickly that we didn't even see which way he went.

"Crap!" I panted once I'd found my feet again. Werther, mopping the sweat from his brow with his embroidered handkerchief, merely shrugged. "I wouldn't say that," he said, cocking his chin at Gregor's head where the idea of the beetle body still shimmered. The thief had not succeeded in stealing it. We'd stopped him. Werther and I grinned at each other. We hadn't managed to catch the scumbag, but at least we'd saved *Metamorphosis*. Hadn't we?

"What if he comes back?" I asked.

"I do not think he will try again here. Everybody is forewarned now, after all." He turned to Gregor's family, who had all come bursting into the bedroom and were staring down at the giant beetle. "You must look after him and keep a very close eye on him from now on."

The family nodded. They were all visibly shocked.

"And we have to think about what we're going to do next," I said. My frustration at having come so close to catching the thief had melted away, giving way to a euphoric thirst for action, which temporarily eclipsed my fears about what might be hidden under that hood. The main thing was that we'd finally managed to stop the thief. We'd been able to save at least one story, and that felt pretty damn good.

Half an hour later, Werther and I had cut across to the neighboring Russian authors and were sitting in the stylish compartment of a nineteenth-century train carriage on the Moscow–St. Petersburg line. A snowstorm raged outside the window and somewhere in the next carriage sat the unhappy Anna Karenina with whom Alexis had once been such good friends.

We, however, were enjoying the cozy warmth and soft seats

of our compartment. A gas lamp bathed the upholstery and plush carpets in a warm light and Werther, who had never ridden a train before in his life, marveled at the rattle of the wheels and the far-off glimmer of the steam engine when it came into view at a bend in the track, twinkling amid the thickly falling snowflakes. For the first ten minutes of our journey he stayed glued to the window and peered out at the passing countryside, which was only dimly visible in the darkness. I left him to it and thought again about what I had found under the sofa in Will's cottage.

"So, if we were to find the core ingredients of the stories," I began at last, "would we be able to . . . er . . . put them back? Would that make the stories start working again?"

"I dare say it would," murmured Werther, without taking his eyes off the window. He whooped like a little kid when the steam engine let out a whistle.

I said nothing for a while. Perhaps I could return the ideas to their stories without anyone noticing. But that wouldn't be enough on its own, if the thief just kept stealing more. "How can we find out where he's going to strike next?"

Werther tore his gaze away from the scenery at last and put his head to one side. He hesitated for a moment, then reached into an inner pocket of his waistcoat, took out the long letter he'd received that morning, and unfolded it. "Well—it so happens that my friend Wilhelm and I have been debating that very question for some time now, and we have come to the conclusion that there must be a specific purpose behind the thefts," he explained.

I sat up straighter. "What purpose?"

"Well." Werther drummed his fingertips together. "I would

naturally have spoken to you of this sooner, Miss Amy," he said, "were it not for the fact that our alliance has acquired a new member of late. . . ." His eyes slid sideways. Was it just my imagination or did he sound ever so slightly hurt? "I was not sure, you see, whether I ought to take the risk, which is why I have preferred to remain silent until now."

I opened my mouth to set Werther straight. I wanted to tell him he was being stupid, that of course we could trust Will. But the words wouldn't come.

Werther looked me straight in the eye and handed me a piece of paper. It was a list, written in his own squiggly handwriting:

STOLEN IDEAS

1. Alice in Wonderland (Rabbit's watch and waistcoat)
2. Sleeping Beauty (long sleep)
3. Picture of Dorian Gray (picture)
4. Elf-King (Elf-King)
5. Wizard of Oz (cyclone)
6. Little Prince (flower)
7. Midsummer Night's Dream (summer)
8. ?
9. ?
10. ?

"What about the treasures from *The Arabian Nights* and *Dracula*?" I asked. "And Elizabeth Bennet's carriage accident?"

But Werther waved these suggestions aside. "No ideas were stolen in those instances."

"Hmm." I read through his list again. "And what do the three question marks at the end stand for?"

"They are part of our theory." Werther leaned forward and clasped my hands in his. The gesture seemed a little uncalled for but I was too excited, too eager to find out what he knew about the thief, to give it much thought. His pale face was very close to mine now. So close that I could make out every single one of his long eyelashes. "We are afraid that a person stealing such powerful core ingredients as these can only have one thing in mind," he whispered. "We are afraid that this person plans to use them to create a new story." A shudder ran through him as he spoke.

"A . . . new story?" I stammered.

"Over the past few days my trusty Wilhelm has immersed himself thoroughly in the annals of our world, and has discovered that it is indeed possible. But only if one succeeds in bringing ten of the most powerful ideas in the history of literature under one's control."

I felt goose bumps on the back of my neck, too, now. "So there are only three to go. *Metamorphosis* would have been number eight."

Werther nodded, but I still didn't fully understand. "But why . . . I mean, if somebody wants to create a new story, why don't they just write one? Why do they have to go helping themselves to things out of other books?"

Werther came even closer. I could feel his breath on my lips— it smelt of peppermint and violets. "Powerful ideas like these do not grow on trees," he whispered. "They are extremely difficult to invent. And not everybody is capable of creating something new. We book characters, for example—"

Something slammed into the windowpane from the outside. Something far too blue to be a snowflake.

We jumped. At last I backed away from Werther's violet-breath and freed my hands from his grasp. I stood up and opened the compartment window to find a tiny fairy clinging to the window frame, flapping about in the wind. She tumbled inside the carriage accompanied by a blast of ice-cold night air and a flurry of snow, and landed on the seat beside me. Her wings were frozen stiff, and she squeaked out her message with such urgency that she tripped over her tongue in her agitation. She had to repeat herself three times before we realized that we had celebrated too soon: while we'd been chugging through the Russian winter, the thief had been carrying out another raid. He'd infiltrated *The Strange Case of Dr. Jekyll and Mr. Hyde*, and made off with no less than Mr. Hyde himself.

Damn it! I bit my lip. Why had we let him get away? How were we supposed to protect the book world when the moment we thwarted him in one book, the thief simply turned his attentions to another?

As Werther took out his quill, crossed out the question mark next to Number 8 on his list and replaced it with the title of the book, my mind began to whirl again. So fast that I felt sick. If Werther and Wilhelm were right, somebody was dismantling the great works of world literature in order to build a new story. But who would want to do that? Betsy? Lady Mairead? I swallowed hard and thought, very quietly: *Will?*

The princess was young and fair.
She had hair down to her heels and she
dressed every day in the finest of gowns. When she
laughed, all the kingdom was entranced.
She was the fairest child in all the land.

15

THE FORGOTTEN GIRL

THE RINGING OF THE ALARM CLOCK on my phone chased away my troubled dreams. My brain felt as though it had been transformed overnight into a wet sponge which was now sliding this way and that inside my head. I groaned as I swung my legs out of bed and blinked in the dull morning light. But at least I could think clearly enough now to know what I had to do. And that the sooner I did it the better.

It was early, not even properly light yet. My book-jumping lesson in the Secret Library awaited me. I staggered into the bathroom for a shower, then picked a few clothes up off the floor at random and slipped them on. I brushed my teeth with one hand and tied my hair back in a messy bun with the other. Having neglected to look in the mirror, I didn't realize until I was halfway downstairs that I was wearing the hideous sweater Alexis had bought me in Lerwick. I didn't care.

On the ground floor I grabbed a slice of bread from the breakfast table as I passed, and headed straight out of the front door. The gravel was wet with dew and crunched under my feet. Cool, damp air filled my lungs. I left the grounds of Lennox House, but I didn't take the path to the Secret Library. No—I hurried out onto the moor. Suddenly I was overcome by such a sense of urgency that I started running. Something—some indefinable feeling—told me there was no time to waste.

I was out of breath by the time I reached Will's cottage. I went in without knocking and made a beeline for the sofa.

Will, who was halfway through putting on a pair of jeans, was so taken aback that he got his foot stuck in one of the legs and fell against the stove. "Amy!" he stammered. "H . . . hello. Has something happened?"

Without even looking at him, I threw myself to the floor. I searched the hiding place under the sofa, feeling around with both hands, peering into every corner, brushing aside the cobwebs. Nothing. I gasped.

"Er—Amy?" Will crouched down beside me. "Is everything okay?"

I leaped to my feet and backed away from him. "Where are they?" If I was going to repair the stories like Werther had said, I would need the core ingredients. But I was too late. I could have kicked myself. "Where are they?" I hissed again.

Will raised his eyebrows. He stared at me uncomprehendingly. "Where are what?"

"The ideas," I whispered. "They were here yesterday, Will, I saw them. So where are they?" With every word, the wave of fear inside me rose higher and higher. It felt like it was about to come crashing down and wash me away.

I didn't even want Will to reply. I didn't want to hear him admit it. I just wanted to find the ideas and take them back to their stories.

Will frowned. "Ideas? What ideas? What do you mean?"

"The stolen ideas," I said flatly. "The ideas that have disappeared from the book world. They were under your sofa."

"Under my sofa?" He knelt down and peered underneath it.

Meanwhile the wave of fear rose higher still, creeping up through my chest and pushing painfully at my throat. Then it broke with a roar that swept away everything in me. My vision blurred. All of a sudden the cottage around us seemed to grow even tinier, the dirty walls closing in on me along with a truth that hurt too much to acknowledge. The next moment I went stumbling out of the cottage.

I slumped down outside the door and hid my face in my hands. I was destined not to have any real friends in this world. It was better to trust nobody. Would I never learn that lesson?

Then I felt an arm around my shoulders. Will had sat down beside me—I recognized his familiar smell. I wanted to shake him off and run away, but I didn't have the strength.

"So you found the stolen ideas in my cottage yesterday and you didn't tell me?" murmured Will. "Did you think *I'd* hidden them there?"

I didn't answer.

Will sighed. "It wasn't me, Amy. It wasn't me, okay? Please believe me—I had no idea they were there."

I looked up. "Really? But . . . then how did they . . . And where . . . ?"

Will thought for a moment, then said: "I think I know who's taken them." He looked me straight in the eye and I could see no hint of a lie in his face as he went on: "When I woke up from one of my nightmares last night, the little girl was lying on the rug by the sofa. I thought she was asleep, so I didn't disturb her. But now I reckon it was her that took the ideas. Remember when we found her messing with my chest of books the other day? She probably left the ideas behind when she ran away from us—and came back for them last night."

I blinked. What Will was saying made sense! It made wonderful sense! And it struck dead all the pain and fear and horrible thoughts inside me with one blow.

I fell into Will's arms and pulled him toward me so hard that I bit his lip when I kissed him. But he didn't complain. We fell backward onto the muddy path. I kissed him and he kissed me back. He loosened the bun in my hair and buried his hands in it, and all the thoughts flew out of my head.

But it wasn't long before they returned. "So the little girl has something to do with the thefts," I mused once we'd got our breath back.

Will nodded. He looked even more disheveled than usual and his lips were red. "We have to find out more about her, and fast."

Half an hour later we were marching side by side across the island.

Stormsay wasn't very big and I'd thought I knew every corner of it already, but I realized now that I'd been quite wrong. Will led me down to the beach and from there northward along the coast. Macalister Castle soon loomed up ahead of us, and I gaped at it. I'd never seen the castle from this angle before. Its formidable turrets looked even higher from here than they did from inland. They scraped the sky like the fingers of an ugly giant. The black stone from which Will's ancestors had built the fortress was porous and shot through with cracks, sprouting clumps of weeds. Facing onto the beach was a wrought-iron gate, beyond which a passageway led deep into the bowels of the castle's foundations. Will explained that this was the tunnel to the old dungeons which the Macalisters had once used for starving prisoners to death—preferably members of the Lennox clan.

But the castle was not the northernmost point of Stormsay, as I'd previously thought. Beyond it were several rugged headlands, like fingers feeling their way out into the slate-gray sea. They were too narrow to build on, and over time the water had carved count-less caves and gullies out of them so that they now resembled mini-ature mountain ranges. All the island's paths petered out when they reached these headlands, and the beach narrowed and eventually dis-appeared altogether. The only things that lived out here were a colony of puffins, who were currently eyeing us with suspicion.

We came to a standstill.

"Welcome to the end of the world," said Will, putting an arm around me.

I sighed. I admired the harsh beauty of the crags, but I was slightly afraid to go on. Surely with my levels of coordination it would be a miracle if I made it to the end of any of these headlands in one piece.

The same thought seemed to have occurred to Will. He cast a glance at my canvas pumps. "We have to be careful. Under the sur-face there are loads of rocks with sharp edges. So if you fall in—"

"Relax," I interrupted him, forcing a smile. "We'll be fine. Fortunately, I happen to be very coordinated."

Without a moment's hesitation I clambered up onto the nearest of the jutting rocks and promptly slipped on a clump of long-haired seaweed. A second later I was up to my knees in the water with grazes on both my hands.

"You're right," said Will, hoisting me back up onto dry land. "This is going to be a piece of cake."

For the next few hours we scrambled along each of the headlands in turn and peered into every cave and behind every ledge we could find. It was a sweaty business. The wind jostled us roughly and the crags did not, unfortunately, get any less slippery. I kept missing my footing and having to be rescued by Will. Once I came so close to falling that if Will hadn't managed to grab hold of my elbow and pull me back just in time I would surely have plunged headfirst into the sea and cracked my head open on the shimmering underwater rocks below.

Will (when he wasn't saving me from certain death) explored the fissures in the rock with his flashlight, illuminating even the very narrowest crevices. But all we found were little pools of still, greenish water and abandoned birds' nests. On the first two headlands, anyway. It wasn't until the afternoon, when we reached the outermost point of the third headland, that the beam of Will's flashlight suddenly fell upon something else. Something that didn't belong there.

The cave lay hidden behind a curtain of seaweed. We would never even have spotted it if one of the puffins hadn't poked its brightly colored beak out through the greenery just as we were passing by the cave mouth. It flew away in fright as I took hold of the curtain. We pushed through the moss and seaweed and left the daylight behind us. It wasn't a particularly large cave—little more than an alcove, really—and the child wasn't there. But there was no doubt that we had found her hiding place.

Will gave a sharp intake of breath.

"What?" I whispered, but he didn't reply.

The roar of the waves was muffled in here, as if it came from far away. The cave walls were damp and almost completely covered in lichens. Only one part of the wall, directly above what looked like a primitive sort of bed, had been scraped clean. The flashlight beam came to a halt on this patch of wall, snagged on the glistening red letters.

I HAVE AWOKEN

Goose bumps ran down my spine.

There were grooves in the rock where the red stuff was, as if somebody had tried to scratch it off. Will stared long and hard at the words. I could see from his face that he was thinking about Holmes.

I left him and went over to examine what I'd assumed was a bed. The first thing I realized was that it wasn't actually a bed at all. It just looked like one. The floor of the cave was carpeted with moss and tendrils, and seaweed and seashells had gotten tangled up in them; they must have built up over time to form a layer as thick as a mattress. In the middle of this mass of plants and sludge was a small hollow, an imprint left by a body. The imprint was the size of a child. And it looked as though the child had lain here on her bed of seaweed for a very long time—so long that the tendrils had started to grow up around her. You could distinctly see the curve of the head, the shape of the shoulders, even the impressions of the hands and feet. As if the body hadn't moved an inch. How long did some-body have to lie still for something like this to form?

I felt among the tendrils and seaweed for the shimmering glass spheres, but the ideas were nowhere to be found. I did come across something else, however—a sort of semicircular metal bar, jagged and overgrown with moss and weeds along one side. I pulled it out of the tangle of plants.

"Give me some light," I said to Will. The flashlight beam darted toward me.

What had looked at first glance like fragments of seashell were in fact stones, which seemed to be set into the piece of curved metal. Dirty stones. As I scraped at the layer of mud that covered them, something gleamed suddenly red beneath my fingers. I dipped the object in a puddle on the ground and rubbed it with the sleeve of my sweater until the dirt began to come away. Rubies appeared. The curved object in my hands was no random piece of flotsam. It was a diadem.

"Is that a crown?" asked Will.

I shrugged. "Could be." I rubbed one of the gemstones with my thumb. "Yes, I think it is."

"What does that mean?"

My eyes were drawn back to the imprint of the little body. The child had lain here in the cave, then—presumably for quite a long time. Years, even? I thought for a while as Will inspected the dia-dem. "She's a book character," I said at last. "She must be. A kind of princess or something. And I think she comes from the same legend as Glenn, Clyde, and Desmond."

"What?" Will exclaimed. "What makes you think that?"

"Well—she stole those scraps of the manuscript. And before that she must have been lying here for a very long time, don't you think? Look how the plants have grown up around her body. Didn't you say all book characters have a long nap once every hundred years?"

"Yes, they do, but—a three-hundred-year nap? Anyway, Glenn, Clyde, and Desmond were the only ones to be rescued from the fire."

"Perhaps in all the commotion our ancestors lost track of who was rescued?"

"Yeah, sure." The corners of Will's mouth twitched. "She escaped without anyone noticing and when she woke up three hundred years later she immediately made a note of it here on the wall and then came and graffitied it above my stove? Is that it?" He lowered himself onto the slippery bed of seaweed.

"Okay—it is pretty weird," I admitted. But I felt as though the puzzle pieces in my head were gradually starting to slot together. "But I still think that's what happened. She's a princess from Desmond's fairy tale and she wants to go back there. That's why she needs the ideas from the book world, do you see? She wants to repair the manuscript!" A wave of relief flooded through me as I finally understood what was going on. Suddenly I knew what we had to do. "If we can find out more about the story that got burned," I told him, "I'm sure we'll be able to see a pattern, and stop her, and then—"

"Amy, what are you talking about?" Will interrupted my torrent of words. "What kind of pattern? And what makes you think there's some way of repairing the manuscript all of a sudden?"

I sat down beside him and told him all about Werther's theory and his list of stolen ideas. "Werther says that if the thief managed to get hold of ten ideas then he—she—would be able to create a whole new story. So surely it would be even easier to use the ideas to patch up an existing story, wouldn't it?"

Will looked at me for a moment, then nodded. "Okay. So, assuming she's found a way into the book world and she's trying to repair the legend . . . if we can find out which two ideas she still needs to steal . . ."

"Then we can get there first, and intercept her."

A look of grim determination settled over Will's features. His stormy-blue eyes glittered. "Let's do it," he said. "And then we'll see what she has to say for herself about what she did to Holmes."

I took his hands in mine and squeezed them. Will's jaw tightened; the muscles in his face twitched. "Come on," I said, and led him out of the cave.

We searched the fourth and fifth headlands for the princess, too, just to be sure. It was possible, after all, that she was hiding from us somewhere close by. But in none of the other caves did we find anything like a bed made of seaweed or a crown of bloodred rubies, or even so much as a child's muddy footprint on the rocks.

It was evening by the time we finally headed home, and every muscle in my body ached. As we walked along the beach, past Macalister Castle and the rusty submarine graveyard, my head was still spinning with thoughts of the princess and her plan. On the one hand I felt relieved that we'd finally stumbled upon a clue we could use, but on the other hand I got the feeling there was still something

I was missing. But what? Hazy images of our hunt for the thief swirled through my mind. There was an insight somewhere in this muddle of thoughts that I couldn't quite put my finger on. And the harder I tried, the further it slipped away from me.

Will, too, looked pensive—his gaze seemed to have turned inward. We probably both needed some time to digest what we'd found out. And there was so much to think about. Important clues that we just couldn't quite seem to make sense of.

At the Secret Library, Will kissed me on the cheek and headed off down the spiral staircase to question Glenn and Clyde about their legend. But I, having bunked off lessons that day, thought it best to stay out of Glenn's way and carried on toward Lennox House to grill Desmond. He'd spent the day with Alexis and was probably still there. Perhaps he'd be able to give me something to go on.

As I crossed the grounds, the sound of Alexis and Desmond talking drifted toward me on the wind. It came from somewhere very high up, and put a stop to my musings for the time being. I followed the voices upward and emerged a few minutes later through the skylight onto the roof of the house. I inched hand over hand across the tiles to the dormer window where my parents had made themselves comfortable.

They smiled when they saw me. There was a picnic basket between them and they were each holding a glass of wine. Sitting there side by side, pink-cheeked and bright-eyed, they looked the very embodiment of happiness.

I sat down beside Alexis, who draped one of the old blankets around my shoulders by way of a greeting and murmured: "Little giraffe! You look tired."

Desmond slid a plate of sandwiches over to me. "Would you like one?" he asked.

I nodded and helped myself—I hadn't realized how hungry I was. I'd had nothing to eat since that slice of bread this morning, after all. Perhaps that was why I was finding it hard to concentrate?

Alexis and Desmond drank their wine while I wolfed down sandwich after sandwich, and the fog that had been clouding my brain lifted a little with every bite. Some of the sandwiches were vegan, with grilled vegetables and hummus, but there were some tuna and some cheese ones as well. I demolished three of each type in quick succession. As I ate I watched the sun setting over the sea and Lady Mairead, in a sweater just as colorful as mine, slipping out of the wrought-iron front gate and onto the moor. At last I felt more or less full, and ready to tell them why I was there.

"Desmond," I began, without beating about the bush, "was there a princess in your story too?"

He choked on his mouthful of food, and coughed. "I beg your pardon? What . . . er, yes. Yes, there was." He cleared his throat. "You know that, Amy, I must have told you: I come from a fairy tale. And in the fairy tale I was a knight, sent by a princess to kill a monster."

The thing about the knight and the monster sounded familiar. But I wasn't sure he'd ever mentioned the princess before. "So you knew her. Was she . . . still a child?" I persisted.

He lowered his eyelids. "Yes," he said softly.

"What did she look like? Did she wear a crown set with rubies? How old was she roughly?"

Desmond set his glass down on the roof, much too hard. "Why

do you want to know all this?" He still wasn't looking at me. "I do not like talking about my home. It . . . it is still very difficult for me."

"And I wouldn't ask you if it wasn't important. But it's to do with the thefts in the book world. Will and I may have found a clue and—"

"This clue leads back to my story?" Desmond raised his eyebrows.

Alexis eyed me curiously.

"It looks that way," I said. "Can't you just tell me a bit more about what happened in your story? This monster, for example—was it a dragon or something?"

"No." Suddenly he fixed me with a piercing gaze. Suddenly he seemed angry. "What have Clyde and Glenn told you?"

"Nothing," I assured him hurriedly, and Desmond's expression softened a little. "I . . . just need to find out a few things. Was there a cyclone in the story, by any chance? Or a metamorphosis? Like when Gregor Samsa turns into a beetle or when Dr. Jekyll turns into Mr. Hyde, I mean?"

"Amy," Alexis broke in, "Desmond's story was a fairy tale from the Middle Ages."

"So?" I said.

Desmond said nothing. He had turned pale, and his eyes were fixed to a spot somewhere far away on the dark moor.

All of a sudden we heard a child crying in the distance. It sounded like the heartrending sobs of a little girl.

When the princess learned of the knight's death, she wept.
She wept bitterly.
Who would protect her now?
Who would fight for her now?
The princess was afraid, and the fear was even
worse than the loneliness. The fear was a monster that
pierced her with its sharp claws.
A terrible monster.

THE PRINCESS

H
E FOUND LADY MAIREAD AT DAWN.

Will had woken suddenly from another nightmare, drenched in sweat, and hadn't been able to get back to sleep. He'd put some clothes on and wandered out into the misty dawn. And he'd considered bringing the Hound of the Baskervilles out of his story to play fetch with him. Though he'd vowed never to set foot in any of Sherlock's stories ever again—for the past few days *Peter Pan* was the only story he'd jumped into—he missed the Hound more than he cared to admit. That was why he was now carrying both books in his coat pockets wherever he went—just in case. Will could feel the books pressing against his chest. He thought of the dog's big wet nose, its faithful eyes, and its saucer-sized paws. Was it time for a reunion?

He didn't get the chance to answer his own question, however, because that was when he saw her. For one confused second he thought it was the dog lying there in the heather close to the cottage, curled up on the ground waiting for him. But it wasn't, of course. Nobody had freed the huge hound from its story—it still stalked its own, fictional moor, not the real one on Stormsay. The body lying amid the tiny purple blossoms was too slim to be the dog's, and it had no fur. It was a human body. It was Lady Mairead.

Will dropped to his knees beside her.

Lady Mairead was motionless, her eyes closed. She looked much smaller than usual—breakable, like a doll. She lay on her back, one hand resting on her stomach and the other beside her face. There was a dark stain on the yarn of her colorful woolly sweater; something wet had seeped into it, something which had once been warm and red and which came from a hole in her chest.

Like Holmes, thought Will. It was all he could think. He dug his hands into the heather and crushed the blossoms, killing them. This time no seashells cut into his skin. This time it wasn't his best and oldest friend he was kneeling beside.

This time it wasn't too late.

Almost imperceptibly, Lady Mairead's chest rose and fell. She was breathing—shallowly, but she was breathing!

Will ran.

He sprinted across the moor to the stone circle. It wasn't far. He took the stairs two and three at a time and raced through the aisles of the Secret Library. Glenn and Clyde, who'd been tight-lipped when he'd asked them about their fairy tale the previous evening, were in their workshop putting a new binding on a book of love poetry. When they saw the look on Will's face they put the book aside immediately. As they ran up the stairs together, Will told them what had happened.

Glenn hurried after him to the patch of heather while Clyde went to sound the alarm at Lennox House.

Lady Mairead was still breathing.

Glenn felt her pulse.

Will didn't know what to do. He rocked from one foot to the other.

Soon the others arrived. Alexis and Amy were still in their pajamas. Desmond had his arm around Alexis, and Mr. Stevens was speaking urgently into an old-fashioned radio. Then they huddled around the pale body and waited. Alexis sobbed quietly, Amy trembled. Will took her hand and squeezed it.

He'd dreamed about her again last night. At least—Amy's name had been mentioned, hadn't it? The memory was already fading, but he still had a vague inkling—Sherlock's dead body had appeared in his dream, as always, but this time Will had not been the only one standing over the dead body. The princess had been there. She'd been holding a dagger, and she'd asked him something about Amy. Will couldn't remember what it was, but the princess must not have liked his reply. Because she had immediately started to cry, loudly and piercingly like a small child.

The helicopter approached from the south. Its rotors clattered in the wind and it circled above the island as it tried to locate them. Then at last it began its descent. The heather parted beneath its skids as it landed a few yards away.

Suddenly everything happened very fast.

The emergency doctor jumped out and immediately inserted a cannula into Lady Mairead's arm. She still wasn't moving. The paramedics carried her inside the helicopter on a stretcher. Alexis and Mr. Stevens got in, too, to accompany Lady Mairead to the hospital on Mainland. The rotor blades began to clatter again, and the helicopter rose into the air.

They gazed after it until it was just a tiny dot on the horizon.

What if they'd found Sherlock sooner? Would he have been taken away in a rescue helicopter too? Would he have survived? Will pressed his lips tightly together.

It was Glenn who finally broke the silence. "Somebody has to tell the Laird what has happened," he remarked, and of course he was right.

Though everybody on Stormsay must surely have seen the helicopter, the Laird would still expect an official report. And he would want to hear it from a member of his own clan. "I'll do it," said Will.

Glenn nodded. "Good. We'll be in the library if you need our help."

He, Clyde, and Desmond left the scene of the accident now, too, and Will was left alone with Amy. The heather was red where Lady Mairead had lain, and Amy was still trembling. Will took off his sweater and gave it to her. Amy slipped it on. Immediately afterward she grabbed his hand again as if it was the only thing stopping her from drowning in the heather.

"Can I come with you?" she asked. "I don't want to be on my own."

"Of course."

Together they made their way toward the castle.

Macalister Castle was just as uncomfortable and drafty on the inside as it looked from the outside. The sea breeze whistled through the cracks in the walls; the windows were dirty and so tiny that they hardly let in any light at all. They were probably former loopholes, now fitted with panes of glass. The muzzle of a cannon would have fitted through them: sunbeams not so much.

Will led me along the corridors of the castle which felt, to me, like a labyrinth of shadows. I still couldn't believe what had happened. My poor grandmother! I began to tremble more violently. But it wasn't fear making me quiver anymore—it was fury. How could somebody just stab another person in the chest like that, in cold blood?

Rage ran hot through my veins, pulsing at my temples. I was sure the princess was the perpetrator—who else on the island would have attacked my grandmother? What the hell was wrong with this child? I pictured myself finding her at last, shaking her till she told me what this was all about. Stealing from literature was one thing. It was awful. But attacking a human being? The mere thought of it—walking up to somebody and sticking a dagger in them! Rage burned behind my eyes and my fists clenched. But the princess, of course, was not here. My anger wasn't helping me right now.

I let out my breath and decided to take a leaf out of Werther's book for once and think logically about what had happened. I concentrated on suppressing my anger as Will and I mounted a long flight of stairs to the top of one of the formidable turrets. It took me several floors, but it worked: the clues made more and more sense to me with every flight of stairs we climbed. By the time we reached the top of the tower I'd made a list in my head, similar to Werther's:

Attempts to kill me

1. Poisoned cake in *Alice in Wonderland*
2. Falling boulder at the stone circle
3. Dagger attack in *A Midsummer Night's Dream*
4. Dagger attack on Stormsay (mistaking Lady Mairead for me)

It had occurred to me some time ago that somebody might have been trying to poison me with that cake in Wonderland. My grandmother had been adamant from the start that food in the book world couldn't go bad, and since it turned out not to have been the only time someone had tried to kill me, it no longer seemed all that far-fetched to suppose that I might have been given the cake on purpose. Only the poison obviously hadn't been strong enough to actually kill me.

After that I'd narrowly avoided being crushed by a falling boulder at the stone circle. The fact that a stone which must have been sitting up there since time immemorial had suddenly fallen off at the precise moment I was standing underneath it seemed a tad too improbable to be a coincidence. I was lucky Will had shoved me out of the way in time.

And thirdly there'd been the dagger attack in *A Midsummer Night's Dream*, which had quite clearly been intentional. As had the attack on the moor last night. The first time the princess had failed to do what she'd set out to do, but the second time the dagger had found its mark—except that the princess had got the wrong person. I didn't know why I felt so sure of it but I was almost certain the attack had been meant for me. After all, my grandmother and I had been wearing almost exactly the same sweater yesterday. And Lady Mairead had been found right next to Will's cottage. In the dark, the princess had probably thought it was me on my way to see Will. What would my grandmother have been doing out there, after all? Wait a minute . . . what *had* she been doing out there? I banished the thought from my mind for the moment. All in all I felt my list made quite a lot of sense, and I decided to write it down when I got home and show it to Werther later on. Only one question remained and that, unfortunately, was the most important one of all. *Why?*

Will and I entered the tower room. It was musty and somber. The walls were hung with portraits of the Macalisters' ancestors. Behind a massive desk sat the Laird with an accounts book, totting up numbers from a pile of receipts which Betsy was handing to him one by one. The Laird grimaced when he saw me at Will's side, but said nothing.

"What's happened?" asked Betsy.

Will told them.

The Laird listened in silence. The look on his face remained grim, but his nostrils flared at the mention of Lady Mairead's name. "I hope she pulls through" was all he muttered when Will had finished speaking, and at these words something inside me plummeted from my chest into the backs of my knees. The fact that my grandmother might . . . that her injuries might be too serious, was something I'd been trying not to admit to myself until now.

Betsy, too, had grown paler and paler with every word Will had spoken. The pile of receipts had slipped out of her hands and fluttered to the floor, and she was now gripping the edge of the desk so hard that her knuckles had gone white.

I looked searchingly into her eyes. "Was Lady Mairead on her way to meet you again?"

Betsy swallowed hard. "W . . . what are you talking about?" she croaked.

The Laird turned his head to look at Betsy, and his eyebrows crept angrily up his forehead like hairy caterpillars.

"I . . . I have no idea what Amy means," Betsy protested, her voice shaking. "I—" She bit her lip.

"You know where she was going," I declared.

She didn't answer. Instead she let go of the edge of the desk and took two unsteady steps toward the door. Then, all of a sudden, she lurched past us and down the stairs. I turned on my heel and gave chase, and as I ran I could hear the Laird ordering Will to pick up the receipts.

Betsy sprinted down the stairs two at a time, turned off into one of the corridors, and went zigzagging through the rooms of the castle. But she couldn't shake me off, no matter how hard she tried. This seemed to dawn on her eventually. At last she skittered into a room with rose-patterned wallpaper from which there was nowhere else to run. She sank breathlessly onto an upholstered stool beside a dressing table, folded her arms, and cocked her chin defiantly as I approached. Her blond hair shone in the illuminated mirror behind her. "What do you want?"

Absolutely exhausted, I stood there trying to get my breath back so I could question her. How on earth had Betsy managed to emerge from this sprint through the castle looking like a candidate for Germany's Next Top Model about to pose for her next photo shoot?

I put my hands on my hips and felt the sharp stab of a stitch in my side. "What . . . what do you know?" I panted.

"Nothing."

"Betsy!" I moved closer until I was standing right in front of her. "My grandmother is in the hospital. Someone tried to *stab her to death*, okay? So do me a favor and stop pissing about." My heart hammered against my ribs. "Why was she out on the moor last night? What are the two of you up to?"

Betsy put her head in her hands and exhaled slowly. "I was helping her," she muttered. "She came to me a few weeks ago and asked me to . . . take care of a few things for her. In the book world. She wanted me to jump there at night and, well, steal some stuff. A bit of gold, a few treasures, just a little bit here and there—so people would hardly notice."

I gasped. "You stole from literature!"

"No, we . . . Okay, fine, we stole the stuff. But only for Stormsay. And we never laid a finger on any of the ideas, I swear. Plus, I only went to the novels and fairy tales where they've got more than enough gold already. The Sultan from *Aladdin* can easily spare a few kilos of gemstones. Have you seen how rich he is? And anyway, we took everything back a few days ago because your grandma suddenly got cold feet."

"Or because she realized how immoral the whole thing was."

"Oh yeah?" sniffed Betsy. "Would you prefer it if there were no book jumpers left at all?"

"What do you mean?"

"Your clan has run out of money. You're bankrupt. How much

do you think it costs to sit around on an island for hundreds of years doing nothing but reading? For a long time the families were very wealthy, but over the years . . . Your family's broke. After your castle got burned down and you had to build a new mansion your finances went downhill pretty rapidly. And my family is in more or less the same boat. We've got a bit more money in reserve because our castle is still standing, but that will run out eventually too. Your grandma and I wanted to secure the clans' future by giving the Lennoxes a bit of a cash injection, and the Laird a little nest egg, too. So that we can stay here. So that we can keep jumping and taking care of the book world, Amy."

I stared at her. Apart from the fact that I'd been wondering for some time now how good it actually was for literature to have us jumping around in it, this whole thing was outrageous! "We can't just help ourselves to stuff from the book world. It's a good thing you took those treasures back," I declared.

"Pff," said Betsy, tilting backward on her stool against the edge of the dressing table. The arsenal of little pots and tubes piled up on it began to wobble. Only now did I realize that this must be her bedroom. It was a lot more homey than the rest of Macalister Castle. Beside the bed were piles of books that wouldn't fit on the shelves, and on the bedside table was a photo of a woman in a blue summer dress who looked exactly like Betsy.

"I thought literature was so important to you. Will said you'd do anything to protect it."

"Would you prefer us to have to leave Stormsay?" said Betsy tonelessly. "That's what'll end up happening sooner or later, Amy. And that will be the end of everything our clans have built up over so many generations. We'll never be able to jump again!"

I shrugged. This wasn't the right time to tell Betsy about my gift. And anyway, the families' financial woes were not exactly top of our list of priorities right now, given that my grandmother had nearly been murdered and might be fighting for her life at this very moment. "If the treasure is back where it belongs, then what was Lady Mairead doing out there last night?" I returned to the issue at hand, and Betsy went white again.

"That was my fault," she said, her shoulders sagging. "I asked her to meet me at the stone circle again. We can't give up Stormsay and the book world—they're my home! I wanted to try to persuade her that we should take a little bit of gold from the fairy tales after all. But she . . . she didn't come."

"Because somebody stopped her."

"Yes." Betsy lowered her eyes.

When Will and I landed in the book world later that morning we could see from Werther's face that something else had happened. In the Inkpot we brought each other up to speed on recent events. It looked as though the princess had made full use of the previous night not only to stab my grandmother but also to acquire the ninth idea, as we now learned that the evil was missing from *Wuthering Heights*. Werther told us it was almost unbearable to see the characters suddenly so polite and kind and completely lacking in vengefulness. There was basically no plot left at all.

We talked for a while about our lists and our suspicions. The princess only needed one more idea, then. But what kind of idea?

Which story would she raid next? Will and I hadn't managed to find out anything new about the burned fairy tale the previous night. All we knew was that it was about a knight who was sent by a princess to fight a monster and who died at the end of the story. Both the knight and the princess had escaped the flames, as we now knew. Both were living on Stormsay.

"What about the monster?" asked Will at last. "If it was burned along with the manuscript, won't she need a new one?"

Werther wobbled his head from side to side. "Perhaps. And unfortunately, literature is only too full of terrible creatures."

"Yes—but it has to be a story where the monster plays a crucial role. She only steals the core ingredients," I reminded him.

For the next half hour we racked our brains trying to think which monster out of which story might fit that description. The more horror stories we came up with the more anxious Werther became— mainly at the thought of having to go inside these stories and confront the princess, as we had done in *Metamorphosis*. But in the end he promised, in spite of himself, to ask around and report back to us as soon as he heard anything.

Will and I, for our part, jumped back to the outside world to look for the princess. At regular intervals as we roamed across the moor we scanned the first page of *Peter Pan*, which was where Werther was to sound the alarm if anything unusual occurred.

The moor—the whole of Stormsay, in fact—felt more deserted than usual today. Perhaps because Alexis and Mr. Stevens were still at the hospital with Lady Mairead. Perhaps because early that evening—just to make matters worse—it began pouring down with rain. The raindrops fell thick and fast, cloaking the landscape in an impenetrable grayness which made every bush and shrub look the same.

In weather like this it was impossible to find somebody who didn't want to be found. Within minutes Will and I were soaked to the skin and we had to accept that it was pointless to continue the search under these conditions. We decided to go back to Will's cottage. As we approached it, however, a figure emerged from the wall of rain ahead of us. I almost screamed in fright.

It wasn't the princess—the figure was too tall and broad-shouldered. He was wearing blue dungarees and a T-shirt with a faded picture on the front, and the fuzzy hair on his cheeks shone like the damp, shaggy fur of an animal. His close-set eyes were fixed on me.

"Amy," said Brock. It was the first time I'd ever heard him open his mouth other than to count something. He extended his huge hand toward me. At first I tried to shake it, but then I spotted the key he was holding out to me. It was large and rusty.

"What's that for?"

"One," said Brock, taking my hand and pressing the key into my palm. The thing was heavier than it looked.

"*One* key?"

He nodded. "One key, one Amy, one princess, one knight. Be careful," said Brock.

"What do you mean? Do you know where the princess is?"

At that he grabbed me by the shoulders and pulled me closer to him, until his rough-hewn nose was almost touching mine. "Be careful," he said again, in a whisper this time. Then he let go of me, pointed to the key, and nodded. Before I could reply he'd turned away and disappeared into the gray haze.

Will and I watched him go, openmouthed.

"What was that?" I asked. My upper arms were tingling where Brock had grabbed hold of them.

Will shrugged. "No idea. But that key looks familiar," he murmured. "I think I know what it opens." He brushed a strand of wet hair off my forehead. "Come with me!"

"Where?"

"To the castle."

So we turned our backs on Will's cottage, which was now only a few yards away, and battled our way through the storm hand in hand. The wind whipped the rain almost sideways across the island and the icy drops stung my face. But I didn't care. The key was a promise. It would lead me to a door, and behind that door there would be another piece of the puzzle. There had to be.

We arrived at Macalister Castle and went in, leaving puddles on the corridor floors. Will marched straight through to the part of the castle that had once been the kitchens, where food had once been cooked over an open fire. There he opened a worm-eaten door to reveal a spiral staircase. A musty smell greeted us, and an age-old chill. We descended the well-trodden steps deep into the foundations of the Macalisters' family seat, where—I soon realized—so many of my ancestors had been kept prisoner.

We were headed for the dungeons.

The deeper underground we went, the more uncomfortable and low-ceilinged the tunnels became as they wound their way through the rock beneath the fortress. There was no electricity down here—all we had was Will's flashlight, its beam dancing ahead of us over the soot-blackened stone. In spite of the thick walls we could hear the soughing of the sea and I thought of the entrance to the castle from the beach, which we had passed only yesterday. Barred doors and windows were set into the walls here and there; the cells beyond lay in compete darkness. The locks were large and rusty. But the key didn't fit any of them.

One after the other, Will shone his flashlight into all of the dungeons. They were all empty.

Why had the Macalisters needed so many jail cells? A chill ran down my spine as the flashlight beam fell upon a collection of strange instruments. The light glanced off something serrated. Something that must once have been used on the prisoners here. Sharp and painful.

I felt for Will's hand and pressed closer to him. The ceiling was so low by now that we had to stoop, but we kept going and at last, as we rounded a corner, the tunnel suddenly brightened around us. Somebody had lit several flaming torches, mounted in brackets on the wall. The flames crackled and bathed the last of the dungeons in a flickering light.

This last dungeon was not empty.

Inside was a thin pallet and on the pallet sat a child in a tattered dress, her dirty hair spread around her like a cloak. Her dark eyes reflected the firelight. Brock had succeeded, then, where we had failed. He had captured the princess. I knew without having to try it that the key would fit.

Will dropped the flashlight the instant he caught sight of the little girl. His shoulders trembled and he gritted his teeth so hard I could hear them grinding against one another. The sound echoed through the dungeons and made the hairs on the back of my neck stand on end. The princess, however, didn't even blink.

For a moment it looked as though Will was going to rush up to the cell door, rattle at the bars, and start screaming at the princess to tell him why she had killed Holmes. But he regained his composure and approached the little girl with unexpected calmness. Their eyes seemed to bore into each other. "Give me the key, Amy," he said quietly, the words trembling in his throat.

The metal of the key had warmed up in my hands. I ran my fingertips over the rusty key bit and thought about my grandmother and the bloodstained heather where she had lain. I thought about the chaos in the book world and the stories that had been so cruelly mutilated. And I thought about the fact that this child had tried to kill me. Then I put the key in my trouser pocket and let out a sigh. "No."

Will looked at me.

"As long as she's in there she can't do any more harm," I explained. "And it'll give us time to think."

"About what?"

"About what we're going to do with her," I said flatly.

Will wove his fingers through mine, almost crushing them. "Okay. Agreed," he said at last with a sigh.

"Agreed," I echoed, just for something to say. The silent princess in her cell was so ghostly, so unreal. But she was there.

For a while we just stood there and stared at the child, who had put her head to one side and was gazing intently back at us. I'd expected hatred to flare up in me when we found her, rage, a thirst for revenge. But all I felt was uneasy. Uneasy and a little helpless. Here she was, then—the girl Will, Werther, and I had been searching for for weeks. Brock had practically handed her to us on a silver platter. But what now?

Again I sensed, somewhere at the edges of my consciousness, that I was missing something.

"Where are the stolen ideas?" I asked the princess. "Where have you hidden them?"

But she didn't answer, of course. She simply lowered her eyes and turned away from us. Her back was so bony, and her elbows jutted out so sharply from her curtain of matted hair. She must be half starved. A touch of pity wormed its way into my thoughts. The key lay heavy against my thigh. Pity?

I pulled Will hurriedly away from the cell door. The flashlight had broken when he'd dropped it, so he took one of the flaming torches from its bracket and we walked back down the tunnel away from the little girl. We could still hear her, however, as we turned the corner.

"She knew," she said in her high, clear child's voice, as if trying to console herself, "that he would stop the monster."

We hastened our steps, running along the stone passageways, up the stairs, through the corridors of the castle. Soon we were stepping back out into the rain.

The storm was fiercer now, whipping up the surface of the sea and sending tongues of lightning flickering across the sky where mountains of dark black clouds were massing. But I welcomed the icy raindrops on my skin—they seemed to wash away my confusion. The wind swept away all my emotions and the thunder silenced the whispering voices in the back of my head. They were replaced by cold, clear thoughts. Thoughts like frozen glass. Ice-cold and sharp. And at last, as I tramped across the moor at Will's side, I realized what it was that had been troubling me since the previous day. At last I saw what it was about all this that didn't fit together.

The thief Werther and I had seen in the book world was not a child.

He was bigger.

As big as a grown man.

The knight had realized too late.

Far too late.

How could he not have noticed the transformation?

What had he done?

THE MONSTER

WE MISSED WERTHER'S ALARM.

Will and I had spent the night in his cottage, where we'd taken turns to stay awake and keep watch in case Werther found out any new information and needed to get hold of us. One of us had slept on the sofa while the other kept an eye on the first page of *Peter Pan*. But at some point this system seemed to have broken down, because when I opened my eyes at daybreak Will was nowhere to be seen.

His copy of *Peter Pan* lay abandoned on the rug by the stove. The book was still open, and I could see at a glance that the action had been interrupted several times by a young man in silk stockings shouting my name.

"Miss Amy! He is back!" he'd yelled, right after the first line about all children having to grow up. *"The Odyssey! It is* The *Odyssey! Come quickly!"*

At this point Werther withdrew into the background of the story but before long (just after the bit about the kiss hidden in the corner of Wendy's mother's mouth) he popped up again: *"Miss Amy! Where are you? Should I go alone?"* A few lines later, Werther began running frantically to and fro. *"Miss Amy?"*

I turned the page. Werther must indeed have gone to *The Odyssey* without me, because on the second page the story continued as normal. But on the third page Werther could be seen flitting about again. He came charging back into the story through the middle of two paragraphs. This time his clothes were wet and he looked bruised and battered.

"Miss Amy!" he shouted. *"It is too late! The thief has stolen one of the two sea monsters, and the other—ah, there it is again! Help!"*

And again he vanished from the book.

I went rushing out of the cottage onto the moor before I'd even finished reading. Where on earth was Will? Why hadn't he woken me up? Had he jumped into *The Odyssey* without me?

As I ran I scoured *Peter Pan* for further clues. And there—on page five Werther reappeared with a long-drawn-out *"Heeeeeeeelp!"* followed by the sound of mighty lizard legs stomping along behind him, coming closer and closer. Then he disappeared from the book completely. Had Will already rescued him and sent the monster back to *The Odyssey?*

I sprinted up to the stone circle, certain that when I arrived I would find an open copy of the ancient epic poem under one of the gateways. But I was wrong. There was not a single book up here— no *Odyssey*, no nothing. Which meant that Will wasn't in the book world either: Werther had been left to fight the sea monster all on his own, and I'd wasted precious time running up here. Why hadn't I gone to Werther's aid right away, straight from the cottage?

Damn, damn, damn!

I threw myself to the ground and slid *Peter Pan* over my face. A moment later the letters swam before my eyes and sucked me into the story.

Will was leaning against the old hearth at Macalister Castle. His eyes were on the door that led down to the dungeons. It was open a crack. Had he and Amy not closed it properly the night before? He moved closer, trying to remember. But wisps of fog clouded his brain.

He walked down the stairs.

The fog was stopping him from thinking clearly. It was making him forget why he'd come here. He couldn't even remember how he'd got here, if he was being honest. . . .

He must have fallen asleep because he'd had a dream, about Holmes—still dead—and about the princess, who had called out to him. Once again, anger at what the girl had done to his best friend sank its claws into him and burrowed into his guts. Had his subconscious driven him to the castle to interrogate the princess again? To force her to look him in the eye and explain herself? To get his revenge?

Will reached the bottom of the staircase. Darkness surrounded him. Without his torch he was forced to feel his way along the clammy walls with his fingers. But he didn't care. The musty breath of the dungeons filled his lungs. Anger sliced through his stomach and ate into his chest, its claws tearing at his ribs.

Why had the princess killed Holmes? Why? What had he known that she didn't want him to know?

Will stumbled through the darkness, ducking beneath the low ceilings. His fingers touched rock and metal bars. Once, something hairy with too many legs went scuttling across his hand. At last he turned the final corner of the tunnel. There was only one torch left burning on the wall—its light hurt his eyes. He wrenched it out of its bracket and spun around, directing the light toward the cell behind him.

Rage was roaring in his ears now, but he resisted the powerful urge to fling the flaming torch through the bars into the princess's gaunt face. Instead he moved closer and shone the firelight into the cell. The pallet was still in place, and in the corners of the cell were the same pools of shadow as on the evening before.

But the princess was gone.

She was gone?

Yes, gone. And the barred door stood open.

Will kicked out at the stone wall. How could this happen? Had somebody set the girl free? Amy? Or had she managed to escape on her own?

The lock looked undamaged, as if it had been opened with a key.

Damn it! Will rubbed his eyes with thumb and forefinger. At least his rage had swallowed up the fog in his head. If the princess had escaped, there was presumably nothing to stop her committing another theft. She might already have gone back into the book world. Werther might already have sounded the alarm!

Come to think of it—why had Will left *Peter Pan* behind? Hadn't it been his turn to keep watch?

His feet flew through the tunnel and up the stairs. He sprinted across the old kitchen, along the draughty corridors and out of the castle gates. A few minutes later he was back at his cottage.

"Amy!" he cried, hurrying inside. "You have to wake up—I—"

But Amy was gone, and so was *Peter Pan*. Will bit his lip and tasted blood. His eyes darted feverishly around the room for an instant, as if expecting to see Amy or the princess behind the stove or by the door. But that was ridiculous, of course. Will turned on his heel and kept running.

Werther must have appeared in the book and called to them. Amy was probably in the book world right now. Without him. What if she needed his help? Why had he gone down to those bloody dungeons? How could he have abandoned her like that? Will headed for the portal as fast as he could. He needed to jump, right away. There was still a chance he might be able to help Amy and Werther stop the princess.

He climbed the hill in long strides and burst into the stone circle. It was just as he'd suspected. *Peter Pan* lay open under one of the gateways—Amy must have jumped in not long ago. But there was somebody else standing at the center of the *Porta Litterae*.

The princess laughed when she saw Will. It was not the laugh of a child, but that of a queen. On her head was the bloodred diadem. "You will come with me," she said, and extended her hand as if expecting him to kneel and kiss it.

The monster that was chasing Werther was the most hideous creature I had ever seen. It looked like a sausage with scales. Unfortunately this particular sausage was the size of a high-speed train and the front end consisted primarily of teeth, set in jagged rows one behind the other inside its enormous mouth. It didn't have any eyes, though—at least not that I could see. And its lizardy legs were tiny, barely capable of supporting its own weight. The creature was clearly more at home in the water than on land.

Even on solid ground, however, it was far from slow. When I landed in *Peter Pan* it was in the process of chasing Werther right across Neverland and into a neighboring story.

"Miss Amy," panted Werther as I joined him. "I am exceedingly glad to see you."

"Likewise," I grunted, through gritted teeth. The smell of the beast's breath was making me feel sick. "We have to take it back to its story."

"That thought had occurred to me, too. But I was somewhat preoccupied with staying alive," replied Werther. The monster took a huge bound toward us and snapped at Werther's head, coming so close that its jaws closed around the velvet ribbon in his ponytail.

We ducked aside, rolled down a slope, and ran on side by side, splitting up and veering off to the right and left from time to time to confuse the monster. Together we reached *The Odyssey* and the ocean strait where the beast lived. But it showed not the slightest interest in its own story. For some reason it didn't want to go home. It was intent on eating Werther.

"I have an idea!" cried Werther at last. We flicked ourselves through the pages of *The Odyssey* from one island to the next, with the monster still hot on our heels. Soon we'd lured it out of the epic poem and into the story of *War and Peace*, to a scene between the enemy lines at the Battle of Austerlitz. Frustratingly, however, not even cannonballs seemed able to make any sort of impression on it.

By this time we were completely out of breath. We'd narrowly avoided being swallowed by the monster several times and the more exhausted we got, the more frequent these near misses became. Werther was panting so loudly that I was afraid he might faint at any moment. On a sudden impulse, therefore, as we passed a series of fairy tales, I dragged a stumbling Werther behind me into *Rapunzel*. We scrambled up the captive girl's braid and into her sky-high tower. And there we sat, watching the monster as it circled the walls and launched itself at them with dogged persistence. Werther, still out of breath and scarlet in the face, told me in broken sentences what had happened before my arrival.

The thief, it seemed, had been less purposeful this time than on his previous forays. He'd been seen roaming around *The Odyssey* for some time, as if unsure whether or not to steal the tenth idea. But in the end he'd made his move and taken one of the two sea monsters (the one he'd stolen, claimed Werther, was even uglier and more terrible than the scaly sausage at the foot of the tower). Werther had tried to stop the thief and pull down his hood, but by that time the second monster had spotted him and he'd had to run for his life.

"I had no choice but to flee, Miss Amy," he explained remorsefully.

"I'm sorry I came too late to help you."

Werther brushed my apology aside. "I am the one who has failed. I had the chance to catch the thief, but I saved my own life instead. Because I am a coward." He sniffed.

"Rubbish," I said. "You're one of the best and bravest friends I've ever had."

Werther's face glowed an even brighter red. "Miss Amy," he whispered. His hand reached for mine.

I beat a hasty retreat and went to lean out of the window where I stood watching the monster. It was making enthusiastic attempts to clamber up the side of the tower, scrabbling at the wall with its little lizard legs.

"Might there be some kind of trick for calming it down?" I wondered. "Do you know much about *The Odyssey*? How do the characters fight the beast?"

"Hmm," said Werther. "I believe Odysseus endeavors to stay as far away from her as possible."

"Her?" I asked. "It's a girl?"

Werther nodded. "Her name is Charybdis, and she causes deadly whirlpools."

The scaly sausage's name was as ugly as she was, then. "She's pretty deadly with or without a whirlpool, if you ask me," I said, pointing to the huge maw full of teeth still snapping in our direction.

"Indeed." Werther sighed and patted the back of his head. Only now did I see that the monster had bitten off not only his velvet ribbon but most of his ponytail as well. "But she will not be able to climb up here. You should jump back to the outside world, Miss Amy, and try to stop the thief from there. Perhaps the last idea has not yet been delivered to the princess's dungeon."

I knew he was right. I'd felt uneasy for a while now, because I was afraid something terrible was going to happen on Stormsay once the princess had got hold of all ten ideas. "But what about you?" I asked. I felt as though I was leaving Werther in the lurch again.

"Well now, I . . . I shall keep this charming young lady company," he said, smiling over at Rapunzel. She waved shyly back at him.

"Okay, great," I said. "I'll be back as soon as I can." I tugged at a loose stone in the wall of the tower. "Take care of yourself, okay?" I called just before the page collapsed on top of me. I took the shortest possible route back to *Peter Pan*, and from there I jumped back to Stormsay.

I knew something was wrong the moment I landed.

". . . with me," I heard a high voice say. Then I caught sight of the princess in the middle of the stone circle. To my left stood Will, his eyes pinned on the little girl. He looked confused, as though he were struggling to think clearly.

I scrambled to my feet and took his hand. "Where were you?" I whispered. "And why is she out of her cell?"

But before Will could reply, the princess laughed aloud. "Wonderful!" she cried. "This is wonderful. Now you can both come with me." She fished a few scraps of burned paper from the depths of her gown and scattered them underneath one of the archways. Then she placed two shimmering spheres in their midst. The Little Prince's flower was suspended inside one of the spheres, and the White Rabbit from Wonderland lolloped about in the other. Both of them melted away into the remnants of the manuscript. All of a sudden several flawless pages appeared on the ground. It was just as we'd suspected: she was trying to repair her story. She'd already started.

My heart began to beat faster.

The princess beamed. "And now come with me," she said, pointing to the new pages.

Obviously, I didn't budge. She'd just implanted the rabbit and the flower into her story without batting an eyelid. And now she wanted us to go with her into her fairy tale of stolen ideas as if none of that mattered? What was she thinking? "If you think we're jumping in there with you, then—"

"That is precisely what I think," the princess broke in. Suddenly she no longer looked like the half-starved child we'd taken her for at first. Her true age was reflected in her eyes. This was no little girl standing before us, but a five-hundred-year-old princess. "I command it." She sounded like somebody who was not accustomed to being disobeyed.

Still, I shrugged. What was she going to do—force me to jump?

"I command it," the princess said again. She was still smiling. "And if you do not do as I say, I will shatter these upon the rocks." She produced several more ideas from the pocket of her gown. I recognized the cyclone and Sleeping Beauty and shrank back in horror. Yes—she was going to force me. And unfortunately, her arguments were pretty damn persuasive.

"They will be irretrievably destroyed," murmured the princess.

"Th . . . then your manuscript will never be any more than a few scraps of paper," I stammered.

"You are mistaken, Amy. The literary world has so many more ideas to steal."

I stared at her. The ingredients in her skinny hands glowed softly. The cyclone, without which *The Wizard of Oz* had practically ceased to exist, whirled round and round inside its glass sphere. Sleeping Beauty looked so peaceful lying there asleep as her bedroom was gradually overrun with climbing roses. There was no way the princess could be allowed to destroy these stories. I squared my shoulders. "Why?" I asked as I wondered frantically what to do. My first impulse was to run at her and try to pin her down. But she would smash the ideas before I got to her.

"Why what?" asked the princess.

"Why should we go with you?" Out of the corner of my eye I tried to sneak a glance at Will's face. He still looked bewildered. Would I be able to give him a signal without the princess noticing? If I distracted her, perhaps he could—

"I need you for my story. It will be too empty otherwise. Now hurry up and come with me."

I tried to think, but the same two ideas kept going round and round in my head: she was going to destroy the stories. We had to buy some time. "H . . . how did you escape from the dungeons?"

The princess did not reply. Instead, she fished another idea out of her pocket. The portrait of a young man floated inside the sphere, staring at us wide-eyed. It must be the picture of Dorian Gray. A moment later the shimmering idea went hurtling through the air and shattered on one of the boulders.

The crash was deafening.

The man in the picture opened his mouth in astonishment.

Then he was gone.

Forever. I stood there as if turned to stone, unable to take my eyes off the shards of glass.

She'd done it. She'd really done it.

The princess was already raising the other ideas above her head, getting ready to throw them. But I still couldn't get my limbs to move. How could the broken glass on the ground look so ordinary? Nothing remained of its shimmering light. No hint of the idea it had once enclosed.

The princess drew back her arm and launched Sleeping Beauty through the air.

It was Will who stepped in. In a heartbeat, he had thrown himself between the idea and the boulder it was about to shatter on. There was a crack as his shoulder slammed into the rock, but he managed to catch the sphere.

"No!" he cried as the princess prepared to hurl the cyclone against one of the other archways. "We'll come with you."

Will got to his feet and tried to pull me toward the archway where the new pages of the old legend awaited us. "We have no choice," he murmured, so quietly that only I could hear. "Just as long as the ideas still exist, there's a chance we can get them back."

At last I managed to snap out of my trance. I followed him across the stone circle to the archway. Will's hand in mine was wet with sweat as we lay down. I couldn't believe we were doing this. We were about to jump into a manuscript that had been destroyed long ago, so badly that nobody could survive in it anymore. This was dangerous. And it was scary.

But we had no other choice.

For a brief instant Will let go of me to pick up the far-too-white pages, and the princess wormed her way in between us. I flinched as her skinny body touched my side. The princess smelled unwashed and strangely musky. Her dirty hair brushed my cheek. I blinked, and when I opened my eyes somebody had slid the words over my face.

Words that nobody had read for a very long time.

Words that began to dance before our eyes and gradually melted into one another.

The fire was still burning.

I smelled the flames before I saw them. The moment I was sucked inside the story my nostrils filled with the stench of destruction. Acrid. Hostile.

We landed in a rugged, hilly landscape that must have been drawn from the Scottish Highlands. Almost every inch of it was burning. Everywhere you looked flames were eating away at rock formations and lush meadows, at flocks of sheep and villages in the valleys. Only the four or five pages on which we stood seemed untouched by the fire. Flowers bloomed on the hilltop at our feet, and to our left loomed a castle with silver battlements and stained-glass windows. It looked ghostly against the black smoke that towered on the horizon.

The princess spread her arms wide, twirled on the spot and shouted for joy. "I have missed you, Valleys!" she cried. "I have dreamed of you, Castle! I have returned at last, do you hear? I have returned! And this time I will stay forever. All three of us will stay forever."

Neither the valleys nor the castle made any reply. The only sound was the fire, spitting and crackling in the distance. It sounded like malicious laughter.

As the little girl proceeded to greet the blades of grass beneath her feet and the sky overhead (parts of which were also ablaze), I seized the opportunity and launched myself at her.

It was easy—ridiculously easy, in fact. The princess went down like a ninepin, the back of her head hitting the ground hard. I held her down by the shoulders with both hands, my knee on her chest. I was so much bigger and heavier than the princess. She didn't even try to push me off.

Instead, she smiled.

Again.

Beneath the dirt on her little face I could see freckles. Her eyes blazed, a very pale icy blue.

I pressed her harder into the grass. "Why are you doing this? Do you know how many stories you've ruined just to save this one? You've destroyed them!"

"Yes, I know," said the princess. "But this one is my home. I can't survive without it."

"Desmond, Glenn, and Clyde can."

A sneer crossed the princess's face. "Desmond, Glenn, and Clyde have betrayed our story. They never even tried to save it—they just surrendered willingly to their fate. They *want* to live in the outside world! They no longer have any right to be part of this story."

"I seem to recall you also spent quite a while holed up in a cave without stealing any ideas, didn't you?" Why had she changed her mind all of a sudden?

The princess shook her head. A thin burn scar ran all the way up her neck and disappeared somewhere behind her ear. "When the accident happened, I only just managed to get out of the burning manuscript alive. Concealed by the smoke I clung to the kilt of one of your ancestors, Amy Lennox. But I was very weak, and I dragged myself away from the people into a cave by the sea, where I fell unconscious. For many, many years my soul drifted in the darkness and I vowed to myself that if I ever did wake up I would do whatever it took to save my story. I hoped that my loyal subjects would do the same—that perhaps they had already found a way back. And then, a few weeks ago, I succeeded at last in opening my eyes. I roamed around Stormsay. I observed the inhabitants of the island and realized that Desmond, Glenn, and Clyde had done nothing at all. That they were living among you. Serving you, even, by giving you book-jumping lessons!" The princess lowered her eyelids for a moment, and when she opened them again there was a strange glint in her eye. "I could see I was going to need a new knight," she whispered.

"What do you mean?"

Her lips curled into a smile as she went on, in a whisper: "I needed a knight to go into the book world for me and steal me a metamorphosis, and catch a monster for me to be afraid of. And a long sleep for that monster, of course. And beautiful flowers, and the summer. And a talking animal to keep me company. And Evil—Evil was necessary too." She laughed in my face, so suddenly and so loudly that I flinched. "I had so many ideas to replace—and for that I needed my knight."

"But—" I stammered. So it was true—the princess hadn't been acting alone. Somebody must have been helping her. That was why the thief had been built like a grown man and not a child. And of course it made sense that she'd got a knight to carry out the thefts for her. In her story she sent him out to kill the monster for her, after all. It was in her nature to get other people to solve her problems. But . . . I swallowed hard.

In the fairy tale, Desmond had been her knight.

Suddenly I found it hard to breathe. Or was it just the smoke, filtering into my lungs and my thoughts?

The princess was still laughing, and my brain was working overtime. I felt the cogs clicking into place one by one inside my head and beginning to turn. The princess no longer saw my father as worthy of being in her story . . . and hadn't she said something about a *new* knight just now?

It wasn't Desmond—no, he wouldn't have been able to get back into the book world any more than the princess herself. A wave of relief flooded through me and I let out my breath. But only briefly. Who was it, then? Who, apart from us, had come into contact with the little girl?

The cogs in my brain grated as they turned. They grated out a single word. A name.

Brock.

Brock, who had locked up the princess and given me the key. Hadn't he said something about a princess and a knight? Had she been forcing him to steal for her? Had he been trying to warn us?

I shifted my weight and felt in my trouser pocket for the key to the jail cell.

It was gone. My pocket was empty.

Was Brock the princess's new knight? Had she ordered him to take back the key from me and set her free? Did he have to do everything she—

There was a crash.

Damn it!

I'd only loosened my hold on the princess for a second, but it had been enough. She'd managed to reach past me into the folds of her gown, pull out another ingredient, and hurl it against the wall of the castle.

The glass sphere shattered just like the one the princess had broken in the stone circle. But this time it was different. Because now we were inside the book world, where ideas never got lost. In literature, nothing and nobody was transient.

Something was rising from the shards of glass. Something that grew larger by the second. At first I thought it was a little plume of smoke seeping from between the fragments. But the plume quickly expanded, bulging outward until it was as thick as one of the castle towers and lengthening skyward until it touched the clouds. And then it began to spin and to roar much more loudly than the fire around us.

My hair whipped across my face and wind tore fiercely at my clothes. A gust caught me and sent me stumbling a few yards backward, away from the princess, who had now got to her feet again and was gazing at the cyclone from *The Wizard of Oz* with shining eyes. She clapped her hands for joy, and not a hair on her matted head stirred.

I, however, was finding it hard to stay on my feet and I staggered backward into something—no, someone—who tried to hold me up. Will. He shouted something, right in my ear, but I couldn't hear him.

The princess's lips were moving, too, as if she were speaking to

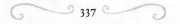

the storm, as if she were giving it an order. Then she pointed suddenly in our direction and sure enough the cyclone began to move, whirling straight toward us.

Will and I ran.

We sprinted down the hill, stumbling over rubble and our own feet. As we ran I tugged again and again at flowers and blades of grass, trying to skip to a different page. But when the page finally did start to turn, all I could see behind it was a wall of flames. Fire, as far as the eye could see. This part of the manuscript had been completely destroyed. I let go of the page and the world fell back into place.

We ran on blindly across the hillside.

The cyclone was very close now. It tore at our clothes. Will and I clung to each other desperately. Somehow we made it to the other side of the hill. This time it was Will who pulled at a stone. But we couldn't skip back a page either. The fire seemed to have eaten away the whole story. The horizon was one big sheet of flame. There was no way we would be able to escape from this book to another part of the book world.

We were trapped, stranded on a lone island in a fiery sea with a lunatic and a cyclone that obeyed her every command.

But perhaps we could jump back to Stormsay?

I dragged Will up the slope with me, back to the castle and the princess. Back to the spot where we'd landed.

Then the princess shouted something and the storm surrounded us, encircled us, whirling so fast that we had to stand very still so as not to be caught up and hurled into the fire.

We huddled as close together as we possibly could. The storm spiraled around us in ever tighter circles. Will's heart beat so hard that I could feel it pounding against my back.

Suddenly the roaring of the wind began to subside. It was as if somebody had turned the sound off. The cyclone still whirled around us, gray and huge and savage. But all of a sudden it was completely silent.

The princess moved closer to us. "See?" she said. "This is my kingdom. Everything and everybody here does what I say." She sounded like a child again now. A child bragging about her ability to rage and scream until her parents did exactly what she wanted.

She gave the storm a signal and it began to shrink. It thinned out until it was only the width of a pencil, then folded in upon itself and rolled up into a ball. A moment later it was a shimmering idea once more, lying in the grass.

The princess stowed the glass sphere in the folds of her gown. "That was just a little taste. Now you know what I am capable of in this world. So you will listen to me more carefully from now on, and do as I say." She cocked her chin. "I am going to repair the story now and then you, Amy, my new—"

"You know what? You can forget it," I hissed.

The princess glared at me. "You do know I can throw you into the fire whenever I want?"

I snorted. "Why don't you, then?" I cried, thinking of the poisoned cake, the falling boulder, and the dagger attacks. "It wouldn't be the first time you've tried to kill me. I'm a bit surprised you've suddenly stopped trying, to be honest."

She shrugged. "I have changed my mind. At first I did want you out of the way, it's true. I was afraid you might thwart my plans. And

I didn't want to share my knight. But I've changed my mind. Now I want both of you for my story."

"What do you mean?" An uneasy feeling settled in the pit of my stomach.

"Where did that stupid rabbit go?" The princess stood on tiptoe and peered down the hill.

But I was not to be deterred. "What do you mean?" I asked again.

The princess sank back onto her heels. "Once the story has been repaired, you two will be the characters. Look, I'll show you." She cleared her throat. "I choose you," she announced majestically. "Kneel."

"Pff," I scoffed. The princess must be even crazier than I'd imagined if she thought we were just going to let her turn us into puppets in her fairy tale.

But there was movement beside me. I only saw it out of the corner of my eye, but that was enough. I spun around.

Beside me, Will had lowered himself to the ground. He was bowing his head reverently.

"Stop it!" I cried, shaking him. What was wrong with him all of a sudden? "Will is never going to be your knight," I hissed at the princess. I was so angry I spat the words at her. "Leave him alone!"

The princess turned to Will as if I hadn't said a word, and spoke to him again. "Do you swear that you will hunt and kill the monster and that you will not rest until I, your princess, am safe once more? Do you swear it upon your life?" she asked, in a strange singsong voice.

Then Will lifted his head and looked at her. His face lit up. He gazed raptly at the dirty little girl. The thief. The miserable, filthy—

"I swear it upon my life," replied Will. He sounded oddly lifeless.

"No he doesn't," I cried, launching myself at him. I slapped him as hard as I could. First on the right cheek, then the left, then the right again. And just as I'd hoped, the veil that had fallen over his eyes lifted. He blinked and looked at me. "Amy!" he whispered. "Is . . . is everything okay? Did the cyclone get us?"

I shook my head and pulled him to his feet. Will looked around as if seeing the hill, the castle, and indeed the whole of the story we found ourselves in, for the very first time.

The princess grinned. "Very well," she said. "Then how about Will the monster?"

Quick as a flash, she pulled two ingredients from the pocket of her gown and flung them at us. The first was the sphere containing the transformation of Dr. Jekyll into Mr. Hyde. It hit Will on the temple, where it smashed. A shimmering liquid ran down his cheek. And then the second idea shattered against his chest. It was the stolen monster from *The Odyssey*.

"No!" I screamed. My first impulse was to reach out and brush the shards of glass off Will's clothes. But desperate as I was to protect him from this lunatic, something held me back. Perhaps it was the sight of Will's face which, from one moment to the next, had stiffened into a kind of mask. Suddenly he didn't look like himself anymore. Was it just my imagination or were his nostrils getting wider?

Will's shoulders trembled. Inch by inch his neck grew longer.

Then everything happened very fast. In the blink of an eye, his stormy-blue eyes turned purple and then blazing red, his nose became a snout, and his teeth grew long and sharp. And two extra heads sprouted from the crook of his neck.

I screamed. Dread coursed through my veins, ice-cold.

"Do you know, Amy—I am glad I didn't kill you," the princess declared. "For if I had, who would my monster hunt? Every story needs a victim. Somebody to terrify. Somebody who dies at the end."

The creature that stood before me was not Will. It was a beast the size of a house, with three heads on three long necks that writhed and snaked in all directions. The monster's body was covered with spikes. Its knife-sharp claws dug deep into the earth and its six blazing red eyes watched me hungrily.

The princess nodded to it in encouragement.

It was him.

It had been him all along.

How could he have failed to see it?

It must be a curse,

laid upon him when he had become the princess's knight.

The curse was a terrible one.

Even now he could barely fight it.

Even now that he knew the truth.

Even now he knew that he himself

was the monster.

The knight was the monster.

The monster was the knight.

Had the princess known all along?

18

THE KNIGHT

"STOP IT!" I SCREAMED. "STOP IT!" I didn't know myself whether I was talking to the monster or the princess.

The monster's three heads dipped toward me. Strings of drool hung from their mouths.

I closed my eyes like a child who thinks that if you can't see someone, they can't see you. But of course the monster would be able to eat me whether I looked it in the eye or not. I felt its hot, moist breath on my face.

But still I kept my eyes closed. I didn't want to see Will like this. I stumbled backward, lost my balance on the slope, and fell. I landed roughly on my left shoulder. Then I rolled down the hill a little way, hit my head on a stone, and lost my bearings for a moment.

The monster plunged down the hill after me. I felt a rush of air as one of its three heads came swooping toward me, its powerful jaws aiming straight for my heart. With the last of my strength I flung myself aside, but I knew it was too late. There was no escape. Sharp teeth pierced my sweater. Nobody could stop the creature Will had become.

Except the princess.

The princess laughed. Then she clapped her hands. "Good boy!" she cried, and "Shhh, that's enough." And: "Well done." And: "Come!"

The teeth released their hold on me.

The monster stamped its clawed feet so hard that the earth shook. But then its rasping breath quietened and eventually fell silent altogether. When I opened my eyes, the beast was gone and the shimmering ingredients were back in the princess's hand.

Will was lying in the grass beside me.

He was asleep.

His nostrils had shrunk back to their normal size and his tousled hair, as usual, was sticking up at crazy angles from his head. And it was just the one head, attached to a perfectly normal neck. I bent over him and touched his cheek with trembling fingers. It felt like Will.

He opened his eyes and stared at me blearily. "Amy!" he yawned. "What happened? Did I . . . fall asleep?"

I stroked his face and kissed his forehead. "No. The little girl changed you."

He sat up. "Changed me?"

"For a while you weren't you anymore—you were her monster. And before that—before that she tried to make you her knight."

"I didn't try to do it," whispered the princess suddenly, right in my ear. "I have already done it."

The uneasy feeling in my stomach intensified, and a bitter taste spread across the roof of my mouth. But my brain still hadn't grasped what she meant. I was too busy spinning around to grab hold of her—I was going to grab hold of her and I was going to—

But she wasn't behind me anymore. She had gone chasing off after a white shadow that was hopping through the flowers a little way away, seemingly in a great hurry.

"Oh dear!" cried the White Rabbit as he glanced at his watch. "I shall be late, oh dear!" He ducked out from under the princess's hands and went bounding off toward the castle gates.

"I command you to stop," panted the princess. "At once!"

The rabbit froze midhop and belly-flopped onto the grass. The princess picked him up and clamped him under her arm. "Good boy!" she told him, in the same tone of voice she had used to the monster a few minutes earlier. The rabbit opened his eyes wide with fear, but didn't say another word.

My knees went weak as the princess turned to face us.

"It was easy to make Will my knight," she explained, fondling the rabbit's neck. He was trying to play dead, and I wished I could have done the same. It was far too absurd to be true. I wanted to laugh but I couldn't. Instead I felt fear clawing at my throat again. The same fear that had come crashing in on me a few days before, the morning I'd suspected Will of being the thief.

"I first met him two days before you arrived on Stormsay," the princess continued as the world fell away around me. Will, the Will I had fallen in love with, was . . . he was . . . the thought hurt too much to think it.

I stared into the rabbit's eyes, the blood roared in my ears, the fire on the horizon crackled. But still I heard the princess's words as clear as glass in my head. Words like blades. "Will was walking on the moor with a huge dog. I hid behind a bush and as he came past I sprinkled my poison on him. I let it seep into his mind and I forced him to obey me from that moment on. The next day I had him kill a couple of geese in a fairy tale, as a test. But the poison had not taken full effect—something inside him was still rebelling. So much so that he wrote something on his wall in the dead birds' blood. As a warning to himself or a threat to me. I don't know. But he wrote the same words on the rocks inside my cave. Perhaps he wanted to show me I did not own him. But there, of course, he was wrong."

I swallowed hard, my fear hardening into a pebble in my throat. It rumbled down through my chest and left a bloody graze on my soul.

Will, I thought. Will, the knight? Will, the thief?

Will, whom I had trusted.

Slowly I turned to face him. He was still sitting beside me. Still looking slightly dazed. Staring into space as if he wasn't taking in a word of what the princess was saying.

"After that I ordered him to steal the first idea for me—my talking rabbit here. It worked beautifully. But then that fool Holmes turned up. He realized at once that it was Will's own handwriting on the wall of his cottage, put two and two together, and tried to help Will. We had to get rid of him," the princess sighed. "Fortunately by that time my knight was entirely obedient to me."

My soul was bleeding, and the loss of blood was making me dizzy. "No," I whispered.

"Yes," said the princess.

"Will would never have done anything to hurt Holmes. And he

helped me look for the thief. Why would he have done that if it was him all along? I don't believe you." I couldn't believe her. I wouldn't believe her.

But I did believe her, and I hated her for it.

The princess clamped the rabbit even more tightly under her arm and bent over Will, who still wasn't moving. She fumbled for a moment with his right boot, then pulled something out from inside it. Something silver. Something with a glittering, jewel-encrusted handle.

The dagger shone with a ghostly gleam in the firelight.

Mechanically, Will put out his hand to take it. His fingers closed around the handle as the princess leaned forward and whispered something in his ear.

The White Rabbit seized his opportunity while the princess was distracted to hop out of her arms and make a run for it.

My feet, however, seemed to have fused with the hilltop so that all I could do was stand there and wait. Wait to see what the princess had come up with this time, where this next whim of hers would take us. Because I understood now: she was playing with us. And she was enjoying it. It was her story and she could do whatever she wanted. In here, she controlled us all.

Me, the rabbit, the storm, and Will.

Will the knight, who was now advancing slowly toward me.

Something told me that this time she wasn't going to tell him to stop at the last moment.

He was having his recurring nightmare.

Holmes lay dead in his armchair and Will chased the murderer.

He chased him across the island and through a bizarre landscape that seemed to be on fire at the edges. This time, though, the murderer didn't have a black cloak but a red ponytail.

It was all very strange.

The murderer had stopped just a few feet away from him. He was staring at Will with large, shining eyes. The murderer was afraid. Will could see him trembling. It served him right.

Will weighed the weapon in his hand—the weapon that was like a friend to him. The metal molded itself to his fingers. It felt good. Strong. Liberating. He could hardly believe it: at last, the moment had come. Soon he would have his revenge.

Will moved closer to the murderer, forgetting the red ponytail. The murderer's eyes, nose, and mouth blurred until he was nothing more than a shimmering silhouette. A flickering shadow who didn't deserve to live.

Will thought of Holmes and raised the dagger.

Then a rabbit came lolloping through his nightmare.

Will blinked in surprise. For a brief moment he was distracted. The murderer, emerging from his trance, took to his heels and ran. He ran through the gates of a castle and into a courtyard, skirted around a well, tried to hide behind the tendrils of a climbing rose-bush. But Will would not let him escape. He ran after him, the weapon still clutched firmly in his hand. The murderer had no chance. He had run into a blind alley and in his panic had got caught up in the thorns.

Will smiled.

The murderer was trying to struggle free of the thorns but was only succeeding in getting himself more and more tangled up in them.

He was shouting, calling out things Will didn't understand. They were not important.

Will was here for one reason alone. He raised his weapon again. Then he lunged, and the blade hummed through the air toward the murderer. Will closed his eyes and thought of Holmes. *For you, Sherlock,* he thought. But the Sherlock in his mind shook his head and said something—a name, very short, only a few letters long. The name felt familiar to Will. It was a name with red hair and large eyes.

The blade stopped just before it reached the murderer's chest.

A . . . M . . . Y, read Will from Holmes's lips. Amy? What did that mean?

"Good boy," whispered a voice beside him, a little girl holding a captive rabbit tightly under her arm. "Do it," she whispered. "Do it now."

Will gripped the weapon with both hands. The tip of the blade touched the murderer, pressing against fabric and skin and bones and a beating heart. The murderer sobbed. Tears rolled down the blurred contours of his face and dripped onto the ground.

"You don't know what you're doing, Will!" cried the murderer. "It's me! How can you not recognize me?"

What was he talking about? Of course Will recognized him. This was the murderer he'd been hunting for so long, wasn't it? The Holmes in Will's mind shook his head even more vehemently.

Will let out a breath. This had happened before in another of his nightmares—a midsummer nightmare. He'd almost done the deed but had faltered at the last minute. He still didn't understand why. But something had stopped him from avenging Sherlock's death. It

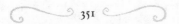

had been a strange feeling, an intuition, which he now felt creeping over him again.

"Do it," commanded the child beside him.

Will's hands trembled. Everything in him cried out to ram the blade into the murderer's heart. It was right. He had to do it, he . . . But still he hesitated.

"It's me—Amy!" the murderer implored. "Amy!"

Amy, thought Will. But—of course! Amy! Like a cool cloth the name slid across his eyes and wiped away the veil that had obscured them. At last he could see clearly again. At last he remembered the significance of those strange three letters. Amy!

He blinked.

Amy stood before him.

She was tangled up in a thorny bush by the wall of the castle. There were bloody scratches on her arms—she must have been struggling frantically to get free. There were tears in her beautiful eyes.

"Will," she whispered.

He stared at her. What had happened? "You," he stammered as his eyes fell upon the dagger in his hands. A dagger? Why was he holding a dagger? And why the hell had he been pointing it at Amy? "I . . . this . . ." He lowered the blade.

What had he done? It was as if somebody had tipped a box full of puzzle pieces into his brain. Puzzle pieces made of blurred memories. Puzzle pieces that showed him plundering the book world.

All of a sudden he felt icy cold.

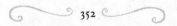

"You must obey me," declared the princess, folding her arms across her chest so that the rabbit was nearly crushed. "You are my knight. If I tell you to kill her, you will kill her."

"Of . . . of course," stuttered Will, but I could see in his eyes that he had come back to me, that he had finally realized. There was horror in his eyes.

"Good," said the princess as she hopped up onto the edge of the well and began to walk along it heel to toe. She pranced away from us, the rabbit in her arms quietly gasping for breath.

Will and I looked at each other. It was over. He was Will again, my Will. Another sob welled up in my chest. He gently loosened the thorny tendrils from around my wrists and eased me out of the bush. I wanted to fall into his arms, but he shied away from me.

"I understand it now," he said tonelessly, his chin quivering. "He's pointing to me."

"What?" I asked. "Who?"

The princess was humming to herself. She still had her back to us. Will fished something out of his pocket, a crumpled sheet of paper—a letter. He unfolded it and handed it to me. It wasn't a written letter but a drawing. A picture of Sherlock's corpse surrounded by the inhabitants of the island. In the foreground stood Brock, pointing at the cluster of people as if he was counting them. But when you looked more closely you could see that Brock wasn't just pointing at random. He was pointing at Will.

How could we have been so blind? How could we have failed to notice? Had Will always just thought he was asleep when in fact he'd been out doing the princess's bidding? Stealing ideas from the book world? I remembered how Werther, Shere Khan, and I had followed the thief from *The Little Prince* to *Pride and Prejudice*. Hadn't I found Will asleep at the stone circle that day? And another thing: how could I not have noticed that Will had never been there, not once, on any of the occasions Werther and I had encountered the thief?

Will appeared to be asking himself the same questions. His jaw clenched. His eyes had become hard and revealed only too clearly that he was thinking of Sherlock. He looked at his hands as if seeing them for the first time.

I swallowed hard. "You didn't know," I said. "You didn't know. The princess bewitched you somehow. She poisoned you. You didn't know what you were doing, okay?"

Will didn't answer. Instead he bent down suddenly and picked up an object that was lying in the grass. It must have fallen out of his pocket when he'd taken out Brock's drawing. It was the key to the dungeon.

"I let her out," he said, with an effort. "I thought I was having a nightmare. But I was actually in *The Odyssey*, stealing a monster, and after that I went and let the princess out of her cell. That's why I was there this morning. I let her out." He bowed his head. "And Sherlock . . . it was *me* who . . ."

"It was a curse. It *is* a curse," I murmured. "The knight is the monster." The princess had abused Will for her own ends just as she had abused Desmond in the fairy tale. But if she'd put the same curse on Will as on Desmond—if it was a fairy-tale curse—wasn't there some way to break it? I cast my mind around frantically, trying to remember everything I knew about this story. What else had Desmond told me about how it ended?

At that moment the princess glanced back over her shoulder and saw that I was still alive. "Oh, my faithful knight," she cried, "I wanted you to do it straightaway. Do it now!"

My breath and my thoughts faltered.

Will nodded jerkily, bent down again, and picked up the dagger. "Your wish is my command," he said, and stabbed the dagger into the rosebush just inches from my face. As he did so he cut a single, particularly beautiful rose from among the thorns and handed it to me. Even as my fingers closed around it the flower turned back into a shimmering glass sphere. It was the Little Prince's flower.

Will smiled sadly, and then all of a sudden his face was expressionless again, his eyes blank. As if of their own accord his hands pointed the dagger at me.

But this time I wasn't tangled up in the thorns: they'd caught fire the moment Will had cut the flower from its stem. And half the castle was now burning along with the rosebush. Flames licked at the walls and windows and made the air shimmer with heat. The roaring fire gave me a few precious seconds of confusion: the princess cried out, and Will's aim was so poor that I was able to dodge the dagger and duck under his arm and away.

I ran. White-hot rage coursed through my veins. How could that devil child have done this to Will? With one hand I clutched the glass sphere and with the other I lunged at the princess, trying to knock her off the wall into the well. I missed, but that didn't stop me trying a second time.

"Help me, my knight! You must protect me!" she shrieked, dodging another of my blows by jumping down off the well onto the cobbles of the castle courtyard. As she ran she rummaged in the pocket of her gown for the other ideas. She was probably planning to send the monster after me again. Or the evil from *Wuthering Heights*. But as she fought to keep hold of the violently struggling rabbit and outrun me at the same time, she was unable to find the idea she was looking for. "This is my story!" yelled the princess as I chased her up a spiral staircase to the top of one of the towers. "Everybody here does what I want. Stop chasing me, Amy! Stop it right now!" And for a moment I found myself ensnared by her words. I tasted her poison on my tongue, felt it trickle into my mind. But it was over as quickly as it had begun. "You have no power over me!" I shouted. "I'm not your knight!"

We had reached the top of the tower by now and the princess cowered against the silver battlements. I launched myself at her, wanting to claw her face, to grab hold of her and—

At the last moment she whirled around so that I only caught the hem of her dress. As I yanked at it the ancient, fraying fabric gave way and ripped. Then there was a clinking sound as the shimmering ideas dropped to the floor. A crack appeared in the glass sphere containing the cyclone, but miraculously it didn't break. It rolled, along with the other ideas, out of the princess's reach.

"So," I said quietly.

The princess stared at me. Suddenly she seemed genuinely afraid of me. "My knight!" she screamed. "Kill her! Hurry up and kill her!"

"With pleasure," replied Will, in the mechanical voice that told me he wasn't Will at all anymore. He'd followed us up the stairs and was now crossing the circular floor of the tower roof. He was still clutching the knight's dagger. He came toward us, faster now, more determined.

I jumped aside, but it was too late. He'd already grabbed hold of me, tugging roughly at my hair, pulling me away from the princess. Then I felt the blade at my throat, cool and sharp.

Will's breath came in short gasps beside my ear. I wanted to look at him but I couldn't turn my head, "Will," I whispered. "Will, come back to me. It's me, Amy. This is not a nightmare, it's the princess's curse."

The pressure of the metal on my neck grew stronger.

"Will, don't do this. I know you don't want to do this."

"No," said Will. "But she's forcing me. I . . ." The words sounded as if they came from very far away.

"You have to fight it, do you hear me? There must a way to break the curse. Desmond managed it, anyway."

The blade broke my skin. I felt a single drop of blood well from the cut and run down my neck. "Desmond died at the end," muttered Will through clenched teeth.

"But before that he killed the monster, Will. Somehow he must have managed to break the curse."

"Before that? Desmond . . ." whispered Will, and suddenly he went very quiet. The pressure of the blade on my neck eased almost imperceptibly. "Amy . . . I think there's only one way to end this," he murmured quietly in my ear. "At the end, the knight has to . . ." He faltered.

"Will!" I cried.

"You have to go, Amy. Go! Take the ideas and—" He broke off. Had his mind lost its battle with the poison?

"And what?" I yelled. "What do you mean? How are we supposed to get out of here while you're still under her control?"

This time he did not reply.

THE END

WILL FELL AND AS HE FELL the world slowed, stopped turning. I saw his knees give way beneath him, infinitely slowly, his body arc backward in slow motion, down and down to land softly on the roof where he'd been standing. As though an invisible current were carrying him gently to the bottom of an unknown ocean. As though it were rocking him to sleep and laying him to rest.

But at last the impact did come and the dull thud of his body hitting the stone roof ripped through the torpor the world had fallen into. It ripped through something inside me too.

"Will!" I heard myself shout, and "No!"

I lurched toward him.

His hands still gripped the jewel-encrusted hilt of the dagger sticking out of his chest. This image was so wrong. It was impossible that the rest of the dagger was buried inside a wound that . . .

Will's eyelids fluttered as my trembling fingers touched his cheek. All of a sudden there was a lot of red. It was even reflected in his stormy-blue eyes.

"Amy," Will whispered. "The . . . story . . . is over."

"Will," I said. "Will, Will."

The patch of red spread further, widening into a pool on the floor, a sea of lost life. "Take the ideas and . . . get out of here. Take them back." Will's voice grew fainter.

"But—"

"Promise me."

"I promise."

"Amy." He smiled feebly. "Now . . . you're shining again . . . like a fairy fl—"

He exhaled. His lips had turned pale. The light in his stormy-blue eyes went out.

The knight died at the end of the story.

The truth gripped me, whether I wanted it or not.

Will was dead.

He couldn't be dead.

Dead.

I heard the words in my head but I didn't understand them.

Instead I cradled Will's head in my lap and stroked his hair. What if Will had just fallen asleep? Yes, that was it—he was asleep. He was just having one of his nightmares and this time he'd taken me inside the nightmare with him. That had to be it. With my thumb I traced the curve of his eyebrow. With my index finger I twiddled the lock of hair behind his left ear. My vision blurred.

The princess was crying too. She crouched between the

battlements and wept bitterly. "Who will protect me now?" she sobbed. "Who will fight for me now?" Out of the corner of my eye I saw her drop the rabbit to the ground and kick it. "Get away from me. I want my knight!"

I wiped my sleeve across my face. I stroked Will's cheek one last time, then stood up. Something sticky welled from the rip inside of me, thick and hot and black as pitch. It filled my chest and throbbed at my temples. "He's not your knight any longer," I said.

"He is," the princess howled. "He is—he has to protect me—he . . ." She took a step toward Will's body, but I stepped forward to meet her. I would never abandon him to her. She had possessed Will for long enough.

I looked around, scanning the battlements and the burning horizon. Somewhere down there, by the foot of the tower—wasn't that where we'd entered the story?

The princess glared at me. "Stand aside!"

"Forget it!" I hissed, and gave a start as something suddenly bumped against my foot.

The White Rabbit had rolled one of the glass spheres toward me. Inside it was the rose Will had cut from the thorns—the Little Prince's flower. I must have dropped the idea in the chaos of the moment. I bent down to pick it up as the rabbit hopped a little farther away and nudged the cyclone, the monster, and Sleeping Beauty's long sleep in my direction.

"We must hurry," it muttered, rolling yet more ideas toward me.

I nodded.

"Stop that!" cried the princess, making a lunge for the glass spheres. But I was faster. I pulled off my sweater, gathered up the stolen ideas inside it, and knotted it so they couldn't fall out. There was only one missing, and that was the rabbit himself. He now turned back into a shimmering idea too.

As I slipped the last idea inside my sweater the story began to fall apart. The princess cried out as the ground beneath her feet went up in flames. The tower crumbled and split in two, and she only just managed to leap across the gap to join Will and me. All that had remained of the surrounding hills was engulfed by the fiery inferno, and suddenly the air around us was filled with heavy black smoke that burned my lungs, stung my eyes, and made me cough. It was as if the fire had only now become truly hot. The heat gnawed at my skin and scorched my eyeballs.

The princess flung herself at me and tried to wrench the ideas out of my grasp. But she was a child. An angry, capricious, malevolent child, yes, but still far smaller and weaker than I was.

I pushed her off me, then turned back to Will and heaved his arm over my shoulder. I put one arm around his waist and held the ideas tight with the other.

The princess tumbled backward, almost falling into the flames. She was beside herself with rage. She cried and yelled. She raged and stamped her dirty feet. Hatred glittered in her eyes. By the time she'd realized what I was planning I had already scrambled up onto the battlements. She ran at me, trying to cling onto me at the last second as she had done to one of my ancestors.

But it was too late. She missed the end of my ponytail by mere millimeters. But she missed it.

I'd already jumped from the tower roof. I plummeted down through the smoke and the flames and the darkness, plummeted toward the burning hilltop and passed straight through it. Back to Stormsay.

The princess was left behind, a prisoner in her own story.

We arrived at the stone circle, me, Will, and the glass spheres. I'd managed to save the ideas. The book world would go back (almost) to the way it had been before.

But Will and I would not. Because he still wasn't moving, and the hole in his chest was still there.

I lay down beside him in the grass and closed my eyes. A river of tears had gathered behind them and now came spilling out from under my eyelids. Our shoulders touched. I felt for his hand and wove my fingers through his. Will's skin still felt warm. Warm and alive and slightly slippery from all the blood. But it was already growing colder. His heart had stopped beating.

Somewhere deep inside me there had been a last vestige of hope. Because it had happened in the book world and Will, after all, was a real person. I'd had this absurd idea that death wasn't real in books, that Will would be okay again once he was back in the outside world.

That idea had been a fairy story.

Will was dead.

Even in the real world, he was dead.

I wanted to cry until the river of tears had run dry and the only warmth left in Will's skin was the warmth flowing from my body to his. But instead I blinked and my eyes fell upon something lying on the ground close by: Will's copy of *Peter Pan*. His favorite story.

Without stopping to think I reached for the book, opened it

somewhere in the middle and slid it over my face. A moment later the words sucked me in and Will along with me, his hand in mine.

We landed on a brig with a rotting wooden hull. It was the *Jolly Roger*, the scourge of the seas, the ship of the infamous Captain Hook.

The pirates, when they found us lying there on the dirty planks, realized at once that something was wrong. The plot came to a temporary halt. The pirates shed their fierce expressions and forgot for a while to be evil and bloodthirsty. Hook himself emerged from his cabin and bent over Will. He touched the wound with his hook, then took off his large plumed hat and bowed his head. He said nothing, but placed his one good hand on my shoulder. Together we stood there in silence.

Somehow, though, the news of our arrival spread quickly throughout the island. Soon characters came running from every corner of Neverland, for everybody here had known and loved Will. The Indians tiptoed onto the deck, the lost boys clambered over the railing, and the mermaids began to circle the ship. Even the ticking crocodile, the one who had eaten Hook's hand and swallowed a clock, made an appearance. It dragged its scaly body toward us and rang the bell of the clock in its stomach. But Will did not wake up, not even when the Darling children, Wendy, John, and Michael, floated down from the sky along with Peter Pan himself.

Peter Pan, the boy who never grew up, dropped to his knees at Will's side. "What happened to him? Was he looking the wrong way?" he asked. The words sounded brusque and a little arrogant, as was his way. But he was crying as he spoke.

Later all I could remember was that I'd tried to tell them what had happened. But my account was disjointed and full of holes because I couldn't tear my gaze away from Will's staring blue eyes.

Perhaps that was why I didn't notice that another character had come darting toward us—not until she landed on the end of Will's nose and pressed her ear to his lips. The fairy Tinker Bell was about the size of my hand. She listened at Will's lower lip and left traces of fairy dust on his skin. Her light flickered and her voice was like the tinkling of a bell when at last she straightened up and told us what we all already knew. "He's dead," she said.

We nodded. Wendy sobbed. The crocodile ticked mournfully.

But Tinker Bell hadn't finished: "He's dead. But a trace of his soul is still inside him. Not enough for him to live, but . . ." She came buzzing over to me and whispered something in my ear.

A tingling sensation flooded through me. I didn't even have to think about her offer—I nodded, straightaway.

Tinker Bell flew straight as a die toward the wound. She flew right inside Will's chest, passing through skin and bone and flesh and muscle. Everything she touched glittered with fairy dust, which came together to form a glimmering golden cloud. And this cloud grew and spread until it encompassed Will's whole body. The fairy dust trickled through his hair, covered his face, settled in every fold of his sweater, and washed the blood away.

Tinker Bell finally came to rest on my head. She laughed her bell-like laugh and as the cloud dispersed, it happened—the thing I had no longer dared to hope for, the most incredible thing in the world, the thing that was possible only in the book world: Will sat up.

He had changed. His arms and legs were less gangling, his facial features were perfectly symmetrical, his hair was glossier, and in his stormy-blue eyes were shimmering gold specks of fairy dust. He was wearing the same clothes as the lost boys, clothes made out of leaves and bearskins. He had become one of them.

Will was a book character.

But he was alive.

I fell into his arms, sobbing his name—and other things—into the crook of his neck. I cried the river of tears now after all, as Will held me tightly. "I love you too," he said. "I love you too, Amy."

Then he kissed me.

A long, familiar kiss.

Will was himself again. My Will.

The mermaids broke into song, Peter crowed like a cockerel, and the pirates lit the cannons and fired several shots for sheer joy.

Will and I, meanwhile, were learning how to fly.

That afternoon we wandered through Neverland together, bathed in the lagoon, danced in the Indian village, and soared starward.

Will belonged here now, in the book world, in this story. He was happy. He'd loved this book since childhood. But it still felt so strange, so final. Tinker Bell had brought Will back to life, but the magic only worked inside *Peter Pan*. He would have to stay here forever. He would always be seventeen. He would never see Stormsay again. But he was breathing. He kissed me. I lost myself in his stormy-blue eyes. And he began, along with Peter and the other boys, to fight Hook.

This was the price. We were happy to pay it.

For a few hours I was able to stop myself thinking about what would happen next. I tried to forget that other stories—and the outside world—still existed. But after a while somebody came flicking through the pages of *Peter Pan* toward us—somebody who, like me, did not belong there.

Werther.

He was riding an enormous monster that looked like a scaly sausage, and looking for me. News of what had happened had spread throughout the book world and he'd come to help me do what I had to do—the thing I'd been doggedly refusing to think about until now.

He found me in the hut on the beach that Peter had lent us to stay in. We were in the middle of dinner when Werther burst in, laddering one of his silk stockings on the door frame in the process.

I leaped to my feet. "Werther!"

"Miss Amy," he greeted me and made as if to kiss my hand, but I just launched myself at him and hugged him tightly. "Oh," he stammered, "I . . . I heard what had happened. Are . . . are you well?"

"Yes," I said. "Very well."

Will had stood up, too, and shook Werther's hand. They looked at each other. Werther saw what Will had become, and cleared his throat. "Welcome to the book world," he said politely, before turning back to me. "Is it true that you were able to recover the ideas?"

I nodded. "They're up by the portal in the outside world."

He looked at me. "Then it is time we returned them to their stories. Come, Miss Amy." He gave me his arm.

I gazed back at him mutely. Then I turned to Will. "See you later," I said, and planted a kiss in the corner of his mouth.

I accompanied Werther outside the hut to where Charybdis,

the scaly sausage, was grazing peacefully. She yelped for joy when she spotted Werther's ruffled shirt.

"It has become apparent that she thinks I am her mother," he explained sheepishly, lifting me onto the monster's back behind him.

A moment later we were speeding through the story. Werther dropped me off by the pirate ship and I jumped back to the real world to fetch the ideas. Then, together, we restored them to their rightful places: the talking rabbit to *Alice in Wonderland*, the long sleep to *Sleeping Beauty*, the Elf-King to *The Elf-King*, the cyclone to *The Wizard of Oz*, the flower to *The Little Prince*, the summer to *A Midsummer Night's Dream*, the transformation to *The Strange Case of Dr. Jekyll and Mr. Hyde*, the evil to *Wuthering Heights*, and the two sea monsters to *The Odyssey*. Only the picture from *The Picture of Dorian Gray* was irretrievably lost, the princess having destroyed it at the stone circle. Luckily the witches from *Macbeth* offered to paint a sort of mock-up of the original picture. Their picture was little more than a sketch, and it sometimes seemed as though there was black magic at work in it. But after a while even this story began to work pretty well, so much so that readers didn't even notice the real picture was missing. In the end, almost everything was back to the way it was supposed to be. Except that Will had disappeared from the outside world forever.

The adult book jumpers especially missed him very much. In the weeks that followed, the Laird and Lady Mairead talked a great deal about Will and less and less about their ancient feud. Will's parents grieved for their son, but consoled themselves with the thought that he would live forever in the story he loved most in the world. And as for me—I traveled back and forth between the real world, which had become so much more important to me over the past few weeks, and my second home, the world of stories. Almost every day I went to visit Will in Neverland.

I tried not to think about what would happen in a few years' time, when I would lose my gift. Nobody could predict when it would happen—I was half fictional, after all. It was possible I'd be able to go on jumping for longer than other people—perhaps even forever. But it was more likely that one day I would have to decide where I wanted to spend my life. With Will in the fabulous world of words, in which everything and everyone was controlled by invisible authors. Or without him in the real world, whose stories were even more exciting because they were written by life.

There were cliffs in Neverland, too. They weren't as high as Shakespeare's Seat, and the wind on the clifftop was only a gentle breeze. The sky was always too blue and always too sunny. But Will and I still climbed up there now and again. We closed our eyes, and as our lips touched we remembered what it had been like the night the princess had stolen the scraps of her fairy tale.

In the days when our love had still been wholly real.

And then, sometimes, the gentle breeze became a storm after all and carried us up, up, up, into the magic of the words.

The princess stood on the highest battlement of the highest
tower and looked out at the sea of flames.
Stories were strange things.
One minute they were over: the next minute you simply
turned back to the beginning and everything began again.
One minute the princess had lost everything,
the next she thought she could already spy a new knight
in the distance, coming to rescue her.
She smiled as she waited for him.